FROST

C.N. CRAWFORD

PROLOGUE

It's a sad truth that most relationships are doomed. Once, I'd thought mine would be an exception, that I'd found *the one*. That unlike most other bright loves, mine would burn forever.

Andrew was a human—unlike me. I was born fae, but I stayed as far away from the rest of them as I could. Most fae were violent, capricious, and *breathtakingly* arrogant. Andrew, on the other hand, made me wildflower crowns and wrote me poems about sycamore trees.

His beauty drew me in first: blue eyes flecked with gold, and wavy chestnut hair. When he smiled, his lips crinkled at the corners in a way that always made me want to kiss him. Andrew's smell was like home, soap and black tea.

But that wasn't what had made me fall in love. It was his kindness.

When I had a long week, he made me tea or cocktails, and I'd fall asleep with my head on his chest. With

Andrew, I could actually feel safe. He was human, and I was fae, but that never seemed to matter between us.

He'd always listened to me, texted back right away, asked me about my day. He had a dachshund named Ralphie, and he drove his mom to her doctor's appointments. On Sundays, we hung out in his tidy suburban condo and read the same books over coffee.

He truly believed that nothing was more important than love. That it should be celebrated. He told me I was his soulmate.

Unlike the others of my kind, Andrew made me feel safe. Secure.

Together, we'd planned a future. The gist of it was this: I'd help support him by paying his mortgage while he finished his MBA. Once he was earning money, we'd work on my dream: opening a cocktail bar named "Chloe's" after my mom. Andrew would help me finance it. We'd live a joyous life together among the humans in a leafy suburb full of backyard barbecues and pillow forts with our kids. Trips to the beach in the summer. A *normal* human life.

Problem was, on the night of my twenty-sixth birthday, I learned it was all a lie.

And that was when I stopped believing in love entirely.

𓊝 I 𓊝
AVA

Standing on a brick sidewalk, I gripped the bag of takeout, already salivating at the thought of chicken vindaloo and Peshwari naan. Royal Bistro made the naan deliciously buttery and the curry so hot, it made me break out in a euphoric sweat.

Since it was my birthday, the manager had let me leave the bar early. I didn't have big plans. After a few hours of mixing drinks for the Friday-night finance crowd, I just wanted to stuff my face and watch comedies with Andrew.

As I walked along the path to our home, I breathed in the scent of chili powder, cumin, and garlic emanating from the paper bag under my arm. It was the first thing we'd bonded over when friends had introduced us—a lust for the hottest food possible.

With a rumbling stomach, I slid my key into the lock and stepped into his home.

My ears perked up at the sounds coming from upstairs. Andrew was clearly blaring some dirty videos, judging from the impossibly loud moaning and gasping —the really fake, high-pitched kind targeted at men. Women would catch the artifice right away.

Interesting. Well, he thought he had a few hours till I got home. Let him watch whatever porn he wanted. But why would he be playing it at that volume when the condo walls were paper thin?

I slipped out of my shoes. As I crossed into the kitchen, I slammed my toe into a sharp wooden chair leg and shouted, "Ow," irrationally irritated at the chair for existing. Scowling, I pulled the vindaloo from the bag. At that moment, I realized the porn had stopped. Andrew was embarrassed to be caught. I quirked a smile at the thought. Surely he must know I didn't care?

"Hello?" Andrew's voice came from upstairs. There was a panicked sound to it. I turned when he said more quietly, "I don't think it's anything."

My breath caught. Was he talking to someone else?

Now, my heart was hammering. Hardly aware of the hot tub of curry in my hand, I tiptoed up the stairs. The high-pitched orgasm started up again, the mattress squeaking.

Dread gripped my heart. I reached the bedroom and found the door slightly cracked.

Very carefully, I pushed it open.

My stomach clenched so hard, I nearly vomited.

Andrew was lying in the middle of the bed, his limbs intimately entwined with those of a blonde woman I'd never seen before. I must have screamed or shouted because they almost fell off the bed as they spun to face me. For a long moment, we all stared at each other, gripped by horror.

"Ava, what are you doing here?" Andrew's face had turned bright red.

"What the fuck are *you* doing?"

"You're supposed to be at work." He was lying beneath a naked woman, but he said that like it was a perfectly reasonable explanation.

"It's my birthday. And they let me off early."

Andrew pushed the woman off him, and they sprawled across the bed, *our* bed, sweaty and flushed. I stared, almost unable to believe what I was seeing, but aware that it was my future disintegrating before my eyes.

"I've been meaning to tell you..." He swallowed hard. "I didn't want it to happen like this. It's just that Ashley and I fell in love."

"No offense," added Ashley, pulling a sheet over herself. "But he's done experimenting. He wants a family. A normal family? Like...a human family."

Andrew swallowed hard, his whole body rigid with tension. "Ashley and I...we just have things in common, Ava. We have a future."

I couldn't breathe. How had I not seen this coming? My thoughts went silent, and there was only the feeling of my heart splitting open.

I hurled the vindaloo at him, and the plastic container hit the bedspread and instantly exploded. Piping hot chicken and chilies sprayed all over them. Andrew and the girl screamed, and I wondered if I'd done something illegal. Could you be arrested for throwing hot curry at someone?

"What are you doing?" shouted Andrew.

"I don't know! What are *you* doing?" I screamed back at him.

My gaze roamed over the room, taking in the laundry bin where our clothes lay mingled together. For some reason, the thought of separating my laundry from his was more depressing than anything else. I always did the laundry and neatly folded it for him... would I be pulling my clothes out of the hamper and doing them at a laundromat?

Holy shit, where was I going to live now?

Andrew was wiping off the curry with the sheet. "You said I had a hall pass when I went on vacation. And the more Ashley and I got to know each other, the more I realized it was meant to be."

"A hall pass?" I stared at him, the two of them hazy through the tears in my eyes. "I said I knew what a hall pass was. I didn't say you had one. And you're not on vacation."

"I met Ashley on vacation. And I couldn't help it. Her beauty called to me."

I blinked and felt a tear running down my cheek. "The last time you went on vacation was nearly three years ago."

Andrew shook his head. "No, Ava. You and I went to Costa Rica last winter, and you stayed in the room the whole time with a UTI. Remember?"

"You met her when *we* were on vacation?"

Andrew swallowed again. "Well, you weren't exactly the most fun on that trip."

Next to him, Ashley was frantically trying to wipe the hot curry off herself with one of my towels. "This is really irritating my skin."

Andrew blinked at me with puppy dog eyes. "Ava. I'm sorry. Obviously, this is just a miscommunication. I never meant to hurt you. But the heart wants what it wants."

My throat felt tight, my chest aching. "What is *wrong* with you?"

"I-I was going to tell you..." he stammered. "We fell in love. And love is beautiful, isn't it? Love should always be celebrated. Honestly, Ava, you should be happy for me. I've found my soulmate." He sighed dramatically. "Can you stop being selfish for a minute and think about this from my perspective?"

The whole world was tilting on its axis. "You said *I* was your soulmate. I suppose you write her poetry, too?" I spun around and had crossed into the hall when it clicked in my head. "Was the poem about the poplar tree for her or me?"

"It was for me," Ashley snapped.

A horrific thought struck me. This wasn't just the end of my relationship. This was the end of my future plans. "Andrew, what about the bar? You were going to help finance it."

He shrugged, giving me a little smile. "Oh, Ava. You'll figure something out. Go to college or something. You'd be a brilliant student."

Panicked thoughts tumbled wildly through my mind

like autumn leaves in a storm. I'd made Andrew my whole life, and now it was gone.

Tears stung my eyes. "You were waiting until you graduated, weren't you?" I said. "Because Ashley's not paying your bills. I was."

She tossed her hair over her shoulder. "I'm an actress. It takes time to build a career."

"And talent. And considering how fake that orgasm sounded, I don't have a lot of hope for you," I retorted.

Ashley yanked the vindaloo off the bed and threw it at me. Red curry splattered over my shirt.

I was already the bitter woman. The spurned. The wicked witch plotting to take down the young beauty.

"Get out!" she yelled.

"He's all yours!" I shouted back. "You two really *do* seem perfectly matched."

I had to leave before I did something that put me in jail for twenty years. I snatched my gym bag off the floor and bounded down the stairs.

And there it was—the moment I decided I would never love again.

Fairy tales? They weren't real.

⚜ 2 ⚘
AVA

An hour later, I was resting my elbows on the sticky wooden bar of the Golden Shamrock. Sipping a Guinness while the TV blared, I watched *Hitched and Stitched*, a reality TV show about women competing to win a groom and plastic surgery for their Big Day. Horrific, yes, but that didn't stop me from tuning in every week.

Maybe that heralded the decline of civilization or something, but none of that really bothered me right now. I was twenty-six years old, with...

What did I have? Nothing, really. Nothing to my name.

Tonight, I just wanted a place where no one would give a shit about the curry stains on my shirt, a place where I could drink a lot on a weeknight and no one would judge me.

The Golden Shamrock was the perfect spot.

It wasn't just the heartbreak, although that did make

me want to curl into the fetal position. This had ruined another of my dreams, at least temporarily—Chloe's. I'd been working day and night on my plans, trying to get permits.

I dropped my head into my hands. I made about thirty thousand a year as a bartender right now, and much of that had gone to Andrew's mortgage. Before I'd met Andrew, I'd been sharing a cramped apartment with an alcoholic who always fell asleep in the bathroom. That wasn't the end of the world, but something really rankled about the way Andrew had just tossed out "go to college" as if I could suddenly pay for it.

Andrew had grown up rich, with parents who earned millions in real estate. He'd decided to make it on his own for a while, which I guess meant I was helping him instead of his parents. Because he'd never truly been broke, he'd cultivated the sort of blithe obliviousness that would lead him to say things like, "You should be happy I'm in love," in the process of shattering several of my dreams.

I sipped my Guinness, licking the foam off my lips. I'd find a way to make it work.

A familiar voice pulled me from my misery. "Ava!"

When I looked up, I saw my best friend Shalini crossing toward me. Her dark, wavy hair cascaded over a figure-hugging red dress that matched her lipstick. She wore shimmery blush over her copper skin, her style in sharp contrast to my food-stained work ensemble.

Shalini slid in next to me and immediately wrapped

an arm around my shoulders. "Oh, my God, Ava. What happened?"

All the emotions I'd been holding back came flooding out then, and I dropped my head into my hands. "I caught Andrew having sex in our bed with a blonde *actress*." When I looked up again at her, my vision had gone blurry.

Shalini's brown eyes were wide, her jaw tight. "Are you fucking kidding me?"

I sipped my beer, feeling numb now. "He said he had a hall pass."

"A *what* pass? What's that?"

I drew in a deep breath and told Shalini everything that had happened: coming home early, the fake orgasm, and then the bit about how I should be happy for him. When I finished, Shalini's expression of utter disgust mirrored my own feelings. Then a smile curled her lips. "You really threw vindaloo on them?"

"It was everywhere."

"I hope he got chili peppers on his balls—" Shalini paused for a second, then grimaced. She was probably trying *not* to imagine what curry might look like all over Andrew's naked body. Shaking her head, she said, "It's unbelievable. I mean, did he really think he wasn't going to get caught?

"I don't know. I guess so. I was supposed to be working late, but it's my birthday." My cheeks were wet, and I wiped my hands across them. "I know most relationships don't last, but I thought we were different."

Shalini gently patted my shoulder. "The cure for a broken heart is a hotter man. Are you on Tinder yet?"

I stared at her. "This just happened an hour and a half ago."

"Right. Well, when you're ready, I'm going to help you. I'm basically desperate for an adventure. Maybe we should go on a cruise! Aren't there cruises for single people?"

I looked down at my now nearly empty glass. Was this my second beer or my third? I was losing count. "No way. I'm done with men. I can be perfectly happy with donuts and movies about Tudor queens."

"Wait a minute. Wasn't he supposed to finance your bar?" Shalini's voice rose. "You've been paying his fucking mortgage. He *owes* you."

I nodded. "And that's probably why he was waiting to tell me."

"What if I invested in your bar?"

It was a lovely thing to say, but I didn't want to ruin a perfect friendship by throwing a steep financial risk into the mix. "No, but thank you. I'll figure something out."

"We could open one together. One of the ones where you can throw axes? And maybe we should invite Andrew to opening night, have some shots, and see where the blades take us."

I nodded over my beer. "We could call it 'Tap that Axe.'"

"Remember when Andrew brought that hatchet thing camping and nearly decapitated a squirrel? What a fucking idiot," said Shalini. "You need an alpha male. Like, someone who can protect you."

I swayed in my seat. "Ew. No, I don't need some alpha twat. I just need to figure out how to get rent money together." I gripped the table. "How dumb am I, exactly, that I trusted him?"

She shrugged. "You're not dumb. He's the one who ruined something good."

I leaned back in my chair. "What's the rent like these days downtown?"

She cleared her throat. "Let's not talk about that now. You can stay with me."

"Okay." I nodded. "That actually sounds kind of fun."

A slim guy with brown hair sidled up to us. He was wearing black Chucks, jeans, and a gray hoodie. His attention was riveted entirely on Shalini—which was how it always went when we ventured out together.

"Having a good night?" he asked, flicking his eyebrows up. He clearly intended the expression to be flirty.

"She's not," said Shalini.

"Maybe I can make you feel better," he replied, his comment entirely directed at Shalini. "Where are you from? I speak three languages."

"Arlington, Massachusetts."

"No, I mean like...where are you *actually* from? Originally."

"Arlington." Shalini's eyes narrowed. "How about a little French? *Foutre le camp!*"

The man laughed nervously. "That's not one of the languages I know."

"Do you know programming languages? How about this—*sudo kill dash nine you?*"

The man's eyes brightened with excitement. "I will if you tell me the admin password." His tone sounded faintly lascivious, and I no longer understood what was happening.

My gaze drifted to *Hitched and Stitched*. The groom had forced his potential brides into a boxing match. Apparently, the best way to choose a wife was to have them punch each other while wearing bikinis. I frowned at the screen, wondering how many of them really would need a new nose after this episode.

When I turned back to Shalini and the random guy, they were arguing about a programming language.

Shalini was absolutely brilliant with computers. She'd been working for some fancy tech startup that had gone public a month ago. I wasn't sure how much money she'd made with her stock options, but whatever it was, she no longer needed a job. Once, she'd been an obsessive academic, insanely driven, but she was burned out, and she just wanted to have fun.

Shalini held up a hand. "Steve, Ava has had a bad night. She's not a fan of men right now. We're going to need some space."

And this was where I made a crucial mistake. "It's just that I caught my boyfriend banging Ashley."

Steve bit his lip. "If you guys want a threesome, or..."

"No!" said Shalini and I in unison.

"Whatever." Steve's face hardened as he looked at me. "Not trying to be a dick, but you're not really that pretty, anyway. Not with the elf ears." He sauntered away, humming to himself.

"Fae!" I turned back to Shalini, touching my delicately pointed fae ears. "Shit. That didn't help my self-esteem."

"You know tons of men say shit like that when they're rejected, right? One second, you're the most beautiful person they've ever seen. The next, you're a stuck-up bitch with weird knees. Everyone knows that fae ears are hot, and so are you. You're just intimidating."

I'd lived among the humans, tried to blend in. I'd like to say it was by choice, but the truth was, the fae had kicked me out long ago. No idea why.

"Is that what all human men think when they see me?" I asked.

Shalini shook her head. "You're fucking gorgeous. Dark brown hair, big eyes, sexy lips. You're like a little fae Angelina Jolie from the '90s. And your ears are hot as fuck. You know what? I'm making it my life's mission to get myself a fae boyfriend. Human men are messy."

I grimaced. "And fae men are terrifying."

"How do you know that?"

A dark memory swept through the back of my mind, but it was intangible, elusive—a wispy phantom in my thoughts. "I don't know. There are a few common fae like me out here, but I don't run into them often. All the High Fae live in Faerie, and I think they have magical powers. But in any case, you can only get into their world through a portal, and that requires an invitation, which I'm certainly not getting."

"What do you imagine the males would be like in bed, though?"

"I've literally never thought about it."

She pointed at me. "Have you ever noticed that the most mind-blowing sex is with the worst trainwrecks of men? The best sex I ever had was with a guy who believed that aliens live in the Earth's core. He lived in a yurt in his parents' backyard, and his only job was trying to make kombucha. Which he never managed, by the way. His shoes were held together with duct tape. Mind blowing sex in the yurt, and that's how I know there is no God. Who was yours?"

"Best sex?" My first instinct was to say Andrew, but no, that wasn't the truth. And I didn't have to be loyal to him anymore. "His name was Dennis. On our first date, he served me cold soup out of a can and tried to beat box for a solid fifteen minutes. He ate weed brownies for breakfast and wanted to be a professional magician. But his body was absolute perfection, and he was insane in bed. In a good way."

Shalini nodded sympathetically. "Exactly. It's too cruel. Is it possible that fae men could be good in bed *and* also normal?"

"Fuck knows. I'm pretty sure they're all arrogant, and I think kind of murdery? But I'm not even *allowed* in the fae world." This was something I never talked about, but all the beer had loosened me up.

"Why not? You never explained it to me."

I leaned forward. "The fae world is all about your family lineage. And since my parents gave me up for adoption at birth, no one knows what my lineage is. I'm an outcast." I looked down at myself, seeing what others must see. "Shalini, I'm not doing much better than Dennis, am I? I'm broke and currently wearing a cat sweatshirt covered in food stains." I reached up to touch my hair, realizing that I had one of those *I've given up* buns with hair sticking out. "Oh, God. This is what I looked like to meet Ashley."

"You look sexier than ever. You look like someone kept you up all night because you're hot as hell." Her eyes moved to my now empty pint glass. "Another round?"

I nodded, even though I already felt dizzy. I could still hear Ashley's high-pitched squeals, and those had to go.

"More," I said slowly, and sighed. "Thanks. Andrew was too good-looking. Too perfect. I should have known better than to trust a man who was so pretty."

Shalini shouted to the bartender, "Can we get a pitcher of margaritas? And can you turn up *Hitched and Stitched*? Someone's getting sent home tonight."

"I hope it's Amberlee," I said. "No, wait. I hope she stays. She's batshit, and that makes her my favorite. She tried to curse Jennica with a curse candle."

As the bartender filled the pitcher, a "breaking news" logo flashed on the TV above the bar, interrupting the video of a *Hitched* contestant drunkenly sobbing. A news reporter was standing on a street corner.

I stared at the screen.

"It's just been announced," said the grinning

reporter, "that Torin, king of the fae, will be getting married this year."

A hush fell over the bar. King Torin was the leader of the High Fae, a lethal group of fae who now ruled our world from a distance. Exactly the type of fae who wanted nothing to do with a commoner like me.

And yet, I found myself staring at the TV anyway, enraptured along with everyone else.

3

AVA

"**A** grand tournament of eligible fae women will be held to choose the bride," continued the reporter. "Not every fae woman will be chosen to participate. Only one hundred will be selected from thousands of possible contestants, hand-picked by the king himself. His bride must demonstrate strength, grace—"

I rolled my eyes. "This is so outdated. Can't he just meet someone and decide if he likes—"

"Shh!" Shalini practically clamped her hand over my mouth. "I love you, but I will *actually* murder you if you keep talking."

Shalini, my completely human friend, was obsessed with the fae. I, on the other hand, was perfectly happy to keep my distance.

The fae had only revealed themselves to the human world about thirty years ago. At first, humans reacted with horror and revulsion—and unfortunately, that attitude had lasted for *most* of my childhood. But now? Humans couldn't get enough of the fae. At some point, the fae had carefully crafted an image of wealth and glamour.

I had a sneaking suspicion they were still fairly terrifying behind the sophisticated façade.

"King Torin," the reporter said, beaming, "was born twenty-six years ago. It's been anticipated for some time that he would choose a queen, in the ancient custom of tournament..."

I'd seen his picture a hundred times before—pale, a razor-sharp jawline, close-cropped dark hair. In this picture, he wore a black suit that accentuated his broad shoulders. King Torin had a devilish grin, and one of his black eyebrows arched.

Maybe it was the beer or the heartbreak, but I felt annoyed just looking at him. You could *tell* he loved himself.

Admittedly, it was hard to look away from his picture.

"Cocky bastard," I slurred. Oh, yeah. I was drunk.

Shalini sighed. "I've heard he's very mysterious. He has this whole tragic air about him, and no one knows why."

That didn't make any sense. "What's tragic about being the richest man in the world? Do you know how many bars he could open if he felt like it? Or schools, for that matter? How many college degrees he could get?" I realized I was shouting.

Her eyes slid to the right. "I heard he has a guilty conscience. Supposedly, he's murdered people...but he feels guilty about it. He's all brooding and tortured."

"What a catch! You know, if he were ugly, no one would be charmed by him, right? Being a murderer isn't usually considered a positive trait." I finished my margarita. That had gone fast. "That's the problem with the rich and powerful, isn't it? And the stupidly beautiful. They never learn boundaries or normal empathy, and then the next thing you know, they're *sticking their dicks* in actresses called Ashley." I was vaguely aware that I'd yelled the last bit.

"Forget Andrew, Ava. Think of King Torin's muscular arms. You're fae! Why don't you join the tournament?"

I snorted. "What, me? No. First of all, I wouldn't be allowed. And second of all, I'd miss out on our fun sleepovers and *Tudors* marathons. And I'm going to get into baking. But maybe it could be, like, Tudor-era baking."

She narrowed her eyes. "We've done two *Tudors* marathons already."

"We can do *Virgin Queen*. Whatever." I grinned. "I'll make hot cross buns."

I stared at the screen, watching the video of King Torin shot from a distance. He managed his public persona very carefully—well groomed, finely dressed, never so much as a stray lock of hair on his forehead—but there'd been a breach about a year ago. A picture had emerged from some dark corner of the internet of Torin rising from the ocean waves like a sea god, droplets glistening off his thickly corded muscles. With his sly grin and perfect features, his overall appearance was much like Henry Cavill in *The Tudors* crossed with Poseidon.

I mean, if you were *into* that kind of thing.

The image on the TV screen cut again. Now the video appeared to be a live feed from a helicopter. On the street below, a silver Lamborghini surrounded by a cavalcade of black motorcycles glided through traffic.

"The king and his host have left Faerie to personally notify each of the winners of the contest," explained the announcer. "In the ancient tradition of the tournament."

"Is that Highway 8?" said somebody at the other end of the bar.

"Whoa," said another patron, "they're close."

I glanced to Shalini. She was staring at the TV transfixed, her mouth partway open.

"Holy shit!" someone shouted. "They're getting off at exit 13."

"That's, like, two blocks from here," said Shalini quietly.

What was everyone on about?

Oh, the fae king and his bride spectacle.

I heard Shalini's voice next to me, breathless with excitement. "Have you ever seen King Torin in person?"

"No. I'm sure he's perfectly acceptable looking, but..." I trailed off, as an icy sense of unease spread through my chest.

I lost focus on what she was saying as the table seemed to wobble before me. My mouth felt unpleasantly watery. The margaritas had been a bad idea.

I dropped my head into my hands, and Andrew's

perfect features bloomed in my mind. "We were going to plant apple trees."

"What? What are you talking about?" asked Shalini.

The sound of motorcycles pulled my attention up again. Outside the windows, the first of King Torin's host roared past. The rumble of the engines was like a small airplane taking off, but if the noise bothered the patrons of the Golden Shamrock, you'd never have known it. They pressed their faces to the windows as one, two, three, four motorcycles drove by.

I was shocked to see that it was still light outside because it felt like the middle of the night. Who got this drunk in the daylight?

"Oh, my God!" Shalini's voice cut through the deafening noise. "He just went by—wait, is he *stopping?*" Her voice had become disturbingly high-pitched.

The entire bar had crowded around the glass, their collective breath clouding it, fingers smudging the window.

"Oh, my God!" Shalini said again. "There he is!"

I found myself stumbling off the stool, moving closer to the window to see if I could get a look. I shoved in between the dork who'd wanted a threesome and a woman who smelled like Lysol.

"Oh, wow," said Shalini, completely awestruck. "Oh, wow..."

Slowly, the door of the Lamborghini slid open, and the fae king stepped out. In the late afternoon, his black hair took on a golden sheen. He was tall and well-built, dressed in a dark leather jacket and black pants. He looked like an otherworldly Calvin Klein model, gilded in the sunlight, his tan skin a sharp contrast to the icy blue of his eyes. A faint hint of stubble darkened his square jaw. His hair had grown longer since the last pictures I'd seen of him. No longer close cropped, it was dark and wavy.

With a twinge of embarrassment, I realized I had my nose pressed against the glass, and I was gawping like all the rest.

He surveyed the façade of the Golden Shamrock, his pale blue eyes glinting in the light. What was he doing here? He couldn't be after me since none of the fae knew who I was.

He leaned against the side of the Lamborghini, arms folded. It took me a second to realize he was waiting for the rest of his host to arrive.

King Torin gestured toward the bar, and two of his guards slid off their motorcycles to head inside.

Next to me, Shalini whispered, "Do you think they're coming for you, Ava?"

"No way. There's gotta be another fae woman in here."

I scanned the bar, looking for another fae girl like myself. We weren't usually hard to spot. Our slightly elongated ears and unusual hair colors were typically a dead giveaway, but as far as I could tell, everyone in the bar was human.

One of King Torin's host pushed open the door, a man with long black hair and bronze skin. He was built like a brick house. You could've heard a pin drop.

"The fae king wishes to stop for a drink."

I stifled a giggle. The fae king was probably used to

centuries-old wines from the finest vineyards in Bordeaux. He was in for a treat at the Golden Shamrock, where the only things aged were the food and the clientele.

I was about to tell Shalini this when King Torin stepped into the doorway of the Golden Shamrock, and I felt my jaw drop.

I'd known he was gorgeous, but in person, his beauty hit me like a fist. Sure, I'd seen his face on a thousand gossip magazines. The square jaw, the devilish smile, the glacial blue eyes that seemed to twinkle with a filthy secret. But those left out some of the details I could see up close: the charcoal black eyelashes, the slight dimple in his chin.

Adonis in the flesh? Godlike? Was this some kind of fae magic?

I'd always thought Andrew was a ten. But if Andrew were a ten, I'd have to invent a completely new scale, because he didn't compare to the fae king.

The king's gaze locked on mine, and I stopped breathing entirely as an icy chill ran down my spine. Suddenly, I felt as if frost were spreading from my vertebrae outward.

Shadows seemed to gather around him as he crossed the bar, and the patrons stepped away instinctively. I'd heard he had this effect on people, that his mere presence was enough to bend humans to his will.

The bartender's hand was shaking as he poured King Torin a whiskey.

"King Torin," the humans whispered reverentially. "King Torin."

Some of them knelt. Threesome Steve pressed his forehead to the beer-stained floor.

"Oh, my God!" Shalini wheezed, gripping my arm so hard I knew she was leaving bruises.

Maybe it was because I was fae, or maybe it was the five beers coursing through my small frame, but I wasn't about to fall to my knees. Even if I could feel the power of a High Fae sliding through my bones, demanding reverence, I'd keep standing if it killed me.

Torin accepted his whiskey from the bartender, his eyes boring into mine. As he started to walk closer, the urge to kneel was overpowering.

A muscle twitched in his jaw. "It is expected for the fae to bow to their king." His low, velvety voice stroked over my skin.

I smiled as charmingly as I could. "But I'm not really one of you. You all decided that long ago." The alcohol was masking the fear I should be feeling. "So I live by human rules now. And humans don't have to bow."

Shalini's sharp, painful squeeze on my arm warned me to be quiet.

I winced and held up my hand. "And I don't really like men anymore after I found Ashley on top of Andrew."

Silence filled the room, heavy and thick.

The king's lip quirked. "Who is Ashley?"

I sighed. "She's not really the problem, I guess. The problem is, I'm not bowing to a pretty, rich man. I've had *kinnndaaa* a rough day," I slurred.

He looked me over then, taking in the stains on my

cat sweatshirt and the empty glass I was white-knuckling. "I can see that."

Again, our eyes met. Behind him, the darkness seemed to gather, and the shadows grew closer. A chill swept through my bones, and my teeth started to chatter.

Honor your king. Honor your king. A voice in my head was commanding me to humble myself before him, and fear danced up my spine.

King Torin's brow furrowed slightly, as if he was surprised by my resistance. But hadn't he heard me say I wasn't one of them?

The corner of his mouth twitched. "It's a good thing I'm not here to invite you to compete for my hand. Your lack of respect would be immediately disqualifying."

I looked into his arctic eyes. King Torin had just explicitly rejected me from a contest I had absolutely no desire to join.

"Oh, don't worry, I have no interest in your tournament. I actually think it's kind of embarrassing."

King Torin's eyes widened, and for the first time, an expression resembling actual emotion invaded his perfect features. "Do you know who I am?"

"Oh, yeah, King Torin. I get that you're royal, from the ancient line of Seelie blah blah..." I was vaguely aware that my slurring took some of the sting out of my rant, but the king was quite simply in the wrong place at the wrong time, and he was going to have to hear it. "I don't really know a lot about you or the fae since you all thought I wasn't good enough to be around you. And that's fine. Because there are amazing things here in the mortal world. But I know y'all think you're better than humans. And here's the thing, King." I was ignoring Shalini's fingernails digging into my arm. "All this pageant...pageantry you're doing, it's not really any better than the *dumbest* side of mortal culture. Your bride tournament? I know they're ancient, and they trace back to the old world when we lived in the forests and wore antlers, and we fucked like animals in the oak groves..."

His jaw tensed, and I felt my cheeks flame red. Where had that come from? And what was I saying?

I closed my eyes for a moment, trying to recover my train of thought. "But how is this whole concept different than *Hitched and Stitched?*" I gestured wildly at the screen. "Your life is basically the *nadir* of human civilization. Your bride tournament is even televised these days. It's all fake, isn't it? And you're not really any better than Chad, the pilot with absurdly white teeth on *Hitched and Stitched*. Just pretty, rich douchebags. Anyone who wants to join in this tournament is after two things: fame and power."

Shalini hissed. "Ava, stop talking."

Underneath my drunkenness, I was aware that I was doing something horrifying. "Okay, fame, power, and your...you know." I waved at him. "Your face and abs. Never trust anyone this hot, ladies. Anyway, I will pass on bowing. Have a good night."

The beer had unleashed a river of speech in me, and I couldn't dam it up.

Behind me, the patrons in the Golden Shamrock

stared, eyes wide as dinner plates. The shadows swirling around Torin seemed to thicken into something almost solid, confirming what I'd always known about the fae: they were dangerous. Which was probably why I should have just fallen to my knees and kept my mouth shut.

The king's eyes seemed to grow brighter, and ice filled my veins. I felt frozen and brittle. I couldn't have moved from my seat if I'd wanted to.

King Torin's voice was smooth as silk, and a faint glint of amusement flickered in his eyes. "As you wish. Clearly, you have your whole life together beautifully." His gaze swept down my body again, taking in the grumpy cat sweatshirt. "I wouldn't want to ruin it."

Then, before I could say another word, he turned and left the bar.

For a long moment, the patrons remained unmoving. Then the spell lifted, and the bar burst into a cacophony voices.

"She rejected the fae king!"

"What does *nadir* mean?"

Shalini grabbed my shoulder. "What is *wrong* with you?"

"Fairy tales aren't real, Shalini," I replied, wincing under her touch. "And the fae? They're not the nice creatures you think they are."

❦ 4 ❧

TORIN

It was nearing midnight, both in Faerie and in the mortal city, when I returned to my chambers after a day on the road.

I loosed a breath as I entered my apartments. The walls were forest green accented with gold, the humid air alive with the scent of foxgloves and the sweet fragrance of the apple tree that grew in my room. Moonlight poured over the tree and plants through a skylight. It was as close to a greenhouse as I could get in the castle.

I dropped onto my bed, still clothed.

Today, I'd personally invited one hundred fae women to compete for my hand in marriage. One princess from each noble clan and an additional ninety-four common fae. No commoner had ever actually won the tournament, but inviting them to participate made them feel included and kept their families from rebelling.

Over the next few weeks, these women would

compete for the Seelie Queen throne and the chance to reign next to me as my wife. And that drunk, ranting woman was probably right—what they really wanted was power and fame.

It didn't matter.

Even if I had no desire to marry, a queen on the throne was crucial to keep our magic flowing. It was the only way to protect the kingdom. And more importantly, it would give me the magic I craved.

If I didn't marry, Faerie and all the fae would die. It was as simple as that, and it really didn't matter what I wanted at all.

My eyes were drifting shut when the door creaked open, and a sliver of light from the hall lit up the room.

"Torin?" It was my sister's voice. "Are you awake?"

"Yes, Orla."

"May I come in?"

"Of course."

Orla pushed the door open and slipped into my room. My sister was twenty-three, only three years behind me, but she looked even younger. Slim and wide-eyed, she hardly looked a day over seventeen, especially in her pale satin frock and silk slippers. Her blonde hair rested loosely on her thin shoulders.

She stood by the doorway, gazing in my general direction, awkwardly waiting for me to speak. Orla was blind, her eyes ruined in childhood. When I remained silent, she went first. "How did it go today?"

"I did what I had to do."

Orla's head shifted ever so slightly towards me as

she followed the sound of my voice. "So you didn't have any trouble?"

I sensed my sister knew the answer to this question. Despite, or maybe because of her blindness, she was very perceptive, and I could never lie to her.

"The only trouble I encountered was a drunken common fae who called the tournament embarrassing, on par with the worst of human civilization."

Orla's narrow shoulders stiffened. "I heard about that."

"She had the slovenly appearance of a beggar, the manners of a fishwife. And yet...she's not entirely wrong about the tournament, is she?" Why was I still thinking about her? Possibly because her words had a painful ring of truth in them. "It's not important."

Orla looked less than convinced. "Brother, your reputation is very important. Our enemies need to fear you. If the six clan kings learn the truth—"

"Don't worry," I said quickly. "Everything is under control. I'll have a queen in a month."

"And you're sure you want to do this now?" I could hear the worry in Orla's voice.

I nodded, feeling the great weight of my position. "A king has to sacrifice for his people. The queen's throne has been empty far too long. You know the people are suffering. The winter drags on, there have been reports of malign magic returning to the land. Without a queen on the throne, the magic of the Faerie is fading. Including mine."

"You know, there's another way." Orla's pale eyes seemed to search my face. "I have a proposal from

Prince Narr. I could marry him, and then you could abdicate. Our line would still rule Faerie. I could sit on the throne."

Fear caught at my heart. Orla could never be queen of the Seelie fae. She was blind and sick, sometimes in bed for weeks. For her, the strain of the role would be a death sentence. But I couldn't say that out loud to her.

So I feigned anger instead. "Marry Prince Narr? Absolutely not. As King of the Seelie, it is my duty and my duty alone to defend the kingdom. The tournament will select my wife. The queen's throne will be filled again. Magic will flow once more into the kingdom."

Orla dropped stiffly onto my bed. "But what if you have to marry someone gorgeous, like Moria of the Dearg Due, or Cleena of the Banshees? Etain of the Leannán Sídhe? I've heard no man can resist their charms. If you should slip up and fall in love, if you kill a princess, it will be disastrous for everyone. Torin, a fissure within the clans could start a civil war. The clans weren't always united, you know—"

"I will not fall in love," I said, cutting her off. "My heart is a vise. Whoever wins the tournament will enjoy all the benefits and luxuries of the position, but I won't curse them with my love. She will be the queen of our people." What I didn't say was that Orla was absolutely right. Any woman near me would be in terrible danger if I started to fall for her.

Orla got up from my bed and began to walk slowly to the door. She'd been in my room a thousand times before and knew every inch of the stone floor, but still it made me nervous, watching her move about on her own. I rose, catching her by the elbow.

"Torin, you know I can walk without your help."

"Humor me," I said, giving her arm a gentle squeeze as I led her the rest of the way to the door.

My footman was waiting for her in the marble hallway. "Aeron," I said, "take the princess back to her room. It's quite late."

I shut the door behind her, then turned around to lean against it, breathing in the vernal air. My hands clenched. I hated to admit it, but Orla was right.

I was cursed, and I had been my whole life. If I ever fell in love with my bride, she would die. And it would be my own touch that would kill her—freezing her to the marrow like the bleak landscape around us.

This was my curse.

Cold webs of grief spread through my chest like a winter frost. I'd been in love before, once. By the old temple to Ostara, I'd held Milisandia's frozen body in my arms as my soul split in two.

My fault.

And every time I began to weaken in my resolve, I'd return to that same temple and remember exactly how Milisandia had looked as her body had turned white and blue...

My fingers tightened into fists.

As part of my curse, I could never speak about it to anyone. I hadn't been able to warn her, to tell her to keep away. The words would die on my tongue. Cursed by the same demons, Orla could never speak of it, either. Only the two of us knew one another's secrets, and that knowledge would die with us.

My love—my touch—is death.

I poured myself a glass of scotch and took a long sip. I'd tried to break it off with her, but she'd followed me to the old temple that night. And I could not resist her...

I would never love again. I *could* never love again. I had only one purpose now—one way to redeem myself for the blood on my hands—and that was to save my people.

And not only would it ruin me completely, but it could mean the end of my kingdom.

Princesses might die in the tournaments, yes. This was always a risk. But a dead princess at *my* hands? Slaughtered by the king himself?

The six clans of the Seelie could turn against a murderous king, as they'd done a thousand years ago when King Caerleon lost his head during a time known in Faerie as the Anarchy. Already, enough rumors had spread through the kingdom of the things I'd done to the women I loved.

Rumors not entirely untrue...

If the clans turned against us, it would be the end of a united Faerie. The first king in thousands of years to let it fall apart.

Unless...I chose someone I could never fall in love with.

I closed my eyes. What I needed was a woman willing to make an arrangement and think of it as nothing more. Someone with repellant manners and no sophistication. Someone who loathed me as much as I did her. Someone lowborn with no sense of morality, who could simply be bought...

My eyes snapped open as the most glorious idea came to me.

5

AVA

For me, the worst thing about getting drunk isn't the hangover. It's that I always end up waking at the crack of dawn. Someone once told me it's because when your body metabolizes the alcohol, it resets your sleep cycles. All I know is that it feels like shit.

This morning was no different. I lay on Shalini's couch, staring at the blinking LED clock on her cable box. It read 4:58 a.m. Far too early to be awake.

I closed my eyes, willing myself to go back to sleep. When I opened them again, one minute had passed.

I groaned. *What did I do last night?*

Oh, right. I'd decided that if I got really wasted, I'd forget about Ashley and Andrew. As much as that had seemed like a good idea at the time, I wanted to go back and punch my earlier self in the face.

I pulled out my phone, and my stomach sank as I saw a text from my boss, Bobby:

Ava I'm sorry your off the schedule. We have been gang threads from fans of the faking.

I stared at the text for a minute, trying to figure out what he was trying to say. But Bobby's texts were always like this because he used dictation and never bothered to correct anything. After a few minutes, I understood. They'd been getting threats from fans of the fae king, and I was fired.

I dropped my head into my hands.

No texts from Andrew. No apology or desperate plea for me to return.

I cringed a bit as I flicked to Andrew's Instagram profile. To my horror, he'd already deleted all the artfully framed photographs of me, along with the wistful poetic captions. Instead, he'd posted a new photo of Ashley standing in a field of wildflowers in the golden light of the setting sun. Beneath it, he'd written, *When someone is so beautiful you forget to breathe...*

During the horror of it all yesterday, I hadn't quite realized how gorgeous she was. *Fuck.*

My hands shook as I stared at it. When had he even taken this photo? We'd only broken up last night.

I rolled over, hoping to get to sleep by hiding my face in the couch cushions. I knew this sofa pulled out into a bed since I'd stayed here before, but I'd failed to manage it last night. I had pulled a blanket on myself, though.

It worked for a few minutes until my stomach twisted and hit me with a nasty wave of nausea. I wasn't sure if that was the alcohol or my life falling apart. Likely both.

I sat up, hoping that a more upright position might settle my stomach. As I did, more memories of last night slowly filtered into my brain.

Five pints of Guinness, the margarita pitcher, a karaoke rendition of "I Will Survive," and I was pretty sure someone had kissed Threesome Steve. And I had the disturbing feeling that someone might have been me.

So many bad decisions.

Still, nothing was as horrifying as the memory of my conversation with King Torin. Had I really said the most powerful fae in the world was nothing more than a pretty, rich douchebag? That he was a fae Chad from *Hitched and Stitched*?

My stomach churned again, and I rose to stumble to Shalini's bathroom. I hunched over her clean, white toilet, my mouth watery. When nothing came up, I stood and rinsed my face in the sink. I looked up at myself—the tangled mess of hair, circles under my eyes, my skin strangely pale.

At 5:03 a.m., I wandered back into Shalini's neatly decorated living room. A box of donuts had been left out on the kitchen island, but the sight of them turned my stomach.

It was clear. Between my throbbing head, twisting stomach, and the horrible memories of last night, I wasn't about to fall asleep anytime soon.

I crossed to Shalini's bedroom and peeked in. She slept under her comforter, her dark hair spread out on the pillow. Passed out, sound asleep.

Rubbing my eyes, I tiptoed back into the living

room. I couldn't find the remote for the TV, and my cell phone was completely dead. I blinked at the sunlight that was already slanting in through the blinds. The hazy mist of memories of last night left me feeling jittery.

Maybe it was time to find a coffee shop, get some fresh air, head home—

Oh, right. I didn't have a home anymore. I turned, surveying the living room, where everything was in its right place, beautifully decorated in shades of caramel and cream.

Everything except my gym bag, which lay on the floor by the end of the couch. I smiled. Seems Drunk Ava actually made a good decision. Maybe I could sweat out the alcohol. Before I met Andrew, I used to have months at a time of depression that would leave me drained of energy, lying in bed, unwashed and barely eating. I didn't want to let myself slide down into that darkness again. And whenever the clouds had started to lift, it was always moving around outside—running, eventually—that had brought me back to life.

Picking up the duffle, I returned to the bathroom and changed into my running clothes. Then, as quietly as I could, I stuffed Shalini's extra set of keys into my pocket and slipped out into the fresh air.

I hurried downstairs, past a row of mailboxes and into a small courtyard. Even in my abysmally hungover state, I had to admit it was an absolutely glorious morning. Not too hot, a pearly pink dawn sky, nearly cloudless. In the grass of the courtyard, a robin hunted for worms. *Focus on the positive, Ava.* I was alive, and it was a perfect day for a run.

And I wouldn't let myself fall into a major depression over some dickhead.

It was only when I'd nearly reached the gate to the street that I noticed a white van with CTY-TV emblazoned on its side in blue letters. As I realized what it was, a bright-eyed man with a microphone clutched in his fist jumped in front of me.

It was the reporter I'd seen on TV the night before. Oh, *fuck*.

"Ms. Jones," he said briskly. "I'd like to ask you a few questions."

I shook my head. "Don't you need consent or something for this? I do not consent."

The reporter acted like he hadn't heard me. "Were you at the Golden Shamrock last night?"

"Maybe?" I tried to slip by him, but he blocked my way. Behind him, a woman had appeared with a large TV camera balanced on her shoulder.

Am I on TV?

"Are you an employee of the Red Stone Cocktail Bar in the South End?"

I felt queasy, and not just because I was hung over. They'd already found out where I worked. What else did they know about me? I pushed past the reporter and tried to run toward the gate, but the camerawoman stepped in front of me.

"Ms. Jones." The reporter was trying to sound pleasant and genial, even as his colleague boxed me in. "Can you tell us about what you said to the fae king?"

Maybe if it weren't five a.m., and they hadn't been trying to corner me, I would have tried to think of a good response. But at that moment, my head was still full of cotton, and I couldn't come up with a single coherent thing.

"I-I'm sorry," I stammered. "I really don't have time to talk to you right now."

The camerawoman didn't budge from the gate, and the reporter stood next to her now. Again, he thrust the microphone in my face. "Is it true you insulted the fae king? With words that we can't play live on TV?"

"I was actually just about to go for a jog." In the back of my mind, horror was dawning that Ashley and Andrew would be watching this. A drunken public meltdown, relived in every household in America. I closed my eyes, wishing the earth would swallow me up.

The TV announcer held up his cell phone so I could see the screen. "Is this you?"

Before I could reply, the video began to play. Even though it was low quality, I immediately recognized the interior of the Golden Shamrock.

"It is expected for the fae to bow to their king." Torin's velvety voice played through the phone, and without the haze of cheap beer, I felt the heavy weight of his voice settle over me.

I stared at the phone as I hurled insults at him, rambling about *Hitched and Stitched*. Worse, the angle on me was deeply unflattering. I was disheveled, red-faced, slurring my words. Sweating. In the video, my eyes were half-lidded, my hair already a mess. The red stains on the sweatshirt gleamed under the bar's warm lights.

"That *is* you, right?" I heard the reporter, but my fight or flight response had kicked in, and he sounded like he was speaking from a distance.

What was the best way to handle this?

Running away.

Ducking past him, I pushed the camerawoman out of the way and practically dove through the gate of the apartment complex. I spun right. I'd expected to sprint away down the sidewalk, but another TV crew was setting up there.

Oh, crap.

Someone shouted my name, and I spun around again, ready to take off in the opposite direction. Already, the first reporter and camerawoman were blocking my path. In hindsight, I probably should have tried to run back into Shalini's apartment, but my thoughts were a blur of confusion. I eyed a gap between the end of the CTY-TV van and the car in front of it, trying to rush through.

My first thought had been to cross the street, but as soon as I stepped into the road, a car horn blared. A giant SUV was barreling towards me. In one terrifying second, I realized I was about to get hit.

Everything seemed to move in slow motion. The black shape of the SUV, the screeching tires, the horrified eyes of the driver. This was *it* for me.

In a fraction of a heartbeat, my life flashed before my eyes. The dark, early years I couldn't remember except for a cold sense of fear. Then the face of my mom came into focus—Chloe's kind smile as she baked me a carrot cake. Fragments of our happiest days together flickered before me: Christmases, birthdays, the time we'd visited Disney World. Her excitement when I finished my bartending course and got hired at one of the best bars in the city...

The memories turned darker.

There'd been the call in the middle of the night—the one everyone dreads. A doctor telling me she'd had a heart attack, that she hadn't made it.

A sharp crack like a gunshot refocused me.

A glass pillar burst from the concrete, and the SUV slammed into it.

In the next moment, another pillar burst from the pavement beneath the news van. The van lurched sideways, then flipped onto its side. I stared, trying to understand what I was seeing.

No, not glass pillars. Ice. My jaw sagged. This certainly hadn't been the relaxing jog I'd been anticipating.

What the hell was going on?

A powerful arm wrapped around my waist and pulled me toward the sidewalk.

"Ava, that was awfully foolish." The smooth, deep tone of King Torin's voice skimmed over my skin from behind me.

I turned to look up at his ice blue eyes, but he wasn't moving away from me. His hand was still on my waist, as if I might run into the street again just for kicks. "What are you doing here?"

His lips quirked in a half-smile. "Keeping you from dying, apparently."

"I was just about to dive out of the way. These

reporters were hounding me because apparently, it's a huge news story if someone is vaguely insulting to you."

His blue eyes blazed with an icy light. "Vaguely?"

A camera lens glinted in the sun behind him.

"The TV people. They're behind you."

"Hmm." Shadows gathered about him, cold on my skin. Torin was shielding me from the view of the cameras. As the reporter called his name, his shadowy magic thickened like heavy fog, swallowing the light and the heat around us.

The reporter's voice faltered. "My sincerest apologies..."

King Torin didn't bother to face him. His eyes were locked on me as he issued a command from over his shoulder. "Destroy the camera."

Through the dark mist, I watched over Torin's shoulder as the anchor grabbed the TV camera from his assistant and threw it on the ground. It shattered on the pavement. I winced. That couldn't have been cheap.

"Can you tell me what's happening?" I whispered.

"I'm getting rid of any witnesses. Today's news is already bad enough without video of you trying to throw yourself in front of an SUV."

King Torin's eyes still pierced me. Behind him, the camerawoman and reporter were stomping the camera into bits.

"How did you get them to do that?"

He arched an eyebrow. "You don't know what glamour is?"

"Should I?"

"Yes."

I jabbed a finger at his chest, which was like pressing a brick wall. "If you people wanted me to know things about the fae, maybe you shouldn't have exiled me. And by the way, I got fired because of you."

"Because of me?"

"Your crazed fans were threatening my boss."

"How is that my fault?" He cocked his head, curiosity glinting in his pale eyes. "We're getting sidetracked. Do you know anything about magic at all?"

His powerful body exuded a menacing chill, and I took a step back from him, breath clouding around my head. "Nope. Why would I? I don't even remember Faerie."

Torin's features softened almost imperceptibly. "Glamour," he said quietly, "is a special kind of magic we use to influence humans and a few weak-minded fae. It allows us to help them forget things."

"Like mind control?"

"Not exactly. More like a powerful suggestion." He turned to face the TV crew, and the icy miasma around him started to thin. The reporter and camerawoman stood among the shattered remains of the camera, their eyes glazed.

The corner of the king's mouth curved. "If they truly loved their job, my magic wouldn't work. They'd want to protect the camera. Instead, the glamour helps ease them past their inhibitions. Encourages them to indulge in their darkest desires. They wanted to destroy it."

I swallowed hard. "How do I know you're not glamouring me right now?"

Torin turned the full force of his arctic gaze on me, and curiosity burned in his expression. "Why? Are you thinking about indulging your dark desires?"

Given how he looked, it was no mystery why he might think that. But I didn't want him any more than I'd wanted the donuts. "No. It's just that power seems ripe for abuse."

"You're certainly primed to think the worst of people, aren't you?" King Torin's eyes narrowed. "Trust me when I tell you that any fae who misuses their glamour is dealt with very harshly. It's what allowed us to remain hidden from the human world for so many years. But we don't see any reason to cause unnecessary problems with the humans by overusing it."

The reporter and the camerawoman stared at each other like they'd just met.

"I'm Dave," said the reporter, smiling faintly.

She blushed. "Barbara."

King Torin caught my arm, pulling me away from them. "I need to speak to you about marriage."

"You *what*? I just rewatched the video of last night. I told you I don't want any part of your tournament, and you said I'd be disqualified even if I did."

Torin's eyes flashed with icy light. "That's exactly it. I don't want to get married, either."

I blinked. "So why are you here?"

"We need to go somewhere more private."

Even if I hated his arrogance, how could I say no to King Torin? I didn't get the sense he was going to take no for an answer. And he had just saved me, I supposed.

"Okay. We can use my friend Shalini's place."

"Take me there."

I wanted to say that I wasn't his subject, and he should stop using that commanding voice with me. But instead, I started guiding him to Shalini's apartment building. When I turned to look back at the reporters, I saw them making out next to their overturned van. Broken glass glittered around them.

A shiver of fear ran over me. Torin's magic seemed very dangerous, indeed.

6

AVA

I led King Torin up the stairs to Shalini's apartment. It felt strange being so close to him. With his lean, muscular build, his piercing eyes, and cut-glass jawline, it was hard not to stare. King Torin was in a whole other category of masculine beauty, of icy eyes and sun-kissed skin. Fae beauty could be otherworldly, almost dizzying in its power, and he seemed to embody that perfectly.

If I hadn't just had my heart ripped out and incinerated, it might have had some kind of effect on me.

Instead, he only irritated me with his absurd confidence. There was no caution, no hesitation when he spoke. He stated his thoughts and expected to be obeyed. He moved with a calculated grace.

When I reached Shalini's door, I glanced at him. His eyes glinted in the gloom of the stairwell, and I felt my muscles tighten. My breath caught, and I hesitated, my body unwilling to slide the key into the lock.

It took me a few moments to put my finger on the

sensation. Last time I'd visited the zoo, I'd stopped by the tiger exhibit. The massive beast had been out, pacing the perimeter of its cage. When I'd made eye contact, the creature had looked right back at me, sending a sharp sliver of fear through my bones. The look wasn't hungry, but it was clear nevertheless: the tiger wouldn't hesitate to rip my throat out if it wanted.

I got the same feeling when I made eye contact with King Torin. The hairs on the back of my arms rose.

Hadn't Shalini said he'd murdered someone? Frankly, it wasn't hard to believe.

"Something the matter?" he purred.

I turned from him, jammed my key into the lock, and opened the door. Torin walked in first, like he owned the place.

I quietly closed the door behind him, my heart racing, and turned to face him. "King Torin? Sorry, how am I supposed to address you?"

The fae king's eyes flashed. "Torin is fine."

"All right, Torin. This is my friend Shalini's apartment. She's asleep in the other room, so we're going to need to be quiet. What exactly is it you want to tell me?"

King Torin paused, scrubbing a hand over the faint stubble on his jaw. For the first time since I'd met him, he seemed hesitant. When he spoke, his voice was quiet, barely more than a whisper. "Faerie is dying."

"What?" This was absolutely the last thing I expected to hear.

I'd thought King Torin and his fae host were immensely powerful. They'd crushed all human opposition in our realm. It was said that within the land of Faerie, King Torin wielded the power of a god. And that was basically how it had looked when he'd summoned pillars of ice from the road.

He frowned, staring at the window. "When a Seelie king sits on the fae throne, he draws upon the magic of the realm to defend the kingdom and conquer new lands. The queen, on the other hand, replenishes that magic. Her magic is vernal, bringing growth and fertility. It will take months to fully return magic to our realm, and after that, we'll need a queen to sit on the throne occasionally."

"So, you need someone else's magic to replenish your own? You're running out of power?"

"Yes." His eyes met mine. "Twenty-three years ago, my mother died. She was the last queen of Faerie. Since then, I've been drawing upon the magic of the realm. I've had to fight the humans and keep the rest of the Seelie clans in line. I've drained a great deal of magic from the kingdom. And now, a cold winter had descended upon the land. Only a queen on the throne can replenish our magic and bring back the spring. And that's where you come in."

I sighed. "Okay. So, you want me to be your wife so your kingdom can drain my magic? Don't be offended, but I'm going to pass on this offer. Why don't you ask one of the many fae women who actually want to do this? There are plenty of them clamoring for the chance."

"I don't want you to be my wife, either," said King

Torin. "That's the whole plan. That's why you're so perfect."

I blinked. "Sorry, what?"

"You'll just need to marry me for a few months. Not for very long. And you wouldn't need to consummate anything. Just sit on the queen's throne and channel your power. Replenish Faerie's magic. Help me save the kingdom. Once things are back to normal, we'll get divorced. And you can go back to"—he surveyed the small living room—"this place. And it can all be over without any messy emotions getting in the way because we don't like each other. At all."

He paused, crossing his arms over his chest like he'd just delivered the deal of a lifetime.

I stared at the king. "Why would I do this? You want me to become your wife, then divorce you a few months later. Can you imagine the impact that would have on my life? I hate being the center of attention, and I'd be all over the news as 'a gold-digger common fae.' Just that ten minutes outside was one of the worst experiences of my life. And after I left Faerie? I'd be all over the tabloids. I don't need this. I have a mess of my own here I need to sort out, Torin. I need to find a way to get my own place. Normal things like rent that you probably don't even know about. Can't you just find someone you actually love?"

For a moment, I thought I saw him wince. Then his expression became unreadable again. "I was planning on paying you handsomely for your role. Thirty million dollars to cover your time and any potential future issues. You'd be set up for life. You can choose to stay in

Faerie, with the understanding that it will not be a real marriage. I should probably add that there is a good chance you could die during the tournaments."

I froze, my eyes widening. "Thirty...sorry I thought you said...did you say thirty million?" As soon as the words were out of my mouth, it occurred to me that I was a terrible negotiator. If he was willing to throw thirty million at me, how high could I get him to go?

I rested my hand on my hip. "I won't have my good name dragged through the mud. And you did mention that I could die."

He snorted. "Your good name? Your meltdown is all over mortal social media. How could it possibly be any worse?"

I closed my eyes, trying not to imagine what the memes were like. Shivers of horror crawled over my body at the thought of everyone sharing the video. Sounds of me slurring about Chad from *Hitched and Stitched* trending on TikTok...

It almost made the idea of running away to Faerie sound appealing.

"Fifty million," I said.

"Fine. Fifty million—if you win. I will do my best to keep you alive."

"How dangerous are we talking, exactly?"

"The tournaments always end in a fencing match, and it has been known to get bloody. But I will help you train."

I let out a long, slow breath. "Besides bartending, fencing is the one thing I'm actually good at." I bit my lip. "But what are the chances I'll win?"

"Assuming you survive, almost certain, since I'm the one who chooses the bride. We just need to make sure it seems believable that I'd choose you, which won't exactly be easy after..."

"The drunken meltdown, yes."

"You must avoid making another public spectacle of yourself in Faerie. My cursory research tells me that until last night, I didn't see any other evidence of public disgrace or scandal. Do you think you can conduct yourself with a modicum of decorum? I'm not expecting much, but my marriage to you has to be at least *somewhat* believable. And the idea of marrying a low-born common fae with a slovenly appearance and a drinking problem already stretches the bounds of credulity."

His insults were sliding right off me now because...*fifty million?* I could probably *buy* my own privacy. I could buy people to compliment me. I could get takeout curry every night. It was a dizzying amount of money; I almost couldn't comprehend what I'd do with it.

I opened my eyes again to find that King Torin had fallen silent and was staring at me. An icy fire danced in his eyes. I sensed that he was studying me. Not in a sexual way, but rather that he was finally taking me in as a person. Assessing my running outfit. The dark circles under my eyes. The rat's nest of my hair. Assessing weaknesses.

"Who are your parents?" he said at last.

"My mother's name was Chloe Jones."

"Not her." He leaned closer. "Who was your biological mother? Your true family?"

A heavy weariness pressed down on me, and I wanted to flop onto the sofa again. A buried memory from my childhood clawed at the hollow recesses of my mind: me, standing before the portal, clutching a Micky Mouse backpack, sobbing uncontrollably because they wouldn't let me in.

"I honestly have no idea. I tried to go back into Faerie one day, but they wouldn't allow me."

He cocked his head. "Why were you trying to get in? Did the human woman mistreat you?"

I felt instantly defensive at his question, and also annoyed he referred to her as *the human woman*. "No. My mother was amazing. But the kids at school thought I was a freak with weird ears and ridiculous blue hair, and they weren't kind. They tied me to a fence post once, like a dog leashed outside a café. I just wanted to see other people like me."

A dark look slid across his eyes. "Well, now you will. If you agree to my proposal, I will help you find your fae family."

"I'm sure they're dead. Why would they let me get kicked out if they weren't?"

But my mind was already made up. Because what kind of moron would turn down fifty million dollars?

Especially someone homeless and unemployable, which was my current situation. With fifty million dollars, I could open an entire chain of bars—if I even decided to work again.

And the truth was, even if they were dead, I was desperate to know more about my birth parents. What exactly had happened to them? Fae almost always lived longer than humans. What were the chances they'd *both* died young?

I took a deep breath. "All right, I'm in. But we should sign some kind of contract."

He reached into his back pocket and pulled out a form. I watched as he held it against the wall and crossed a few things out, then signed his name in an elegant calligraphy at the bottom.

He handed me the form, and I scanned it.

Generally, when given paperwork, my eyes just sort of glaze over, and the words seem to blur. Then I assume everything is fine, and I scribble my signature. But this was too important to half-ass, so I forced myself to focus. He'd added in the amount I'd be paid and initialed next to it. There was a clause about secrecy, and a stipulation that I'd forfeit the money if I told any other fae about my role. And if I lost the tournament, I got nothing.

I licked my lips, realizing there might be no point to a contract with the most powerful person in the world. "Who, exactly, would enforce this?"

Surprise flickered over his features. "If a fae king breaks a contract, he will grow sick and die. I can't break it. Only you can."

"Right. Okay. I guess that's binding, then." I signed it, then handed it over to him.

"Are you ready?" he asked. "It starts soon."

"*Now?* I haven't even showered."

He scrubbed a hand over his jaw. "Unfortunately, there is no time. But we'll try to make you presentable in Faerie."

"I volunteer as tribute!" Shalini stood in the doorway of her bedroom wearing a hot pink bathrobe. "Take me to Faerie. I'll be a contestant."

Torin exhaled sharply. "You're not fae. And Ava has already agreed."

"Don't some of the women have advisors?" asked Shalini. "Someone as counsel? In Ava's case, someone to stop her from any more outrageous drunken episodes?"

I should have asked about an advisor, but I was so caught off guard, I stammered, "Shalini, what are you doing?"

"Helping you." She beamed. "I'm not letting you go alone. Who knows what these people are like in their own realm? I heard him say it's dangerous."

Torin shrugged. "So is your world."

Of course—Shalini was desperate for adventure.

Torin turned, already heading for the door. "I don't really have time to argue about this, but maybe it's not the worst idea. You may need emotional support to keep you from falling off the rails and someone to help negotiate any duels. Let's go. Now."

I felt my stomach drop.

Duels. Neat.

But if anything could take my mind off the crushing heartbreak of last night, maybe it was a looming threat of death.

King Torin insisted I didn't have time to shower. But no doubt, all of Faerie had seen the video of me covered in food and beer, and I supposed their impressions of me could only go up from there. I grabbed my gym bag and followed Torin out of the apartment.

As we went down the stairs, Shalini gripped my arm, whispering, "Ava, I'll be one of the first humans to ever go to Faerie. This is so much better than a cruise."

My pounding hangover added an extra layer of surreal to the situation. I bit my lip, trying to think clearly. This *was* the right decision, right? Really, it didn't feel like I had much of a choice. A broke person doesn't turn down fifty million.

When we stepped outside, the sunlight burned my eyes. The reporters had left the shattered camera and overturned van behind, and police sirens blared in the distance—no doubt on their way here. I realized I was shaking as I walked along the pavement. Maybe I should eat something?

"Do you think you'll get to learn magic?" Shalini asked.

"Common fae can't conduct magic," I said. "I mean, I guess the throne can suck some kind of queen energy from me, but I can't do magic on my own."

"How do you know you're a common fae? What if you're the long-lost daughter of the High Fae king?"

My nose wrinkled. "Then this marriage would be very awkward because Torin would be my brother. And I know I'm not High Fae because they'd never let one of us go missing. A common fae they could easily kick out into the human world."

Instead of his Lamborghini, Torin led us to a gray Hummer. Flashing us a big smile, he opened the doors for us. For a moment, I imagined that he was actually heroic and honorable, and that he hadn't just bribed a woman he hated.

Not that I was really in a position to be on my high horse, considering I was gladly taking the bribe.

I slid into the front seat, my gaze roaming over the fine leather upholstery. I ran my fingers across it, dizzy with the thought that I'd be able to buy something like this. Assuming he fulfilled his end of the bargain.

Torin slid into the driver's seat. I'd hardly buckled my seatbelt when he turned the key and leaned on the accelerator. Nausea climbed up my throat as we started to speed down the road.

Of all the days to get an invitation into Faerie...

I swallowed hard, still trying to come to grips with

what was happening. "What exactly does this tournament entail?"

Shalini leaned forward. "May I answer? I've been following this for months."

"Please," said Torin.

"Okay. There are a hundred women—"

"A hundred and one in this case," Torin interrupted.

"Right, and they all have to compete for Torin's hand. This has been a tradition for thousands of years at this point. So, there are several different competitions. After every competition, some of the competitors are forced to leave. And this year, for the first time, it will all be televised."

I frowned, trying not to imagine all the people who'd be scrutinizing me through their living rooms.

Outside the Hummer's windows, the world whipped by as we turned onto the highway.

At the bar, he'd been surrounded by his host, with a helicopter following overhead, filming the whole thing. Now, I saw only the usual morning traffic. I had a very strong suspicion that Torin had made this visit in secret.

The Hummer's motor growled as he pressed the accelerator to the floor, my stomach lurching as he wove in and out of the traffic.

My mouth felt dry and watery at the same time. Glancing at Shalini, her expression told me she felt similarly queasy.

I gripped the door handle. "Torin, do you need to go this fast?"

"Yes."

"Would it make a difference if I said this kind of

wild driving was a breach of decorum?" I asked in desperation.

"Not at this moment, no."

The car was like a rocket now, barreling over the asphalt. Outside, the buildings whipped by in a gray blur. What was his problem?

"Torin!" I shouted. "You're going to get us killed!"

Shalini grabbed my shoulder. "Look!"

I followed the path of her outstretched finger. Outside, the blur of concrete faded, the expanse paling. Torin began to slow the Hummer, and the exterior came into focus.

We were no longer on Highway 8. Rather, we were driving down a narrow lane in what looked like the sixteenth century. Thatched timber-frame houses stood clustered by one side of the road. On the other, the sun shone brightly on fields thick with snow until we passed through a small copse of trees. Smoke drifted from chimneys into a frosty sky.

My breath caught with an uncanny sense of having seen this place in a dream.

"Oh, my God," Shalini breathed. "Ava."

Around us, the Hummer itself began to transform, making my head swim with dizziness. The seat belts disappeared, and I found myself sitting on velvet across from Shalini. White curtains had appeared in the windows. When I turned to look in the front, I caught a glimpse of Torin from behind, holding the reins of half a dozen horses.

I gripped the side of the carriage, trying to get my

bearings. We were traveling in a horse-drawn carriage, and I had a hangover from hell.

Shalini's eyes looked glazed. "This is real, isn't it?"

"I think so," I whispered.

"This is the most exciting thing that has ever happened to me," she murmured.

WE RODE THROUGH FAERIE'S WINTERY LANDSCAPE, passing icy hamlets with steep-peaked houses that cluttered the road, and shops with warmly lit windows. The carriage rolled past forests and frozen fields. Smoke rose from distant chimneys, and snowflakes sparkled in the air.

But that dark cloud of sadness was starting to settle over me, and when I closed my eyes, I was back at home, wrapped up in Andrew's arms. My chest felt like it was cleaving in two.

Sighing, I closed my eyes, thinking of some of the beautiful photos I'd taken of Andrew, photos I couldn't see right now. Andrew, lying down in bed. Golden skin, his hands folded behind his head, he smiled up at me. I'd always loved that picture.

There was the image Shalini had taken of us at a party... I remembered that night. He told me I looked gorgeous, that every other guy there would be jealous. And yet, in between those nights, he was snapping photos of Ashley in fields of red flowers... Loneliness was splitting me open, and a wave of tiredness crashed down on me. I wanted to curl up in bed, pull the covers over myself, and never leave.

Shalini glared at me. "No."

"No, what?"

"I'm not having you mope over this loser when we're in Faerie." Her jaw was set tight, and she pointed at the glass. "Look out the window, Ava. You're missing it. And he's not worth it." Shalini's breath clouded the glass as she looked outside. "I mean, I'd always heard it was amazing, but I never expected it to look this beautiful."

The thing about heartbreak was that I knew how to cover it up so I didn't bring everyone down with me. I plastered a smile on my face and stared outside. "It really is amazing. We're so lucky to be here."

Shalini leaned in, whispering, "I overheard what Torin said...about Faerie dying? It seems hard to believe."

My chest felt tight. "I guess that with a queen on the throne, the snow will melt, and spring will return once more." I shrugged. "And then I return to the human world, where I will get takeout every night and cappuccinos in the morning."

She stared at me, frowning. "Fifty million dollars, and the best thing you can think of is takeout and coffee?"

"It's gotten very expensive. Anyway, I don't really know what to do with all that money."

"Darling, you're going on a vacation. The Maldives, or—"

Shalini stopped short as the carriage began to slow. We'd turned off the lane onto a private drive. Enormous trees loomed on either side, and their dark trunks towered far above us.

Between the trunks, I could just make out vast snow-covered fields and the white-capped peaks of a distant mountain range. I hugged myself, teeth chattering in the cold. I'd dressed in running gear appropriate for seventy-degree weather, and the chill bit at my skin.

When I turned to look out the front, my breath caught at the sight of a castle on a hill. The place seemed to exude a malign presence—formed of dark stone and sharply peaked towers, with gothic windows that glittered under the winter sun. My breath misted around my head as I stared at it. Had I seen this place before?

We rolled closer, and my heart started beating faster. Was it possible the king was actually bringing me here for a public execution for the crime of insolence? Treason? The castle loomed over us as we approached.

We pulled up slowly, gravel crunching under the carriage wheels. One of the horses whinnied as we finally came to a stop. Outside my window, fae guards in immaculate white uniforms approached. One of them hurried to the door.

As the footmen opened the door for us, his eyes widened with surprise—likely because I was showing up to a gothic castle in a wintry kingdom dressed in a tank top and running shorts, with the hairstyle of someone who'd given up on life long ago.

The frigid air slid down to my bones when I stepped outside.

Shalini wasn't dressed any better in a baggy T-shirt, a pair of men's boxer shorts, and sandals with socks. Still, her smile was gorgeous enough to pull attention away from her attire.

"Miss?" the footman said.

"Ava," I said quickly. "Ava Jones."

"All right, Ms. Jones. I can help you down."

I took his hand, feeling unnecessarily awkward, since I was in sneakers and didn't really need the help.

As I stepped down, I caught sight of King Torin. The magic of this place had changed his outfit, too. Now, he was dressed like some sort of medieval warrior in black leather armor studded with metal. A dark cloak hung over his shoulders, and there was a rapier at his waist with an obsidian hilt.

He did not look anything like Chad from *Hitched and Stitched* right now. He looked like some sort of warrior god, more intimidating than ever. Hard not to think of him bluntly telling me that he didn't like me at all.

When his preternaturally bright eyes met mine, gleaming like a deadly blade, a shiver ran through me. I hugged myself as I shivered in the icy wind. This had seemed like a great idea an hour ago, but now I felt completely vulnerable.

I wrenched my eyes away from him, forcing myself to take in my surroundings. A large stone awning stretched over head—a porte cochère, I was pretty sure it was called, though I had no idea how to actually pronounce it. Gargoyles leered from above.

"We wait here," he commanded. "I need to speak to someone about your addition to the tournament."

Footmen lined the wide castle steps, which led to a pair of wooden doors inset with dark metal spikes. With a groan, they swung open to reveal a hall of stunning stonework. Pointed arches soared above us, and candles flickered in high iron chandeliers. Skilled stonemasons had carved wicked-looking creatures beneath the arches—demons and dragons hewn from the rock in such a way that in the dancing candlelight, they almost seemed to be moving. But the most unsettling thing in this place was a set of ivory stag antlers jutting above the entryway, gleaming with ice. I couldn't explain why, but as soon as my eyes landed on them, a sense of dread slid over me. Somewhere in the recesses of my mind, I knew the castle didn't want me here.

Here, I was an abomination. I tugged my gaze away, wondering if that was the hangover speaking.

It wasn't, though, was it? I *really* didn't belong here, and I had the most desperate desire to run back outside. I felt as if the castle wanted to expel me, to eject a poison from its veins.

Shalini was clutching my arm, and I found myself clutching hers right back.

We'd hardly moved at all into the hall, even if the wintry wind stung our skin in the entryway.

"Ava," she whispered, "did we make a bad decision?"

"Fifty million," I whispered back.

The sound of gravel crunching made me turn my head.

A carriage was now rolling over the frozen stone. This carriage was entirely gilded, from the rims of the wheels to the bridles of the horses. A driver perched in the front, dressed in immaculate black wool. He hopped down and began shooing away King Torin's footmen.

Still gripping my arm, Shalini exhaled sharply. "I think it's one of the princesses."

I had the disturbing feeling that I was about to feel *a lot* more out of place.

We stared as the driver placed a gold step by the carriage door. Slowly, the door opened, and an elegant leg extended into the winter air. The foot, shod in a pearly white shoe, had nearly reached the step when it stopped.

A woman's voice spoke sharply. "Too far."

"I'm sorry, madam," said the driver quickly.

I winced as his knees crunched audibly in the gravel as he knelt to push the step closer. With the gilt step repositioned, he stood, and the woman's leg extended again. This time, she took his hand and allowed him to guide her down.

The first thing I noticed about her was the dress—a dark swirl of satin and silk that moved like smoke. Not pure black, I realized as she straightened. It shimmered with dark silver and deep red.

When she caught my gaze, I drew in an involuntary breath. I'd never seen a woman like her before. Her hands and forearms were sheathed in silk gloves, but her upper arms and chest were an otherworldly porcelain white. In contrast with her pale skin, she'd painted her lips a deep red. But nothing compared to her hair. It hung down to her shoulders in thick waves, a deep burgundy, the color of a bruised rose petal.

Torin said he'd chosen me because I was someone

he could never love, a "lowborn common fae with a slovenly appearance." And *this* woman, I imagined, was just the kind of woman he *could* love. Shockingly gorgeous, and with an apparent penchant for ordering people around. Two peas in a pod.

Her plum eyes swept over me, and I turned to see King Torin stalking closer. His dark cloak trailed behind him as the icy wind swept in.

She lowered her chin. "Your Royal Highness. I didn't expect to see you until later this evening."

"Welcome to my castle, Princess Moria." King Torin's deep voice echoed off the stone.

"Oh, there's no need for formality," Moria laughed. "I believe we're on a first-name basis."

King Torin arched an eyebrow. "Is everything in order, Princess?"

"Oh, yes," said Moria lightly. "It just took a little while to get here. You know how things can be, packing up. My help simply can't do anything on their own."

Really, a perfect match for him. But then, if he chose her, he'd have the distasteful problem of a messy emotional entanglement. Couldn't have that.

Princess Moria's eyes moved on from the king. I expected her to look at me, but instead, her gaze latched firmly onto Shalini. She stopped speaking, and her nose wrinkled like she'd just sniffed a fresh pile of dog shit. "Oh! How open-minded of you to allow humans into Faerie. Things really have changed, haven't they?" Her gaze swept down my body.

"She's not the only one," said King Torin. "We have

a few with the news organizations to film the competitions."

Moria's eyebrows rose. "She's a reporter?"

"She is my counsel," I said with a smile. "My advisor."

Finally, Princess Moria's gaze moved to me, and an involuntary shiver ran down my spine. Her eyes were a plum color, like venous blood. They narrowed as she assessed me. Her gaze swept down, and a look of horror crossed her features as she took in my appearance.

"Your advisor?" she said, not bothering to hide the incredulity in her voice. "You're competing in the tournament?"

"I am."

She laughed again, trying to make it sound light, but I could hear the strain in her voice. "Most open-minded, indeed. And to offer her your carriage, King Torin, when such an unfortunate creature could not afford her own. I admire your generosity to those in need."

Ouch.

"Princess Moria." King Torin bowed slightly. "The opening ceremonies are to begin in twenty minutes."

If Moria sensed she was being brushed off, she didn't let on. "Of course, Your Highness. I look forward to spending time in your company once again."

❈ 8 ❈
AVA

Moria veritably glided into the castle, and King Torin turned back to Shalini and me. "We don't have much time," he said. "The opening ceremonies of the tournament begin in an hour."

I shook my head "It's just after six a.m."

His hand rested on the hilt of his sword like he might need to slaughter two poorly dressed interlopers at any moment. "In Faerie, time moves differently than in the human realm. It is supper here now. All of the competitors have been waiting for nearly an hour, and you'll need to look—"

"Less slovenly and common?"

He nodded. "Exactly."

I'd been sort of joking, but Torin was not.

He turned, catching the eye of one of the footmen outside. "Aeron, bring these ladies to see Madam Sioba."

Without another word, he stalked off, his cloak billowing behind him.

I looked to Shalini, and she shrugged as the footman gestured for us to follow after the king.

The footman walked in front of us, his boots echoing on the flagstones as he led us deeper into the hall, until we reached a doorway with a set of stairs that curved upward. We climbed the stairs, the darkness illuminated by warm candlelight.

Even the footman was beautiful, his body broad and muscular, his hair dark blond, wavy, and slightly wild. When he glanced back at us, I caught sight of his eyes. They were an otherworldly shade of gold.

Shalini smacked my arm, then nodded at the footman. She grinned at me, and I already knew what she was thinking. He was gorgeous.

But his beauty wasn't enough to distract me from the sinister feel of this place. I was struck again by a lacerating feeling of being unwanted here, as if the dark stone itself were rejecting me. Shadows danced on the walls around me, making me jump.

The stairs seemed to stretch on forever. How big was this place?

"I'm regretting skipping my leg day," Shalini said from behind me. "I mean, like, every leg day."

At last, the footman led us into a hall, where tawny light slanted through narrow windows, casting diamond-shaped shadows onto the suits of armor lining the opposite wall. Even though the hall seemed to stretch on forever, not a single other fae was up here. The castle itself seemed to be almost entirely deserted, only the shadows moving across the stones.

I desperately wanted to ask the footman for a snack,

but I didn't imagine that was on the agenda for now. "Where are you taking us?" I asked quietly.

He turned with a hint of a smile. "Just a little further."

As we walked, I grew increasingly confused how the interior of the castle could be so large.

At last, we stopped by an oak door inset into the wall. A small brass plaque beside it read MADAM SIOBA'S FINEST in curling script.

The footman knocked, the sound echoing down the hall.

A woman answered. She had the pointed ears of a fae, which stuck up through loose hair of a wiry gray. She looked exhausted, with bags under her eyes that could have rivaled my own. But her clothing was exquisite, a long robe of crimson silk embroidered with gold threads.

"Aeron?" She tutted. "Don't tell me he wants another one. What am I supposed to do with this mess...and her human?"

"Listen, Sioba. You don't want to get in the way of the king's will, do you? Of what's best for Faerie?" He nodded at me. "I thought not. So she'll need a dress."

Madam Sioba's lip curled as she looked me over, but she pulled the door open wider. "Better get on with it."

We entered a dimly lit workshop with a black and white tiled floor. Aeron entered behind us but stayed by the door, arms folded. His blond hair hung rakishly before his eyes.

I surveyed the room. Rolls of fabric were draped over every surface: taffeta, silk, satin, velvet, chiffon, and brocade. Bundles leaned against the walls, were stacked on shelves, and had been stuffed into large wicker bins. Skeins of thread and yarn littered the place, tinged red in the light of the sunset.

But my gaze slid to a plate of scones, by far the most appealing thing to me right now. It wasn't so much that I was hungry, since the heartbreak had destroyed my appetite, but a buried instinct knew I needed calories. When was the last time I'd actually eaten?

"You're Ms. Jones?" Madame Sioba's voice snapped me out of my hunger-trance.

I blinked at her. "How did you know my name?"

"It's not important." She planted her hands on her hips. "Now get up there, and let me get a proper look at you," she ordered, and gestured to the enormous ottoman.

I started forward, but Madam Sioba caught my arm and pointed at my feet. "Not in those hideous things."

"Oh, right." I was still wearing my Nike running shoes.

I started to bend over, but Madam Sioba flicked her wrist, shooting a flash of yellow flame at my shoes. They ignited, and I jumped, my muscles clenching in anticipation of the burning pain that was sure to come. It took me a moment to realize I wasn't on fire, just barefoot. The acrid scent of burning plastic hung in the air. My shoes and socks had been completely incinerated, but my skin was untouched.

My eyes met hers, and my mouth hung open.

She tutted. "I can see you are unaccustomed to

magic. That's fine. We are welcoming of *all sorts* here. Even the common fae." Her voice dripped with disdain.

Why was it that whenever they claimed to be welcoming here, it sounded very much like the opposite?

Madam Sioba ignored me, muttering to herself as she poked around in a large hamper full of scraps of satin. "Simply unbelievable. I specifically told Torin that they need to be here at least a day in advance. And these two, dressed like common whores."

Shalini and I exchanged looks.

"You do realize we can hear you?" I asked.

Madame Sioba either didn't notice or didn't care.

"Every single time"—she shook her head as she tossed pieces of fabric onto the floor—"Torin thinks I'm going to fix his problems for him. As if I don't have any life of my own." She turned back to us, holding up a lustrous piece of satin in an antique cream color. "What do you think of this?"

My eyes flicked back to the scones. "It's beautiful. Sorry, is anyone going to eat those?"

"It's perfect," Shalini added.

Madam Sioba's gaze moved to Shalini, and her right eyebrow twitched up. "Who, exactly, are you?"

"I'm Shalini, Ava's official counsel. I believe I'm supposed to get a dress as well." She smiled hopefully and handed me one of the scones.

No one had said anything about a dress for her, but she couldn't keep running around in her pajamas.

Madam Sioba grunted dismissively and yanked a piece of emerald taffeta off a table. Then her gaze returned to me, and she grimaced, clearly irritated. "Why aren't you on my ottoman? For the fitting, I will need to see you properly."

I hopped up on the velvet surface, and Madame Sioba glared at me. In my bare feet, nylon running shorts, and thin running shirt, I felt strangely naked.

She walked around, muttering to herself as she took my measurements. "Nice hips. That's good. Torin likes a bit of curves. Not that you really have a chance." Her gaze had moved to my face, and I felt myself blush. "Good bone structure, pretty face. I suppose that's why you're here. Skin will do, apart from the eye bags. Then there's the bloodshot eyes, and the hair's an absolute fright—"

Given that she was pointing out all my flaws, I no longer cared about being polite, and I took a bite of the scone. It was buttery and delicious, but I only had two bites before she snatched it away from me and tossed it on the floor.

From behind us, Aeron muttered, "For gods' sakes, Sioba."

I'd nearly forgotten he was here.

"Madam Sioba?" Shalini said. "King Torin said the banquet starts in only twenty minutes—"

"Do you want Ms. Jones to look like a slatternly harlot?" Sioba shot back. "Is that what you want? My work takes time. Designing, fitting, hemming." She shrugged with an exaggerated sigh. "What I do is an art, and it cannot be rushed. Especially in tragic cases like this."

Shalini pressed her lips together and glanced at the footman.

Madam Sioba walked around a few times before she stepped back to appraise me once more. "Aeron," she barked, "you will need to leave the room now."

Aeron flashed me a devilish smile like he was about to say something flirtatious. But the smile faded as quickly as it had arrived—probably when he realized I could be his next queen, and he'd be wise to keep his mouth shut around me. With a shrug, he stepped out, closing the door behind him. Shalini and I were left alone with the dressmaker.

Cocking her head, Madam Sioba flicked her wrist again. A flash of flames and heat engulfed me. I gasped, nearly falling off the stool.

"Stop thrashing about," tutted Madam Sioba. "You're fine."

"Wow," said Shalini. "That's quite a party trick."

I looked down to find my skin unmarked by fire. That was the good news. The bad news was that I was completely naked.

"What happened to my cell phone?" I asked.

"You're standing here, naked as the day you were born," said Sioba, "and that's your concern? Those contraptions are vile things. We never should have allowed them here."

I supposed it was for the best because I wouldn't be able to stare at it anymore, hoping that Andrew would text.

White puff sponges ran over my skin, making suds.

I was reasonably comfortable being naked around

other women, but I'd only just met Sioba, and we hadn't exactly bonded. I covered myself with my arms. Warm water ran over me, streaming down my hair and dripping down the floor. Sioba had created a shower for me, here in her workshop.

The warm water stopped, and I felt hot air blast over me, drying the water from my skin and hair. When I opened my eyes again, my skin was dry—and the ottoman, too. My hair hung down in shining waves, and when I reached up, I felt a crown of flowers on my head.

Now I could taste lipstick on my lips, though I was still uncomfortably naked. Awkwardly, I covered my boobs.

"Stand still," she hissed.

She muttered under her breath in a language I didn't understand, and a cream-colored lace floated through the air as if blown by an unseen wind.

Madam Sioba directed the silk around me, and it slid around my breasts, hips, and ass. This felt...awkward.

When I looked down, I realized she'd just used magic to create racy, transparent underwear for me. It was surprisingly comfortable.

But that was when Madam Sioba's door cracked open, and she and Shalini spun to face the intruder.

"Hey!" said Shalini. "We're not finished in here!"

I expected to see Aeron skulk out of the room. Instead, I found myself staring at the ice blue eyes of King Torin. He was gazing right at me.

"You can't be in here right now," Madam Sioba snapped.

The king had gone stock-still, and icy shadows gathered around him. I waited for him to apologize and back away, but he seemed strangely frozen in place.

"Do you mind?" I said.

He pulled his gaze away, his body rigid. "I was just coming to see if you were ready. What is the delay?"

Madam Sioba jumped in front of me. "I'll be done with her in a minute, Your Highness. Please wait outside."

With his eyes on the floor, Torin crossed out of the room.

"Oh, my, oh, my, I must have forgotten to lock the door," said Madam Sioba, tsking under her breath. "Well, I suppose you'll have an advantage if he liked what he saw."

Turning back to me, she raised her hands, and a bolt of satin slid from a shelf. Hanging in midair, it unspooled as if guided by invisible fingers. As the cloth stretched and extended, I stared at the gorgeous rose-gold silk knitting itself into the shape of a dress before my eyes. A swathe of tulle slipped over it, covering the silk to form a sort of bodice. Pearly threads flowed through the air, embroidering a sort of delicate belt with tiny shimmering beads. For an instant, the dress hung before us— one with a plunging neckline and a rather daring slit up the side. A swath of fabric hung down the back like a cape. It looked very 1930s movie star, which I loved.

Then, with a flick of her wrist. Madam Sioba sent it

flying towards me. Soft tulle brushed my bare legs and satin clutched at my ribs as it wrapped round my body like a glove.

Shalini gasped. "It's beautiful."

A knock sounded on the door.

"Just one more second," Madam Sioba yelled, turning back to me. "What shoe size?"

"Seven."

Sioba flicked her hand again. I barely had time to duck as a pair of cream-colored heels appeared. She spun them around, then directed them to the foot of the ottoman.

As I stepped into them, Madam Sioba called out, "Okay. She's ready."

The door cracked open again, and I saw the now-familiar flash of King Torin's blue eyes on me.

"Ava's ready, but I need to make her advisor's outfit," said Madam Sioba.

King Torin glanced at Shalini, who remained dressed in pink slippers and an oversized T-shirt. "Aeron will wait for you," he said. "I'll take Ava. The opening ceremony starts in ten minutes."

Truth be told, I felt amazing as I slipped off the ottoman and crossed toward the hall. Torin held the door open for me, and it closed behind him.

The corner of Torin's mouth quirked as he looked down at me. "When we enter the ceremony, it would be best if you didn't draw too much attention to yourself. Understood?"

My eyebrows shot up. "I told you, I hate being the

center of attention. What makes you think I would try to get it on purpose?"

He stopped, then turned to face me with an eyebrow raised. "It's just that the first time I met you, you were screaming about Chad from *Hitched and Stitched*. I think you called me a 'pretty douchebag' and said something about my teeth."

I sucked in a sharp breath. "That wasn't a normal night for me."

"I'm glad to hear it." His dark magic coalesced around him as his expression grew more serious. "But when we reach the great hall, I do not want you to speak to any of the six princesses."

This was starting to feel a bit insulting. "Look," I whispered, "I'm on your side, here. I'll keep my end of the bargain, and I'm not going to make a scene. Have you seriously never gotten trashed and acted like an ass?"

He held my gaze. "I don't like to overindulge, and particularly not around people with whom I'm not extremely well acquainted."

When he said the phrase "extremely well acquainted," a hot shiver ran up my spine. Ignoring it, I flashed him a wry smile. "Of course you don't like to overindulge. Your hair could get rustled in public, and that would be dreadful. What can we expect from the opening ceremony?"

His expression darkened. "It will be a room full of people vying for my attention in their finest clothes, drinking champagne. Talking to each other about absolutely nothing."

"You mean...it's a party. Do you actually hate parties?"

A line formed between his brows. "I'm afraid I don't see the point of them. At least, not *this* kind of party."

"Right. Parties are fun, and fun doesn't seem like your thing." Truth be told, fun wasn't my thing right now, either. But maybe needling Torin was the *tiniest* bit of fun I could wrench from the world.

He shrugged slowly. "Not *this* kind of party, anyway."

"Is the castle party with princesses not fancy enough for you?"

"It's not Seelie enough for me."

I had no idea what that meant, and I suspect he'd done that on purpose—a little reminder that I didn't belong here, didn't know about my own people.

He arched an eyebrow. "When we have time, I will ask you what you do, Ms. Jones, besides scream at men you've just met at a bar. I suppose you must also leave time in your schedule for forming brutal snap judgments concerning people about whom you know nothing."

"But I know plenty about the fae hierarchy, Torin," I said. "It's the whole reason I spent my life in exile. And so far, you've confirmed everything I've thought about it."

"Well, that's good, darling, because as I said, I'm looking for someone I can't love, and so far, you are the perfect match."

That's right, Torin. I'm not super lovable. His words stung a bit after Andrew's rejection, and without entirely realizing, it, I found myself flipping my middle finger at him.

He glanced down at it, looking baffled.

Feeling childish, I shoved my hand back in my pocket. "So, that's it? It's just a party?"

"And after the pointless small talk over canapés, I will explain the rules of the tournament."

I bit my lip. "Tell me something. Why would someone who loathes being undignified invite a television crew to broadcast this whole charade?"

He pressed his hand against the wall, and as he leaned closer, I smelled his earthy, masculine aroma. "Because I'm a man who does what he must. And in this case, my kingdom is starving, with the winters growing longer every year. Faerie is enduring a famine, and for the past twenty-three years, we have been forced to buy food from humans. But I can't keep taxing my people to death to pay for it all. The network is paying me one hundred fifty million dollars an episode to make this show, and I will be able to settle my debts with the humans."

I stared at him. "Is that why the fae decided to come out of Faerie? You needed our food?"

"That's precisely it. We just need to get through this one last winter, and then our magic will return with the help of a queen." He pulled his hand away and shrugged. "It seems that what humans desire above all else is entertainment, so that is what I will give them."

"That seems accurate." My gaze roamed over his pointed ears—so strange to be around others like me, after all this time. "But if you're so desperate for money, why are you wasting it on me and this whole charade instead of just finding someone you love?"

"Because love isn't for me, Ava."

I narrowed my eyes. "We have something in common. What happened? Did someone break your heart?"

He turned and started walking, and I hurried to keep pace with him. "You know, for all the vitriol you unleashed on me about the falseness of human entertainment, I note that you are not immune to its charms."

"Nice evasion of my question."

"You seem to know a lot about Chad and his teeth," he added.

I shrugged. "Guilty pleasure. The romance is bullshit, but it's fun when they fight. There's always a crazy one."

He cut me a sharp look. "And why do I have a feeling the crazy one in your cohort might be you?"

"Because you like forming snap judgments about people you just met? Oh, shit. Do we have something *else* in common?" I shuddered. "We should probably stop talking before we get involved in a messy emotional entanglement."

"Right." A smile ghosted over his lips, just for a moment. "Faster, Ava."

And with that abrupt order, he'd picked up the pace, his cape billowing behind him.

9

AVA

King Torin strode down the hall, moving at a clip so brisk, I had to run to keep up with him. I kicked off my heels and carried them, getting out of breath as I hurried after him.

I felt dazed, my mind flicking back every few moments to Andrew and Ashley. What were they doing right now? Cooking in our kitchen? Fucking in our bed? Planning *their* wedding?

We'd always planned a forest wedding. Secretly, I'd started the plans on my own, but he'd been on board with the general idea. I knew he'd be popping the question any day, so I'd picked out a gown, the table settings. I wanted to wear a crown of wildflowers, and to have live music.

Holy shit.

How fucking sad was I?

Maybe this little adventure wasn't the worst thing for me. Beautiful castle. Beautiful people. Plenty to take my mind off the wedding that would never happen.

I played my new mantra again in my head: *Fifty million dollars.* That was the most important part of this.

I could feel my long cape trailing behind me as I ran. We hurried through the castle, and he was somehow able to walk at a pace faster than my typical jog. But as I moved, I took in the sights. The beautiful courtyards, ruddy in the setting sun. The tall windows and ornate carvings. A winding stairwell that seemed to spiral on forever.

Just when I felt my lungs were going to explode, Torin slowed and stood before towering oak doors in the vaulted hall. Heaving for breath, I touched my chest. My skin glowed with a faint sweat.

Torin nodded at the doors. "The contestants are through there, but I'll be entering separately. And remember—" He lifted his finger to his lips, arching an eyebrow.

He *really* didn't have much faith in my subtlety.

With that, he turned from me and crossed to a narrow stairwell that led upward.

I slipped on the heels again and pulled open the door. Before me, under soaring gothic arches, I found an ocean of silk, satin, tulle, and taffeta. Many of the women had wildflowers braided and threaded into their hair, and wreaths of leaves on their heads. These gorgeous women chatted to one another to the dulcet sounds of a string quartet. Torin's footmen mingled among them, carrying gilded platters of hors d'oeuvres.

To Torin, of course, all this was positively dreadful.

I eyed the triangular cucumber sandwiches with a dim realization that I should eat. And the food, honestly, looked amazing: shrimp skewers and cocktail sauce, blini topped with crème fraiche and caviar, and hot dates wrapped with bacon. If I got my appetite back, this deal would be worth it for the food alone.

The women didn't seem to be eating much, but they weren't holding back when it came to drinking. Champagne goblets sparkled in their hands. Normally, I'd have been all about a glass of bubbly, but not after last night. Instead, I popped one of the hot dates into my mouth. Oh, *gods*, it was delicious.

I walked the edges of the hall, keeping to the shadows. Great tapestries hung on the stone walls, and my gaze roamed over the verdant scenes, the forests and gardens embroidered before me. As I stared at the exquisite art, I felt a tap on my shoulder. "Hey, Ava."

I turned to see Shalini and smiled at how gorgeous she looked. The loose T-shirt had been replaced by a sleeveless silk jumpsuit in rose gold, like my dress, but somehow far sexier. Especially with her sleeve tattoos on display. With her plunging neckline, it was hard not to stare.

"Madam Sioba said an advisor should wear a suit, but she didn't object to a jumpsuit."

"You look amazing!"

She looked down at herself. "Are you sure?"

"Would I ever lie to you?"

Shalini brightened. "No. You're totally shit at lying —" Shalini cut short, catching my elbow. "Ava, look."

She pointed through the crowd to a small group of fae women at the far end of the hall. Far more opulently dressed than the women near us, they wore gowns that glittered with pearls and gemstones. Instead of wreaths of flowers or leaves, they wore small silver crowns.

"The princesses," said Shalini breathlessly. "There are six of them, each from a different clan."

She started to pull me toward them, skirting the main crowd of contestants.

I wasn't going to speak to them, as instructed. But I found myself following. These were the women I was supposed to beat.

Though apparently, Torin would do everything in his power to help me win, since he desperately needed someone...unlovable. I tried not to get too offended by that thought, since the man hated everything.

Shalini stopped short again, catching my arm, and I followed her gaze.

On the other side of the princess clique stood a small group of humans—the news crew who'd accosted me outside Shalini's apartment, now with a brand-new camera. The reality show host spoke excitedly to the camera, gesturing at the princess we'd met earlier. "And the woman in the magnificent dark gown is Princess Moria, the eldest of the Dearg-Due. We will have to keep a careful eye on what she drinks this evening." He raised an eyebrow, giving the camera a knowing look. "As we all know, the Dearg-Due prefer a fluid of the sanguine sort."

My eyes widened in surprise. She drinks blood?

The reporter sucked in a sharp breath as another beautiful fae princess crossed in front of him, wearing a shimmering golden gown that accentuated her black hair and rich mahogany skin. Motioning for the camerawoman to focus the lens on her, he spoke in breathless tones.

"Now, here is Princess Cleena of the Banshees. *Vanity Fair* has described her as the most beautiful woman on the planet."

The princess was standing a few feet away, but if she heard the reporter, she gave no indication.

He was right about her beauty, though. Her dark hair hung in beautiful ringlets down her back, but it was her eyes that drew my attention. Widely set and a deep golden amber, they demanded attention. Princess Cleena's gaze moved languorously around the room. She was all composure.

When the reporter's eyes met mine, my breath caught. For a moment, we stared at each other, and then he was moving toward me with a hungry look in his eye.

Torin had glamoured him to forget me—hadn't he?

"Ava Jones?"

Fuck.

The camerawoman focused her lens on me.

"Now, this *is* something, our final contestant," he said. "The whole country watched the conflict between these two in the bar. And boy, did sparks fly! Except I'm not sure they were the right kind of sparks. I think none of us were expecting to see this fiery fae here as a contestant, but this is an interesting turn of events."

I stepped away, and Shalini touched my back for support.

The reporter's eyes narrowed, "And who is this with you, Ms. Jones?"

I sighed. "This is my advisor, Shalini."

He stared at her, nodding. "A human advisor in Faerie. Wow, I bet a lot of people would love to have your job." He thrust the microphone in her face. "Are you going to keep Ms. Jones in control, or can we expect more fireworks?"

Shalini glanced at me. "She's perfectly composed. It was just a bad night, that's all."

Around us, a murmur was growing, and I sensed that the crowd noticed the attention on us. I desperately wanted to shrink back into the shadows.

A trumpet sounded, saving me from all the attention. The doors swung slowly open at the end of the hall, and a footman stepped into the entryway. He was dressed in an exceptionally extravagant suit festooned in gold embroidery. "Ladies and gentlemen," he said in a booming voice, "dinner is served."

More food? Fantastic. I wasn't sure I ever wanted the tournament to end.

The reporter shoved his microphone in my face, asking me what had caused my meltdown in the bar with the king, but I slipped away from him, blending into the crowd. After an entire life as a fae among humans, I'd learned something about the art of going unnoticed.

Embedded in the crowd of taller fae, we crossed into a new hall where tables were arranged in a semi-circle around a pair of giant thrones. Constructed from gray granite, they seemed to have grown from the stone floor itself. The floor was white marble inlaid with a magnificent bronze stag. The lofty ceiling was formed of entwined tree branches. Hundreds of tiny, glittering lights flitted among the boughs like fireflies.

I glanced at Shalini, catching her enraptured expression. Awestruck, I gazed at the ceiling again.

Aeron caught my elbow, recalling my attention. "This way," he said, nodding at one of the tables.

The contestants were already taking their seats, and the princesses sat among the rest.

My gaze snagged on a princess seated near me. She wore an elegant green dress that sparkled like the sea under the sun. Her brown eyes were enormous and fringed with long lashes, and a wreath of seaweed was nestled in her white hair. Her pale skin had an almost iridescent hue that shimmered under the lights. "Aren't we all lucky to be here?" she said to her neighbors. "One of us will find true love. We might bear the king's children."

She beamed, but no one answered her.

True love. *You poor, naive thing.*

"Who's that?" I whispered to Shalini.

Shalini leaned close so only I could hear. "That's Princess Alice. She's a kelpie—a lake fae. They can be very weepy, but she seems thrilled with all this."

"Oh." I had only a vague memory of what that meant. Something to do with horses, I thought.

"And next to her, Etain of the Leannán Sídhe."

I followed her gaze to see a woman with tawny skin and hair the color of a sunset, periwinkle and coral. She wore a delicate crown of pearls and a pale violet dress—and she was presently giving the middle finger to Moria.

"Don't think you can order us all around here, blood-drinker."

"What's a Leannán Sídhe?" I asked.

"A seductress of some kind, I think," she whispered back. "And that"—she pointed to a green-haired beauty—"is Eliza, princess of the Selkie clan."

The warm lights shimmered off Eliza's green hair and bronze skin. "I have been told that the king's generosity is unparalleled," Eliza said, lifting a crystal flute. She smiled, but her expression seemed forced. "And this fine champagne certainly lends credence to that opinion."

"Selkie?" I whispered.

"They live by the sea," said Shalini. "The clan symbol is a seal. And to her right is Sydoc the Redcap. Just...maybe just stay away from her. Redcaps are terrifying."

Sydoc wore a bright red gown and hat, the color a startling contrast to her pale skin, and her long raven hair cascaded over bare shoulders. She spoke to no one, just drank her wine, her eyes flitting from one side to another.

At this point, I was wishing I'd paid more attention to my fae history.

As the only fae kid in my town, I'd stood out. I'd done everything I could to be like the human kids—watched their TV shows, listened to their pop music, grown my hair out to cover my ears, dyed it brown to match the other kids. I wasn't even entirely sure what color of blue my hair was anymore, since I got the roots done every three weeks.

The only properly fae thing I'd done was learn how to fence in high school, just when the fae were starting to become fashionable among a few of the cooler, edgier humans. And fencing was a fae thing. With my little fae-loving clique, I'd learned the art of the foil, the épée, and the sabre. It had come more naturally to me than anything I'd done before.

Finally, by my sophomore year of high school, some of the kids *actually* thought I was cool, and no one was tying me to fence posts anymore.

In the past few years, humans had become increasingly obsessed with us. Now, news reporters and the paparazzi followed our every move, and fae dictated the fashions. Pink and purple hair dye sold off the shelves, and colored contact lenses now went for thousands of dollars on eBay. Plastic surgeons had begun adding silicon points to human ears.

But that was five years ago; I hadn't touched a sword since then.

The sound of a blaring trumpet snapped me out of my reminiscences, and I looked up to see King Torin enter the room, dressed in black. His pale gaze slid over the crowd. Striding across the marble with his contingent of footmen and soldiers, he looked every bit the king.

He wore a long cloak, inky black with silver embroidery. At his hip, I could see the glint of his onyx-hilt rapier. But what really caught my eye was the crown of antlers on his head—a dark silver color, sharply pointed.

He stopped in the center of the room with his back to the granite thrones. His host stepped away, and a hush fell over the ballroom. For once, even the reporter was silent. All eyes were fixed on King Torin.

His regal magic seemed to command us to bow. *Honor your king.*

Heads around me lowered, but I kept my eyes on him. I guess I still resented being exiled.

Torin's eyes met mine for an instant, but his expression betrayed nothing. "Welcome to my home. I appreciate that all of you have come on such short notice. It is important that we—that I—select a queen to rule Faerie, to strengthen the power of the six Seelie clans. My mother's throne has been empty for too long, and the kingdom needs the strength of a high queen."

There was a murmur of appreciation from the audience.

"Before things begin, I want to explain the rules of the tournament." King Torin's eyes moved around the room, and they seemed to linger on me just a heartbeat longer than the rest. "According to the ancient writings of the great Seelie historical chronicler, Oberon, these trials have been a custom for centuries. Every time, they end with a sword fight in the arena. Their purpose is to identify those possessing traits of a true fae queen: strength and agility, wit, intelligence, and of course, skill with a blade. And at times in the history of the fae, when we blended with the human world, we have incorporated elements of their culture. As High King of the Seelie, ruler of the six clans, I must see that the humans continue to revere us."

Interesting. I supposed that was the TV bit.

"The first contest will be a race, to identify those of

you who are strongest and fastest. To gauge wit, intelligence, charm, and poise, I will host parties, and we will spend time together, one on one. Those who make the final cut will compete in a fencing tournament."

"Your Highness?" The princess with white hair and porcelain skin raised her hands. "How will you determine who is the most witty and charming?"

"That," King Torin said with a smile, "will be up to me."

❧ 10 ❧

AVA

After Torin's speech, a servant appeared at our table with plates of salmon, rice, and a wild-flower salad.

If I had been hungry, this meal would have been delectable. The salmon was perfectly cooked, with a light glaze. I took a tiny bite. As I ate, someone filled my glass with a zesty white wine. Sauvignon blanc, maybe?

Gods, this was amazing. Had the cooks enchanted the food?

King Torin moved through the room, taking time to speak with each of the princesses and some of the common fae. He approached our table just as I finished the last bit of salmon.

"Did you enjoy your meal?"

"Yes, it was delicious." With a shock, I realized I'd managed to eat the whole plate. That never usually happened when I was heartbroken. "I didn't have any dinner last night, and I guess I was starving."

Torin leaned in and whispered, "Yes, as I recall, most of your dinner was on your shirt."

And with that little comment, he was already moving on to Princess Alice's table.

My empty plate was replaced with a fresh blueberry tart topped with whipped cream. The footmen filled delicate porcelain cups with tea and coffee.

As I was putting the last forkful of tart into my mouth, Aeron leaned closer to speak to us. "The king has retired for the night. I'm supposed to take you two lasses to your rooms. No idea where I'm supposed to put you, though. Torin never quite mentioned that."

"We don't have a room, Aeron?" Shalini's eyes were wide.

His dark blond hair hung before his eyes. "I'll need to speak to the king. Give me a moment, please."

He hurried off, and I stared as his broad form disappeared through the doorway.

Shalini leaned in, whispering, "Maybe Aeron will let us stay with him."

I took a sip of my coffee and watched as the other women filed out of the room. A number of them stared at me as they passed, and I caught hints of their whispers. *Drunk...insane...ranting lunatic.*

Moria cut me a sharp look as she passed, saying loudly enough for everyone to hear, "How lucky for you that the king was willing to entertain a sluttish tavern wench."

Her friends burst out laughing, and they crossed out of the hall.

Maybe that explained the sense of unwelcomeness

that seemed to hang over this whole castle like a dark miasma.

But those women hadn't paid a bit of attention to me before. Perhaps Torin's whisper in my ear had raised their hackles. A sign of favoritism.

I held the coffee cup to my lips and slid my gaze to Shalini. "Awkward."

"Ignore them," she murmured. "They know you're competition. And there's nothing wrong with being a sluttish tavern wench, anyway. Some of my best friends are tavern wenches."

I snorted.

At last, we were alone in the ballroom, and the lights dimmed.

Shalini looked to me. "So, we just wait here?"

I shrugged. "I don't know what else to do." A dark thought slid through my mind, making my muscles tense. "Do you think Andrew watched that viral video of me? God, do you think his parents saw it?"

"I don't think about Andrew at all, and neither should you."

Aeron returned to the dining room once more, carrying a lantern and looking pleased with himself. "Guess who sorted something out for you two, then?"

Shalini sipped her wine. "Was it you, Aeron?"

I rose from the table. "Thank you for looking after us."

"My pleasure," he said, his amber eyes on Shalini as he spoke.

He led us through the doors and into a gloomy hall. Dark forms seemed to loom in the shadows. I slowed to survey the taxidermied heads of animals—a stag with great horns, a giant bear's head, and an enormous reptile with sharp teeth, which caught my eye. "What is *that?*"

Aeron paused, squinting into the darkness. "Oh, that?" His tone was nonchalant. "Just a dragon. They're extinct now."

I gaped at it. *Just a dragon.*

Aeron's lantern cast warm light over the green scales. A plaque under the beast read, FOREST DRAGON, SLAUGHTERED BY KING SEOIRSE.

The light danced over more trophies, a massive boar and a creature that resembled a lion. Shalini gasped, and I turned to see her standing by what appeared to be a grotesque human head.

"Watch it, there. Back up a bit." Aeron grabbed her by the elbow, pulling her away.

"I didn't touch it," she said hurriedly.

I moved closer, my lip curling with distaste. The head was wrinkly and gray, his hair long and white. But most disturbing of all, his eyes had been sewn shut.

A shiver danced up my spine.

"What is this?" I asked.

He stared at it, his jaw set tight. "That's the Erlking. Killed by Torin's father."

In the light of the lantern, the shadows writhed over the gruesome display.

"So he was a king?" Shalini asked.

A muscle twitched in his jaw. "No, not a real king. The Erlking was a fae, but one who'd gone feral—like a demon or a wild beast. He lived deep in the forest." He met my gaze, his expression haunted. "Once, the forests were littered with the bodies of those he'd killed. A mass grave of fae, their bodies strewn among the oaks."

I shuddered, wanting to get away from this thing.

"When King Torin's father brought the Erlking home," Aeron went on, "they left it to dry in the sun until it was completely mummified."

AERON LED US THROUGH SHADOWY CORRIDORS, THEIR dark stone walls hung with weapons and armor. On the top floor, he began to slow, and my gaze roamed over magnificent portraits of fae in regal clothing and furs. The portraits seemed to go on forever.

"Is this the royal family?" I asked. "Why are there so many of them?"

Aeron stopped walking and gestured at the paintings. "These are King Torin's relatives. His lineage extends nearly five hundred generations, all of it carefully chronicled. Painting in the fae realm developed long before it did in the human world, so you can see realistic images going back thousands of years."

"Wow." I studied a painting of a man wearing black fur and a bronze circlet crown with a twisting golden torque around his neck.

"Would be amazing to see your ancestors like that, wouldn't it?" he said.

"Or even my birth parents," I muttered.

Aeron led us another hundred yards until we reached a large doorway—one of oak, carved with flowers. A brass doorknob shaped like a rose jutted from the door. He twisted the knob and gently pushed it open to a breathtaking gothic room, one in the shape of an octagon.

Shalini grinned. "Oh, my God, this is amazing."

A vaulted ceiling arched above us like that of a Gothic cathedral. Stone carvings of roses adorned some of the peaks. Towering windows with pointed arches rose twenty feet high, flanked by crimson velvet drapes. Tapestries hung on some of the walls—forest scenes and mossy stone ruins. Two doors stood between the tapestries.

A four-poster bed awaited in one corner, opposite a fireplace with velvety chairs and a sofa. Crystal decanters and glasses sat on a mahogany table, and books with faded spines were tucked into alcoves around the room. An embroidered rug had been spread over the flagstone floor.

Aeron quickly crossed to one of the other doors, beckoning me to follow. "In here is the bath." He pushed open the door to a stone room with a clawfoot tub. A star-kissed sky shone through a window, and a mirror hung on another wall.

I turned to see Shalini flop onto the bed. "Oh, my God, Ava. This mattress is divine."

Aeron crossed to the next door. "Well, you can sleep where you want, but we have an advisor's quarters here."

He pushed open the door to a room that looked like a small library, with books and a dresser lining two of the walls, and a fireplace on the third. A bed rested next to tall windows that gave a view of the stars, and a black fur blanket covered it.

"Oh, my God, Ava!" shouted Shalini from the bed. "This place is amazing."

I turned back to see her making herself comfortable with a book in her hands.

Aeron looked around the room uneasily. "This room isn't normally used anymore, but..." His voice trailed off.

"Why?" I asked.

He frowned at me. "Bit nosy, aren't you?" He cleared his throat. "Listen, if you win this, please forget I said that."

Shalini tapped the bed next to her. "Come sit next to me, Ava. This is the most comfortable bed I've ever sat on."

As I plopped down beside her, Aeron gave us a dazzling smile. "You'll find clothes in the drawers and wardrobes." He inhaled deeply. "The curios—" He seemed to stop himself and cleared his throat. "The human news crews in Faerie have insisted on some human technology as part of our deal. We have recently outfitted brand new electrical charging stations for your human telephones, and the..." He trailed off. "Whatever it is that makes the telephones get the videos and images through the air."

"Cell phone reception and internet," I said. "Thanks!"

I did not add that Madame Sioba had dissolved my freaking phone.

Then again, whatever kept me from obsessively

checking for messages from Andrew was probably a good thing.

Aeron smiled, his cheeks dimpling. "Since you ladies seem to have made yourselves comfortable, I will see myself out."

As the footman crossed the room, I called after him, "Thanks Aeron. I really appreciate all your help this evening."

"Oh, no problem." Aeron met Shalini's gaze. "As I said, the pleasure was all mine." His deep, velvety tone made the word "pleasure" sound positively filthy.

As soon as Aeron left the room, I nudged her. "He likes you."

"We'll see."

A knock sounded at the door, echoing in the large, stony space. "See? He came back for you."

The knock was louder now, impatient.

"Coming!" I called.

I pulled the door open to find Torin leaning against the door frame, his ice-blue eyes focused on me. "You did well."

"I didn't do anything." I frowned. "Oh, you mean I didn't cause another spectacle. What are you doing here?" I asked. "It's quite late."

"It is important that we talk before tomorrow." He crossed into the room. "Will you be prepared to run a race in the morning? You do run regularly, right?"

On the bed, Shalini had pulled out her phone to watch an old season of *Hitched and Stitched*.

"I think I'll do all right," I said. "But I don't have any running gear. Madam Sioba burned it all. I'll need new running shoes. Size seven, Nike preferably. And a shirt and shorts, both size small."

He nodded. "Fine. I'll come by early to show you the course and bring you the gear. Though the other fae will be dressed more traditionally in bare feet and animal skins."

"Sounds like I'll have an advantage then."

"You are fast, Ava. It's why I chose a race to start. Usually, it's a traditional fae dance or musical instrument, but I thought you'd have the advantage at running."

I cocked my head. "How do you know I'm fast?"

"I was testing you earlier when we moved through the castle. You kept up with me well."

I stared at him. "But you were walking the whole time. How is it impressive that I could run at your walking speed?"

He shrugged. "I'm the king, Ava. You must expect me to be naturally superior in most things."

I blinked at him. "Do you really not hear how you sound?"

I actually thought the corner of his mouth quirked up a little bit with amusement. "Good night, Ms. Jones."

He turned, and the door shut behind him.

S halini was lost in her phone, and I crossed to one of the bookcases. My gaze roamed over the spines—classics like *Pamela; or, Virtue Rewarded*, *Jane Eyre*, *Pride and Prejudice*, and *Wuthering Heights*.

But my gaze started to grow unfocused.

I felt completely disoriented here, and even with Shalini, I seemed to be lost in a fog.

Here was the thing about routines—I missed mine. When I was little, I'd get home from school and do my homework while Chloe cleaned the house. She always had a snack for me. We'd have dinner together, then TV, and a bath. There'd been something soothing in always knowing what was happening.

Long after I left home, Andrew and I formed our own routines. We'd open a bottle of wine, make some popcorn, and read books or watch movies together under the blankets. We'd alternate cooking for each other after work. Weekends were the best, with coffee and newspapers, and pajamas until noon.

And now the routines were gone, and the people I'd enjoyed them with.

Ava, you should be happy for me.

I blinked, clearing my eyes.

I glanced at the beautifully rendered tapestries on the walls. The one closest to me depicted a crumbling castle with overgrown gardens. Hiding in the undergrowth were strange creatures—unicorns, centaurs, and satyrs.

And there were fae, too. Lords and ladies at leisure. Picnicking, bathing, playing music on ornate instruments. In one part of the scene, a hunting party chased a boar. The leader wore a silver crown shaped like stag antlers—the fae king and his host.

I crossed to another tapestry, this one much darker, a shadowy forest filled with monstrous insects—giant spiders and enormous butterflies. Even the trees were sinister, with craggy boughs and trunks carved with leering faces.

In one corner, a group of figures gathered round a small fire, some with butterfly wings. Others had heads shaped like insects; a few were covered in mossy fur. In the middle stood what appeared to be their leader—a woman wearing a thorny crown and holding a staff that glowed with a greenish light. All of them had the pointed ears of the fae, but not any fae I recognized.

The image was strange and beautiful, and I couldn't take my eyes off it. It entranced me, and yet, as I stared at it, a corrosive sorrow pooled in my chest. A sense of loss I couldn't name.

"Shalini?" I called out. "Have you ever heard of fae with wings and fur? Or horns?"

"No." She slid off the bed. "What are you looking at?"

"See?" I pointed to the tapestry on the right. "Those are normal fae. There's even one wearing a crown just like Torin's. That must be the king."

"Right."

"But what are these other guys, then?" I indicated the strange figures in the opposite tapestry "Do you think this is what fae looked like thousands of years ago? In prehistory, maybe?"

Shalini shook her head. "Honestly, I don't know. I've never heard of any fae that look like this. Maybe it's just artistic license." She turned to me. "Is it weird for you, being here among your own kind after all this time?"

I nodded. "Weird as hell, but I'm getting paid for this. What made *you* so desperate for an adventure?"

She stared at me. "Work was my whole life. And before that, it was studying. I never went to a prom, never went on dates. Never went to parties. And now, I don't need to work, and I feel like there's a whole world I've missed. Ava, I feel like I've woken up at last. But I don't quite know what to do with myself. Because the Tinder dates have been shit, and there's only so many nights you can spend at fancy bars before it gets boring. I just know that I can't stop and be alone with my thoughts."

"Why?"

She shuddered. "Reality TV staves off the anxiety. There's a lot of shit to be afraid of in this world. In both worlds, probably, but at least this one is new and distracting."

I nodded. "Whatever happens here, I'm pretty sure we won't be bored. There will be plenty to distract you from your own mortality."

"Perfect."

Another knock sounded at the door—lighter this time.

"Who is it?" I said, opening the door a crack.

A tiny fae woman stood in the doorway, dressed in a silk bathrobe. Her pale blonde hair hung in loose waves to her shoulders. When she looked up at me, I saw that her eyes were milky white.

"Are you Ava?" she asked quietly.

"I am," I answered cautiously.

"Oh, good." Her face brightened. "I'm Princess Orla."

She looked far too young to get married. "Are you part of the competition?"

Princess Orla laughed, her voice tinkling in the dark hall. "Oh, no. King Torin is my brother."

Shalini slipped up next to me. Though the princess was clearly blind, she seemed to sense Shalini's presence. "Who is this?" she asked, lifting her chin.

"I'm Shalini. Ava's advisor."

Orla bowed slightly. "It's my pleasure to meet you."

"Is there something you wanted, Princess?" I asked, hoping I didn't sound rude. "It's quite late."

"Oh, sorry," said Princess Orla. "I have the hardest time knowing the hour. I just noticed that someone was in the Rose Room, and I was curious. But I didn't realize it was so late. I'd best be off. Good luck tomorrow," she said softly.

Before I could reply, she walked down the dark hall and was swallowed by the shadows.

The Rose Room? I looked to Shalini, but she only shrugged. "I didn't even know he had a sister," she said. "They're very secretive."

I glanced at the dark windows, and a mantle of weariness enveloped me, making my muscles ache, my eyes heavy. But I dreaded going to bed when sorrow had its icy grip on me.

Shalini headed for the smaller room.

"Oh, no," I said. "The big bed is all yours. I'll take the little one."

Her eyes brightened. "Are you sure?"

"I feel more comfortable in a cozy room."

Shalini leapt back onto the four-poster and immediately snuggled under the blankets.

I returned to the library room, pulling the door shut behind me. I leaned against it for a moment, trying to collect myself. The week had been such a whirlwind.

My comfortable life had been ripped out from under me. I'd been homeless and rejected. Then, within hours, I was living in a magnificent Faerie palace dressed in silk.

None of this seemed real. The one thing I didn't quite understand was why I didn't feel more of a sense of homecoming here. I'd always imagined that if I got back into Faerie, it would feel more familiar.

I peeled off the ball gown and hung it on a hook on the door.

The fire was still burning in a stone fireplace, bathing the room in warmth.

I flicked off the light and crawled into the bed. It was small but surprisingly comfortable, and I pulled the covers up to my neck.

I left the curtains open, however, and moonlight spilled in through the multipaned windows. I sat up, peering through the glass. It felt cold and drafty, and little webs of frost had spread over some of the panes, but the fur blanket warmed my legs. I couldn't make out the grounds of the castle through the window, only a distant line that might be treetops. Tonight, the moon was full, and stars twinkled in the distance.

As I studied the moon, a shadow flew over it, circling the dark sky. My breath caught at the silhouette of massive wings and a long, sinuous tail. For an instant, the sky was illuminated as a great gout of fire bloomed in the darkness.

I held my breath. Dragons *were* real.

I lay down, hoping the dark mist of sleep would wrap around me, pulling me under the surface.

And if I couldn't fall asleep, I had a beautiful view while insomnia kept my heart racing.

12

AVA

I rubbed my eyes, still groggy as I followed Torin through the shadowy halls.

He'd woken me before the sun had risen, bringing me running clothes, leggings, and something like a tunic in muted shades of forest green and brown. The clothing fit perfectly, but I was struggling to wake. I'd only slept about an hour, and I was fighting the urge to curl up in some creepy castle alcove and fall back to sleep.

"When does the race start?" I asked through a yawn.

He shot me an irritated look. "You look half dead. Were you up drinking again last night?"

I opened my mouth to argue and changed my mind. I didn't want to tell him I'd lain awake crying over Andrew and Ashley. That was far more pathetic than a night of drinking.

"Yes, but I'll be fine. But is the race really starting this early?"

"Three hours," said Torin.

I closed my eyes, marshaling patience. "So why are we up here now?"

"Because parts of the race are dangerous, and I'm going to make sure you get through them without dying."

I blinked. "Dangerous?"

"We'll get to that. I have a plan."

At last, he pushed through an oak door into a gleaming, wintry landscape of snow-encrusted trees and fields. As I stepped outside, the icy air bit my face and hands.

The stark, crystalline beauty of the place made me catch my breath, and the rising sun stained the snowy world in stunning shades of gold and peach. My breath clouded around my face. The wind stung my skin, and I wrapped my arms around my chest, shivering. My feet were already growing cold and wet in the snow, the damp seeping through my sneakers.

Torin turned to look back at me and pulled two things from beneath his cloak, a small paper bag and a thermos. Tiny wisps of steam rose from the metal container.

I took it from him, grateful for the warmth, and inhaled the fresh scent of coffee. Oh, thank *God*.

I took a sip and felt my brain finally turn on.

He removed his thick black cloak and stepped behind me, wrapping the garment around my shoulders. I pulled it close. It had retained some of his heat, and instantly, my muscles began to relax. I inhaled his scent, picking out the particular notes that identified him: moss, wet oak, and the faintest hint of pine straw.

"I don't even feel the cold anymore," he said softly.

When he stepped in front of me, I saw that he was wearing black wool trousers and a deep navy sweater that hugged his athletic body.

With the coat over my shoulders, I was better able to take in my surroundings. The castle stood on a small, snow-covered hill that overlooked white fields, which gently undulated to a row of trees in the distance, a dark forest that stretched on either side.

He handed me the little paper bag. "I have fresh croissants with blackberry jam."

I pulled out the pastry and took a bite, savoring the rich, buttery flavor and the tartness of the berries. It tasted absolutely amazing.

If Torin wanted to charm me, he certainly knew how to go about it.

He stared out onto the landscape, his eyes flecks of ice. "The frost is descending upon us, but Faerie is as beautiful as ever."

I blinked in the bright light. "I've never experienced anything quite like this. Waking up to the most perfect winter morning with an unsullied landscape." I breathed in, letting the cool air fill my lungs. "I never get up this early."

"It has its advantages," said Torin.

"Is an early morning part of your sacrosanct routine?" I asked.

He turned to me, flipping up his middle finger with the ghost of smile.

I blinked.

"Did I do that right?" he asked.

"You did, yes. Impressive."

"As for my sacrosanct routine, in my mornings, while you're sleeping off your late nights, I get up at dawn to train. A Seelie king, above all, must be powerful and lethal." Another faint smile. "And so must his queen."

He started walking, leading me past the snowy fields to a path that curved around the castle. My damp shoes crunched over flattened, frozen grass. "If you're looking for powerful and lethal," I said, "you've got the wrong fae."

"I knew that when I offered you the deal. But we're going to fake it, and that's all that matters."

"You don't mind cheating, then." I sipped my coffee, still endlessly grateful that he'd thought to bring it.

King Torin's eyes glinted. "Not when it's necessary. We had to get out here before anyone saw us. If I'm caught giving you an unfair advantage, you could be disqualified." He met my gaze. "And I need you to win."

We rounded a corner, and I glimpsed the starting line: two maypoles, the frozen wind whipping at their colored ribbons. A silk banner strung between them was labelled *START*.

The path curved down to a ridge of barren trees.

"How long is the course?" I asked.

"Just three miles. The trail was cleared last night. It's about a mile in the forest and two in the fields. For the final mile, you'll be coming back up toward the other side of the castle, and the crowd will be waiting there to identify the winner."

A broad path of frozen grass cut straight across the rolling fields. As we walked, my shoes crushed on the icy ground. When we crossed the fields, I was inundated with a multitude of new smells: the raw earth, the sun warming the wool of his jacket, and the faintest hint of woodsmoke. What would I have been like if I'd grown up here?

Snowflakes fluttered in the air, and ice glinted off distant thatched roofs.

We walked deeper into the snowy field, and I looked back at the castle. Despite its enormous interior that seemed to stretch for miles, it didn't look that big from the outside. Intimidating, yes, with its sleek black rock and sharp-peaked towers, but not miles long. I wondered if there was some sort of magic or enchantment at play.

It gleamed in the morning sun. Flying from the tallest tower was a white flag emblazoned with a dark blue stag's head.

When I glanced at the distant cottages and the smoke curling from their chimneys, curiosity stirred. "Tell me about Faerie," I said. "What do people here do? Besides the tournament."

He inhaled deeply. "Farming is important. If I weren't born a prince, that's what I would have done. Farmers are crucial members of fae society. They grow the crops that feed our people. Without them, we'd all starve. But with the frost encroaching, their job is becoming more difficult than ever."

"And what do people do for fun?" I sipped my coffee. "Oh, you wouldn't know, would you?"

"I do know, as it happens. In Faerie, the summer season starts on what you would call May first. And that's when we celebrate Beltane."

"What happens then?" I asked.

The look he gave me was incredulous. "You *really* don't know? Even the humans celebrate it."

I shook my head. "Not anymore."

"Well, they should. It's when the veil between the worlds thins. Once, humans offered us food and drink. I suppose I never see it these days. No wonder we're starving here." The wind whipped at his dark, wavy hair. "Beltane is a fire festival. The children decorate the trees of the forest and thorny bushes with yellow ribbons and flowers, like flame. And after they go to bed, we sacrifice to the old gods. Usually, it's one or two humans who have trespassed in our realm."

My stomach swooped. What the hell had I gotten myself into here? "I asked you what you did for fun, and your answer is human sacrifice? How do they die?"

"We burn them." He slid me a sharp look. "It's not quite as terrible as it sounds. They're drugged ahead of time, and there are drums to drown out the screams."

I must have had a horrified expression because he added—somewhat defensively, "It's our ancient tradition, and we still have a sense of the sacred here in Faerie. A reverence for the primordial forests, the bounty and mercilessness of the earth. To ask the blessing of the old gods, we lead the cattle between two bonfires. It helps to protect them. Then there are the forest rituals. Our gods are very important to us, and stags are, too."

I glanced back at the castle's flag. "Is it some kind of masculine thing?"

"A stag can move back and forth between the realms

of the living and the dead, the human and the fae. They're powerful, dominating. They're like nature itself —mystical, beautiful, and brutal at the same time." He met my gaze. "They take what they want. And for this one festival, this one night a year, the old god Cernunnos blesses us. The mists twine through the forest oaks. For one night, the Horned One transforms the worthy males into stags. We race through the forest and fight each other. Sometimes to the death. If I ever lost a fight in my stag form, I'd be dethroned."

Okay. Maybe the king had a darker side than I'd imagined. "None of this sounds...fun. It sounds sort of horrific."

When he met my gaze, his eyes burned with a cold intensity. "But that's what we're like. The fae. We are creatures of the earth and mists. We are warriors. And when we are at our best, we transcend our bodies and commune with the gods. When was the last time you really felt alive, Ava?"

Not anytime recently, I'd give him that. "I have no idea. Probably yelling at you in the bar."

"That's quite sad."

I sipped my coffee. "Just so I'm clear, it would be better if my 'good time' involved murdering people in the woods?"

"There are more pleasurable sides of Beltane," he said, his deep voice turning sultry.

I felt something coil tight inside me, but I ignored it. "Do you batter baby animals to death with clubs or something?"

He turned to me and tucked his finger under my

chin, lifting it so I couldn't look away. His pale eyes burned with a dominating ferocity that made my heart race—an otherworldly power that transfixed me and made me want to drop my gaze at the same time.

"No, Ava. We fuck each other hard up against the oak trees, rending the forest air with the sounds of our ecstasy. We fuck around bonfires, bathed in their flames." He leaned in closer, his finger gently stroking the side of my face. With his lips by my ear, his earthy, masculine scent wrapped around me like a forbidden caress. "When was the last time you lost yourself in a pleasure so intense, you forgot your name? That you forgot your own mortality? Because that is what it means to be fae. I could make you ache with pleasure until you forget the name of every human who made you think there was something wrong with you."

He stroked a delicate tip of his finger up my pointed ear, so light, and yet such a forbidden thrill that it made me shudder and clench tightly inside.

His eyes met mine again, and I felt that illicit, electric jolt of excitement at the unexpected intimacy. That close studying, like he was reading me. And that I was failing some sort of test.

"You fuck each other around the bonfires..." I repeated, like an idiot.

He traced his thumb over my lower lip. "And if you think I can't see how much that excites you, if you think I couldn't hear your heart racing, Ava, you are mistaken. Because if it were you and me, in the oak grove on Beltane, I would have you screaming my name. Calling me your king. I would have your body responding to my every command, shuddering with pleasure underneath me, until you forgot the human world existed at all."

I couldn't remember how to speak. "I see," I managed at last.

"If I could," he purred. "I would teach you what you really are, and I would make sure you never forgot it." His gaze lowered to my mouth like he was going to kiss me, and I was surprised at how much I wanted it. And even more horrified at the disappointment I felt when he didn't. "But that won't happen, of course. Because nothing can happen between us."

My breath hitched as he turned to walk away from me, and I muttered, "What was that about," feeling like I'd already lost the trial.

His lips were faintly curved in a smile. "That was about you being astoundingly judgmental even though you are no better or worse than the rest of us. And now you know it. You belong here, fucking at Beltane like the rest of us."

My pulse was racing out of control, and I felt as if I'd just lost some sort of battle against him. Particularly since I couldn't stop imagining bare skin in the forest, his hands cupping my ass, bodies sliding against each other. I could envision myself glowing and clenching as the King of the Fae made me moan toward the heavens, my nipples hard in the forest air. Slick with desire, shameless, on all fours...completely unable to control myself.

So *that* was a real Seelie party...

"No worse than the rest of you?" I repeated, gathering my thoughts. "It seems your estimation of me has gone up, then."

"It went up when you woke sober and on time." The king led me toward the dark line of trees.

"I can see why you wouldn't want a real wife. You'd miss out on the post-sacrifice orgies. I'll bet all the fae women are clamoring for a chance to get a crack at the handsome king all covered in blood from the stag fights."

His gaze slid to mine. "That is the second time you called me handsome. Is this why you have to pretend to hate me so much? You can't stop thinking about how I look."

I'm sure he already knew he was handsome. It wasn't the kind of beauty that went unnoticed.

He reached for my thermos of coffee and took a sip. I guess we were on "sharing thermos" terms now, even if we didn't like each other.

We'd nearly reached the tree line, a dark row of evergreens, their branches thick with snow and needles. Mist swirled between the trunks, and it was impossible to see more than a few feet into the interior of the forest. A chill ran down my spine.

The fae were so beautiful and refined, it hadn't occurred to me exactly how brutal they could be. And that made me wonder *exactly* how much danger I'd be in during these trials.

Then, out of the corner of my eye, a flicker of pale skin slipped between the trees.

I turned to see a beautiful woman with long, black hair and silvery skin washing a cloth in an icy stream.

Crimson blood seemed to stain the fabric. She was singing quietly, a mournful song in a language that I couldn't understand. Nonetheless, it made my heart clench and brought tears to my eyes.

I'd stopped walking to stare at her.

Torin leaned in, whispering, "The bean nighe. She's more spirit than fae."

"Amazing," I breathed.

She seemed to hear me, and she turned, her black eyes locking on me. Her lips were the same blood red as the cloth she washed, and her hands were stained with blood. She wore only the thinnest of white gowns. Black as coal, her eyes turned to the king. "Your Majesty?" she called out in a low voice. "Death is coming to Faerie."

"It always is. Do we have permission to enter the forest?"

She glanced at me, then back at the king.

"Of course, Your Majesty," she said at last. "That one belongs here in the wild."

King Torin inclined his head respectfully. "Thank you, mistress."

He led me deeper into the icy wood, and the fog enveloped us.

The creepy woman was right. I *did* feel like I belonged here.

13

AVA

As soon as we crossed beyond the first few trees, King Torin held up his hand, motioning for me to stop. "Okay," he said. "This is the first mile mark. Until the forest, there's not much to worry about."

I took in the billowing mist around me, and a cold sense of dread started to dance up my spine. "So what do I need to worry about here?"

"It's here, in the forest, where I expect people to be severely injured. It's the other contestants you need to worry about."

I hugged myself under the cloak. "You didn't mention this when we signed the contract."

"Would you have turned down fifty million just because of a little danger?"

No. "Maybe. What, exactly, will we be doing? Fighting each other like stags?"

"It's a race to select the strong and lithe. Every

contest will involve subterfuge, deceit, and lethal aggression."

My jaw tightened. Five years of slinging cocktails for humans hadn't exactly prepared me for lethal aggression.

It seemed I'd been wrong. This was nothing like *Hitched and Stitched*.

"These women will do anything to win," he went on, "and there's nothing barring violence in the rules. A fae queen must be ruthless, so it's really expected. They will use magic to try to bring down anyone in the front. And this is why it's always a princess who wins. Common fae like you don't have any magic."

My stomach was twisting. "Are you going to get to the part where you explain how I can win?"

He turned to me with a dark smile. "Fortunately, not all magic requires that one cast a spell." Torin reached into a pocket and withdrew three small glass vials. He handed one to me. "Be very careful with this."

The little vial hummed unnaturally in my hand. Inside, the glass swirled with dark orange gas. "What is it?" I asked.

"It's an ampule of purified magic."

"What am I supposed to do with it?"

"That one," he said, pointing to the vial with the glowing orange gas, "contains a very powerful vapor that will burn your nose and eyes if you inhale it. Throw it behind you as you're running, and the glass will shatter. Anyone within ten feet will be overwhelmed by the vapor, and they won't be able to see for at least five minutes."

Brutal.

He handed me two more glass vials. One was nearly opaque, containing a white vapor, while the last held a pale green liquid. It had a screw cap on it, as opposed to being a single glass ampule.

"What's this one?" I said, holding up the opaque container.

"That's basic magic fog. Just like the spice vapor, you throw it on the ground. The difference is, it's a smoke screen. It won't hurt anyone, but no one will be able to see a thing. It's a hundred times thicker than what you see now. Might help you escape in a tough situation."

Seems useful. "And this other one?" I asked, holding up the green.

"Anti-pain potion. Pretend you're doing tequila shots at Golden Shamrock and drink the whole thing down in one gulp. If you're hurt, you won't feel any pain for at least ten minutes. Be careful if you drink it, though. You can easily injure yourself further because you won't feel a thing."

"Let's hope I don't have to use that one."

King Torin's expression darkened, and I got the distinct impression that he didn't think that was likely.

He nodded at the forest. "Let's keep going, shall we?"

He started into the woods, and I followed. The path narrowed, and the temperature dropped as a thick evergreen canopy closed in overhead. Moss carpeted the path between the snow. From the forest floor, massive trees rose, their trunks covered in craggy bark. Though

I looked carefully, I didn't see any faces carved onto them.

The dense canopy of pine needles completely obscured the sky. In a few places, shafts of light filtered down and dappled the floor with golden flecks. Where the light shone brightest, little clusters of shimmering blue and purple butterflies flitted about in the wintry air.

"What did she mean?" My breath clouded around me. "When the washerwoman said death was coming?"

"She never explains, but it could be anything. An old fae could be dying right now. The kingdom itself is in the deadly throes of winter unless I find a queen." He glanced at me. "Or, of course, someone may die during the race."

"Cool."

The air was completely still, and I felt myself holding my breath. It was beautiful, but at the same time, I sensed something wasn't right. The back of my neck prickled with an uncomfortable sensation, like I was being watched.

"Torin?" I asked, "what sorts of animals live in this forest?"

"Deer and boar. Maybe a few bears."

"No dragons?"

He frowned. "No, dragons are extinct."

I took a sip of my coffee, wondering if I'd dreamed up the soaring dragon. But I was sure I'd been awake. "Are you sure they're all extinct? I saw something in the sky last night that might have been one."

King Torin stopped short and turned to look at me.

His eyes shone pale blue in the dim forest light. "Tell me exactly what you saw."

"It flew across the moon," I said. "It was large, with wings. I'm pretty sure it breathed fire."

He exhaled a cloudy puff of breath. "Did you see where it went?"

I shook my head. "No, it was just a shape against the stars."

King Torin glanced over my shoulder, then leaned down to speak in a whisper. "And this is part of the death returning to Faerie. It's not just the winters. Without a queen to generate new magic, evil creatures and destructive forces are bleeding in from the shadows again."

"Like the dragon?"

"Exactly. It would never have been here ten years ago, but darkness is filling the magical void." Shadows slid through his eyes. "And unfortunately, Ava, there are worse things out there than dragons."

❦ 14 ❦

AVA

We walked on through the icy forest, and the thick trees started to thin. Sunlit, snowy fields showed through gaps in the trees until we reached the final mile of the race, a clear, frozen path that ran back to the castle. As we approached the wooden stands, I noticed that a few people were already sitting in them.

"Torin," I said, "I think there are already people out here."

He glanced at the newly built tournament stands. "Damn. What are they doing up at this hour?" He sighed. "Well, it can't be helped now."

He started towards the grandstands at a fast clip. As we neared the bleachers, my stomach sank. Moria and Cleena sat right at the front, dressed in tight animal skins. I tried to avoid eye contact, but the two women glided into my path.

Moria's stunning burgundy hair hung around her shoulders, and she studied me with obvious hostility.

"Out for a walk with the king?" Her tone dripped with venom.

"We ran into each other," I said quickly. "Seems we're both early risers."

We were out of Torin's earshot, and Moria went for the jugular. "What are you wearing under that cloak?" She turned to Cleena. "You know, Princess, most females will do *anything* to get the attention of males. Showing off their thighs like Ava, trying to catch the king's attention. Trying to distract from the fact that under the surface, she's an empty shell." Her gaze snapped back to me. "But women like Cleena and me don't need to engage in those kinds of tactics. Not when we have the keen, sharp minds of men to keep a king engaged. And the appetite of a king, as well, for food and war. A tumble in the woods might provide a momentary diversion for him, but quick-witted conversation with a woman who is his peer won't be so quickly forgotten."

My eyebrows rose. "Please do let me know if you're ever going to display this wit of yours. Sounds *very* unique. For a woman, I mean."

Moria's eyes narrowed. "It seems you found an unfair advantage for yourself this morning. If you think he'll choose you just because you rutted with him, I'm afraid you're mistaken. He can find plenty of common fae to mate with every Beltane, but he'd never remember a single one of their names."

When I glanced at Cleena, I saw that she looked more bored than out for blood. I wondered if I should bother trying to explain that zero rutting had occurred

—but I was pretty sure the princess's mind was already made up.

I composed my features. "I got lost in the woods, and the king helped me find my way out. That's it."

Snowflakes had crystalized on her long, black lashes. "Just like he happened to give you a ride last night?"

"Life's full of coincidences," I said.

I began to walk away, but Cleena touched my arm. "What's your name, common fae? And who are your parents?"

"Ava." I let the silence hang in the air. I wasn't going to bother answering about my parents.

"Well, Ava," said Moria, "playing with fire will get your fingers burned."

"Oh." I widened my eyes. "Like this one?" I flipped her off, which seemed to be my new, very mature habit.

And with that, I hurried off around her, hoping to head back into the castle before I got into any more arguments.

But before I got to the castle door, a hand reached out from under the shadows of the grandstand, and Torin pulled me into the darkness beneath the seats.

He did not look amused. "I told you not to speak to the princesses."

"They were impossible to avoid."

His eyes flashed. "If they see you as a threat, they'll work together to eliminate you. I'm afraid you could be in danger now."

"They saw us together. I'm already in danger."

He stood close to me, one arm on my elbow, the other close to my waist. His blue eyes roved over my face, inspecting every inch of me, my forehead, eyebrows, nose, lips, and chin.

"What are you doing?" I whispered.

"Trying to decide how to glamour you."

"So they don't beat the shit out of me?"

"You won't last ten minutes otherwise."

Before I could ask exactly what the glamour would look like, he began to whisper in that same fae language Madam Sioba had used to create my ballgown. A delicious warmth spread over my skin, and the hairs on my arms tingled as the sensation moved to my shoulders.

King Torin's eyes were closed tightly with concentration, but I found myself unable to look away. I studied the dark sweep of his lashes, his thick black eyebrows, and his furrowed brow. It must have been the magic, but it felt like a powerful bond connected us. For just a moment, my gaze drifted down to his lips.

The warmth of his magic spread to my stomach and hips.

An unexpected scent filled the air, and it took me a moment to recognize it—strawberry ice cream.

His magic hummed up my neck, brushed my eyelids, and swirled about my lips until at last, he opened his bright blue eyes. "There," he said in a low voice, "that should do it."

Torin reached out and pulled a lock of my hair before my eyes, and I gasped. My hair had faded from brunette to a pale violet at the ends. "Now you look fae."

I took a deep breath, trying to be positive. "It's...pretty."

"Glad you like it, because you're stuck with it for a while."

"You can't un-glamour it?" I asked.

"No, but it'll fade in a few weeks, and you'll be back to normal." Torin pulled a small dagger from a leather sheath at his side and held up the blade, showing me my reflection in the bright surface. In addition to the violet hair, Torin had darkened my eyebrows and painted my lips a deep red. My eyes were now the same violet color as my hair.

I stared at myself in his blade. "Will the lipstick and eyebrows last for weeks?"

He shook his head. "Just the hair. But Ava, keep yourself out of sight until the race starts. Once they've got you in their sights again, it'll all be over."

🎰 15 🎰

AVA

As I stood by the starting line, no one gave me a second look. The icy winter wind rushed over us, and I kept my face tilted down, my violet locks whipping around my face.

The news crews stood at the edges of our throng, cameras trained on the princesses at the front. They'd formed their own little clique near the starting line, while the rest of the common fae milled around behind them. I was happy to hang back for now.

Moria and a few of the others had decorated their faces with bright blue war paint, which didn't help ease my nerves. Clearly, we were going into battle, not for a Sunday fun run.

At last, one of King Torin's footmen strode to the front of the starting line, a man with long red braids over his blue uniform. He carried a silver staff that he banged twice on the frozen earth. "Thirty seconds from now, at the sound of the trumpet, the race will begin."

His words sent my nerves juddering, and I clenched my fists, repeating my mantra to myself.

Fifty million dollars. Fifty million dollars.

Around me, the contestants were jostling for good positions, though no one seemed to be moving toward the princesses. I found myself about a row back, sandwiched between a muscular fae with pink hair and one who was mysteriously soaking wet.

I glanced to my right. A footman marched toward the starting line with his trumpet. He put it to his lips, and I held my breath, waiting for the sound.

When the horn blared, my heart thundered.

The contestants surged forward in a mad rush, pushing past the starting line and down the hill. I kept a decent pace behind the princesses, but they were running at an all-out sprint. How were they going to keep up that pace? We were all fae here, and I doubted they spent more time running than I did. They were going to burn out in half a mile.

As the distance stretched between us, a bit of concern twisted in my chest. What were they planning with this sprint?

While I raced down the hill in the stinging winter air, the sun came out from behind the clouds. Golden light shone off the stone, glinting on the drifting flakes around us and turning the iced tree branches into glittering crystals. Clouds of breath puffed from the princesses ahead of me as they ran at the maximum of their capacity.

A cameraperson raced alongside us in a little vehicle,

an image that seemed bizarrely out of place here. But they were mostly focused on the frontrunners.

I'd been saving some energy, waiting until I knew what they were up to. At the forest's edge, they sprinted even faster and in unison, without saying a word to one another.

They'd planned something ahead of time, and maybe I shouldn't be in the front lines when the plan came to fruition. Because it wasn't just a race, but a battle.

I drifted back into the pack of runners, remembering Torin's warning about the forest being the most dangerous part of the race.

We crossed into the shade of the trees, and an unnatural, icy fog billowed around me until I could no longer see a thing. All I could hear was rhythmic breathing and the pounding of feet against the ground.

A few women sprinted ahead of me, out of my sight maybe five seconds before agonized screams pierced the quiet. My heart skipped a beat, and I hung back a little. Didn't seem like a good idea to run *toward* the screaming.

Ahead, another horrified scream pierced the air. None of us could see what was happening, but it sounded brutal.

Clearly, the princesses had laid a trap for the rest of us. Around me, the other common fae stopped at the edge of the mist, and I could just about make out their silhouettes in the fog.

"What the hell is going on?" someone nearby asked. "What are we supposed to do here?"

No one—including me—seemed to have an answer,

but time was running out. If I waited too long, there'd be no chance to catch up, and it already felt like I'd lost the race. I had to beat at least one of the princesses to make the cut, and they'd all slipped far ahead.

I considered my choices. The mist stretched into the woods. Running around the fog wasn't an option.

The potions weren't helpful. Gas, fog, anti-pain...

Maybe I could climb a tree?

It was at that point that I heard the low, mournful song of the bean nighe. I moved toward the sound and found her standing by the stream. She stared at me, her eyes black as coal, skin shining with silver like she was bathed in moonlight. My breath caught in my throat at her unearthly beauty.

She turned, slipping into the fog—a smudge of darkness in the cloud around me.

Wind howled loudly around us, drowning out the song of the bean nighe. When I glanced up, I saw the wind blowing the snow from the trees and shaking the branches. The freezing gale swept away the fog, too. But the wind also carried with it the sounds of torment. Screams floated between the boughs.

Had the bean nighe done this?

As the mist cleared, I caught a glimpse of four injured fae, and my stomach turned. One of them lay crumpled in the middle of the path, clutching her right ankle. I sucked in a short breath as nausea roiled my stomach. Her foot had been hacked clean off, and blood stained the snow around her. Her face was gray with shock.

"Oh, my gods," said a woman next to me.

My gaze slid to the other contestant writhing in the bloodstained snow. Both of her feet were missing, her legs ending in bloody stumps.

I stared with dawning horror. This place—these people—were fucking barbaric.

The runners around me screamed in panic.

The princesses stood just beyond the injured runners, catching their breath. Just as I'd predicted, the early sprint had knocked the wind out of them, and they'd burned themselves out completely.

"Fucking psychopaths," I muttered. I wanted to run, but I still didn't know how the trap worked. And the fact that the princesses were still there—watching—made me think it wasn't over yet.

I scanned the bloody ground, trying to figure out what had severed their legs. It took me a few seconds, then I noticed a faint shimmer in the air, a narrow line strung across the path. A few red beads of blood dripped from it, perfect round drops of red against white, like holly berries in the snow. The princesses had set up some sort of razor-sharp magical trip wire.

The screams of pain still filled the icy air.

With a grunt, I leaned down, snatched up a thin tree branch, and threw it on the wire. It sliced clean through the wood, and I heard the princesses tittering on the other side.

"Do you think this is funny?" I shouted. "Injuring and disfiguring people?" I turned. "They've set up a razor wire!"

Around me, the other fae were shouting curses at the princesses.

The princesses fell silent, and Moria's smile slipped. She turned, stomping off through the snow. I watched as she started jogging again, though her sluggish gait suggested she was tired from her earlier sprint.

I could simply leap over the wire, but I had no idea if everyone had heard me. Did I want fifty million? Hell, yes, I did. But even that much money wasn't worth a ton of severed limbs on my conscience.

I glanced at a mossy rock by the edge of the path. I snatched it up, took several steps closer, and hurled it at the wire. The wire snapped with a sharp twang.

I broke into a sprint, hoping they hadn't set up any more. I scanned the ground while I ran, desperately trying to catch the faint sheen of wire.

Up ahead, the princesses looked fatigued. I was starting to gain on them. When we broke from the woods, I was no more than five yards behind the princesses.

With a burst of speed, I pumped my arms hard and passed the hindmost princess, a delicate beauty with dark skin who was gasping audibly. I ran past the ravaged corpse of a fae with white hair, her head ripped from her neck, staining the snow with claret.

Up ahead, a red-haired princess was raking her long claws through another common fae, tearing through her chest.

Holy shit.

But I was still moving faster, catching up with the princesses. I listened to the sound of their wheezing.

Ahead, the finish line was maybe two tenths of a

mile away. With a final sprint, I could pass them all. I dodged past another one, closing in on Moria.

But as I narrowed the gap, she turned to look at me. Her elbow slammed into my chest with a force that knocked me flat on my back. I scrambled up, but another foot caught me in the side. Something snapped, the disturbing sound of breaking bone...

Oh, *fuck*.

It was a weird sensation, not immediately painful, but then a shooting pain lanced through me. As I started after the princesses, agony tore at my side. Up ahead, Moria crossed the finish line, her burgundy hair flowing behind her, arms over her head.

I shambled forward, trying to run.

Pain engulfed my chest, and something was wrong with my breathing. I coughed, and blood spattered into the snow. I stared with horror at the red droplets.

They'd punctured my fucking lung.

I staggered forward, spitting hot blood on the ground. Gasping, I looked up at the stands in the distance, and the princesses jogging up the hill toward the castle.

I was about to lose.

From up ahead, I heard a woman yell, "Can't run with a hole in your lung!"

I stumbled forward, clutching at my side. Two tenths of a mile to the castle that towered over the landscape, but I could no longer walk, let alone run.

I slipped my hand into my pocket, feeling for the vials of magic Torin had given me. Did I want to run into a cloud of gas? Absolutely not. Was it the only way to get past this trial and closer to my fifty million? Probably, yes.

Shaking, I jammed my hand into my pocket and drew out one of the vials, staring in a daze at the faint orange light glimmering between my fingers. Precisely as Torin had told me *not* to do, I hurled it ahead of the princesses who'd taken the lead.

The vial exploded, and an orange mist billowed into the air.

Even from here, the inhalation hurt like crazy and breathing it in with a broken rib and injured lung was a blinding, maddening sort of agony. Based on the screams from in front of me, it was worse just twenty feet away.

Fortunately, I had another vial, one that would ensure I wouldn't feel a thing.

I reached into my pocket removed the anti-pain potion. Shaking, I swallowed the contents, a slightly nauseating mixture of sickly sweet and medicinal herbs. I closed my eyes, feeling the warmth spread through my chest, and the pain disappeared immediately.

Up ahead, the runners had stopped, falling to the ground in the cloud of poison.

I started moving again, not at full speed, but putting one foot in front of the other. Tears streamed down my face as I dragged myself through the rosy cloud. The haze cleared, and the other fae—those with two functioning lungs—were passing me again. I shuffled forward, trying to keep up, dragging myself closer to the black castle on the hill and the waiting camera crews.

As a raven-haired princess passed me, she shot me a withering look, but she looked far too tired for any more attacks at this point.

One by one, the other contestants passed the finish line, someone calling out each of their names in a booming voice. A trumpet sounded, and the crowd screamed.

My feet thudded on the icy earth, and my gaze homed in on the stands.

The king sat calmly on a raised dais, claret silks above him, a silver crown on his brow, and guards all around.

Even if I couldn't feel the pain from my punctured lung, my breath was rasping. Whistling. My head swam from a lack of oxygen.

A droplet of blood fell in the snow from my lips, but it seemed so distant, layered with shadows.

Darkness filled my vision as I collapsed onto the ice.

As if from a distance, I heard the TV host shout "— the only common fae to make the cut to the next round!"

AVA

When I opened my eyes, I was being carried. Strong arms cradled me, and my head rested against a man's chest. He smelled nice, like an ancient forest and the faintest hint of a mountain stream.

Distant screams floated through the air. Not agonized, like before. Jubilant.

Had I lost?

These thoughts were floating by like dandelion seeds on the wind, because the anti-pain potion was beginning to fade. What had been a distant ache now turned hot and agonizing.

I coughed, and my vision flashed white.

Breath warmed the side of my face, and a low voice whispered in my ear, "You'll be fine. I've got you."

That rich timbre...I recognized it, but it couldn't be Torin, right? I opened my eyes, and my blurred vision focused on a perfect face—cheekbones sharpened by shadows, pale eyes staring straight ahead.

"Torin?" I rasped.

"Don't talk," he said. "They beat you, just as I was afraid of. You're badly hurt."

I tried to form the words to ask if I was still in the running for the fifty million, but my next breath was like swallowing shards of glass.

In this very moment, I was starting to think maybe this wasn't worth the money. Maybe this was all another very bad decision in a lifetime of bad decisions.

Torin's gaze swept down over me, and if I didn't know any better, I'd say his forehead looked creased with worry for me. Which made me wonder if I was about to die, and he'd lose his best-laid plans.

When he cupped the side of my face, his skin making direct contact with mine, I could already feel his magic sliding over me. Quietly, he murmured in the Fae language, a low and hypnotic purr that thrummed over my skin. There was something rhythmic about the way he chanted, his skin glowing with magic. It was entrancing, bringing to mind beating drums, fires burning under a starry sky.

His eyes locked on mine, and his hand traced down from the side of my face to my chest, just between my breasts. My heart fluttered. If circumstances were different—if I didn't know this was all fake, and if my life weren't a complete mess—I would absolutely fall for this man.

And with every quiet word he uttered, with every light stroke of his fingertips, the pain began to ebb, my muscles growing more supple and relaxed. I felt as if the Seelie king were in complete control of my body now, orchestrating my healing like an artist. And I didn't hate that as much as I should.

I wondered if he could hear my heart racing again, because this type of magic he possessed had a disturbingly sensual edge, making my body feel full, even if he was hardly touching me.

He lowered his face, his gaze tracing over mine. Studying me again. Reading my body's reactions. He wasn't just taking the pain away from me—his magic was flowing *into* me. From the point where his hand met my body, tendrils of heat slid into my chest, sliding down into my core.

My mind flickered with images of Faerie—then uninvited images of what I imagined he'd look like without his shirt on, hunting in the woods. Not hunting to kill. Hunting to fuck, to make women moan and fill them with the power he drew from the land.

Gods, the raw *power* of him, like tapping into the earth itself...

I closed my eyes, growing acutely aware of how my wet clothes felt against my skin, clinging to me, and I had the disturbing sensation that I wanted to tear them off. That I wanted him to see *me* naked, to use his mouth on me instead of his hands...a real *Seelie* party.

But I refused to accept the ache that was building in me, because I wasn't falling for assholes anymore.

Andrew. Think of Andrew. But in my mind's eye, I could only see Torin ripping through my underwear, spreading my thighs, and taking me hard and fast up against an oak until I forgot my name.

Freaking hell, I'd only been with him one day, and

that was all it took to fall under the spell of a beautiful man. What about the pledge I'd made to myself?

Gritting my teeth, I sat up, knocking his hand off me. "That's enough," I said, catching my breath. I held up the covers over my chest like I was naked, even though I was still fully clothed. As I was trying to gain control of myself, my voice came out sounding furious. Imperious, even.

Torin arched a surprised eyebrow. "I wasn't quite finished."

"I feel fine now. You can get away from me." I nodded at the door. "I need sleep, thank you."

Never in my life had I sounded this prim and proper, like an irritated librarian in a convent.

Freaking hell. Maybe he was right about me being judgmental.

My mind flicked back to our conversation earlier, where I'd been making fun of him for hating parties. But who was the prude now?

He'd said, "A real Seelie party."

And now I understood exactly what he meant.

※

I WOKE ON SOFT, CLEAN SHEETS AND TOOK A DEEP breath. A cool breeze whispered over my skin. Shalini sat slumped in a silky arm chair, sunlight washing over her.

She looked up at me, and her eyes lit. She slammed the book in her hands shut. "You're awake!"

I touched my chest, my gaze roaming over the

books lining the small room. I'd been brought back to the chamber where I'd slept last night. I inhaled deeply, relieved to find the pain was almost gone, then winced a little, feeling bruised around my ribs. "I think I'm better.

She rose. "Hang on a second. You can speak to the medical expert." She crossed to the door and beckoned to someone.

A moment later, Torin was crossing into the room, and his piercing gaze landed on me.

I swallowed hard. "You didn't tell me yet if I made the cut."

"Just barely," he said. "Two broken ribs and a punctured lung. It had nearly collapsed by the time you crossed the finish line. You could have suffocated or bled to death." He quirked an eyebrow. "Last one to make the cut. You barely got over the line in time, but you did it."

I let out a long, slow breath. "Oh, thank the gods."

Torin sat next to me on the bed, and I felt the mattress depress with his weight. "Tell me if anything hurts when I touch it."

Oh, gods. There goes my restraint. "Okay..." I said slowly, not sure if it would send me into some kind of unwanted lust spiral. I started to push up on my elbows, but he raised a hand, signaling for me to stay down.

Torin pulled back the sheets, and I glanced down at my sweat-dampened shirt. He traced his fingertips over my ribs on my right side. A line formed between his eyebrows as he concentrated. "Does this hurt? You didn't let me finish healing you for reasons I'd frankly love to examine."

I wouldn't.

"That does," I said wincing as he touched my ribs below my breast. He was trying to be gentle, but I still felt a stab through my chest. "Are you training to be a doctor or something?"

"Here in Faerie, the one with the strongest magic is the best doctor, and I have the most powerful magic of any fae in this realm. You must have felt it."

"What about the women with the severed limbs?" I asked.

"They did not make it over the line in time, so they will be recovering in whatever common fae towns they hail from."

My eyebrows shot up. *Ice cold.* As soon as I got my money, I would be out of this place. I'd always been suspicious of other fae, but never before had I fully understood how terrifying they were.

He paused, a wicked glint smoldered in his eyes. "Unless there's some reason, Ava, that you are afraid of me being near you."

"Don't be ridiculous. I just don't need someone fussing over me." It was my *prim and proper* voice again, one that I'd never before used in my life. I was now a deeply repressed Victorian governess.

He cupped my side, and his magic slid into me. A flash of heat flared in my core, and I sucked in a sharp breath. A soothing sensation washed over me, like warm water trickling down my skin, making my muscles relax.

Then his magic slipped into me, making my body feel full and ripe with his essence, his primordial power...

It was a divine feeling that made my limbs feel languorous and supple, and despite what the Victorian governess was saying out loud, the real me didn't want it to end.

"You should be fully healed now." He gave me a half-smile, then pulled that delicious magic from me. "I'm impressed that you dragged yourself over the finish line."

I nodded, and a dark image unfurled in my mind—the two women with severed legs, screaming in pools of their own blood. "A good day for both of us, then. I could still win the money, and you have a potential queen, with no messy emotional involvement."

His expression was unreadable. "Exactly the way it should be for a king."

"That whole thing was brutal today," I said. "Have you ever considered banning mutilations and murder attempts during the trials?"

He pulled his gaze away, staring out the window. "That is not the fae way, Ava. Do not try to change us just because you lived a few years among insipid humans, with all the comfort their culture entails. We are creatures of the Wild Hunt, and we could never be anything else. If you feel we go too far, it's only because you are living a lie about your true nature." The corner of his mouth curled. "Because underneath it all, you are as vicious as the rest of us."

And with that, he stood and crossed to the door. I shot Shalini a nervous look, and for the first time, I saw her looking unnerved as well. She gave me a casual shrug, but by the furrow of her brow, I could tell she was wondering if we'd made a bad decision in coming here.

Torin paused at the door to look back at me. "I'll return for you later. We must prepare. Because if you thought the competition today was brutal, I don't know if you'll survive what comes later."

A fog of cold dread wrapped around me, and I clutched at my blankets.

At least I wasn't thinking about Andrew anymore.

❧ 17 ❧

AVA

When I awoke, it was late in the day. The afternoon sun poured in through the window, filling the room with a honey-hued light. It bathed the old book spines and the black fur blanket in gold, and cast long, deep blue shadows across the stone floor. Here, even the light seemed enchanted—richer, more vibrant.

Slowly, I rose from the bed, running my hand over my ribs to check for sore points. The pain had faded, feeling like a faint bruise at most.

I glanced down, slightly disgusted to find that I was still in my running clothes. But I supposed no one was around to judge me.

Blinking, I entered the larger room and found Shalini sprawled on her bed, reading a book. She looked up at me with a grin. "Look at you, already better."

My head was pounding like I was hungover. "Almost." I flopped down on the bed next to her, closing my eyes. King Torin's healing appeared to have worked, but it had left my muscles and the cartilage between my ribs painfully sore. "Have you heard anything about the next trial yet? Torin suggested it would be more brutal than the first."

"Shit. No, I haven't heard a thing. Aeron came by earlier with food, but that was it."

My stomach rumbled, and I sat up. By the door was a small wooden table laden with silver cloche–lidded platters.

"There's chicken and some kind of herbal salad with flowers," said Shalini, adding, "Surprisingly tasty."

Swinging my feet over the side of the bed, I approached the table and removed one of the domed covers. The food looked exquisite, the salad riotous shades of spring and sunsets—green, violet, carrot, canary yellow, and plum. I pulled a plate from the table and crossed to a desk to eat, then popped a little yellow flower into my mouth, which was flavored with a tangy orange vinaigrette.

Worry danced in the background of my thoughts.

Let's hope Torin keeps me alive until this is over.

WHEN I'D FINISHED EATING, I WENT INTO THE bathroom and turned on the water in the copper claw-foot tub. Outside, a lurid crimson sunset stained the sky, tinging the snow with red. I stripped off the filthy running clothes and dipped my feet into the hot water.

I slid into the bath, my skin turning pink as steam coiled around me. I didn't belong here. Even the dark castle stones made me feel that way. Despite my ears and genetic makeup, I was a human through and through—Chloe's daughter.

When I closed my eyes, I kept seeing visions of blood seeping into snow.

Forcing those images out of my mind, I stretched my arms over my head, letting the hot water run over me, remembering the feel of Torin's magic. Now I could feel the knots and the tightness in my chest loosen. The skin over my ribs was unblemished, unbruised. Torin's healing touch had been miraculously effective.

I grabbed a bar of soap and ran it over my body. It smelled of evergreen trees and petrichor.

Only when the water started getting cold did I drag myself from the tub. I dried my hair and body with a towel. Still damp, I crossed into the main room to find we were no longer alone. Torin had returned and draped himself over a velvety armchair. "We need to train." He pulled out a silver flask and took a sip. "Are you ready?"

I stared at him. "Does it look like I'm ready?"

"Get dressed, Ava. Let's try to make sure the next trial goes better than today's." He nodded at a pile of tidy white clothes, neatly folded on the table where the food had been. He rose from the chair and slid his flask back into his pocket. "A half mile east of the castle, you'll find a clearing in the woods. A cemetery. Look for the lit torches through the tree branches, and you'll find me there."

When the door closed behind him, I turned to Shalini, still clutching my towel, and frowned. "He's awfully bossy."

"He *is* a fae king with nearly unlimited magical power, so...I think that's expected."

"A cemetery, though?" I snatched the pile of clothes from the table. "Did he say what we'd be doing?"

"Not a word." She jumped off her bed and pulled on a cloak. "But I'm coming with you."

"Why not stay in the warmth?" I knew Shalini well enough to drop the towel and start dressing.

"Because I came here for adventure, and I won't get it reading books. Although some of the smut is really quite good." She smiled brightly.

I pulled on a pair of white pants, a matching shirt, and a white woolen cloak. Perfect for blending into the snow outside. "If I die during the next trial, do you think you could stay and ask Aeron out?"

"How about we don't find out?"

I frowned at Shalini's red cloak, thinking of the medieval English queen who'd escaped a winter siege camouflaged in white. "If you want to come with me, you need to dress the part. All white. I don't think anyone is supposed to see us, or the princesses will be kicking my ribs in again."

Shalini cocked her head, and the warm light shown in her dark brown eyes. "Listen, Ava, it's a bit scarier here than I imagined, but I think you just need to go with it. You are fae, after all. I watched clips of Moria and the princesses online. They're taking no prisoners. You've got to be as brutal as they are."

"I *did* poison a crowd of people with mustard gas or something today," I admitted. "Which is something I never expected to do with my life."

"Good. If they come for you again, go for the jugular. Because it's you or them, and I *really* prefer you."

I HUGGED MY CLOAK TIGHTLY AS WE CROSSED INTO the dark landscape and the icy wind stung my cheeks. Shalini had found a white cloak several sizes too large, and she trudged by my side. I could hear her teeth chattering, but she didn't complain once. We entered the dark forest. Moonlight streamed over iced tree branches.

"What do you think the princesses are doing now?" she asked.

"Hot bath, maybe. And some champagne. Celebrating their wins."

"And that's what we'll do after your next win," she said brightly.

There was a note of false cheer in her voice, and I appreciated her effort. I could tell she was worried about where this would all go, but she was doing her best not to show it.

Between the dark trunks, warm light flickered. As we drew closer, I glanced at the ribbons and baubles decorating the tree branches. I stopped to look at one of the glittering charms swinging in the breeze. A small golden frame encircled a portrait of a beautiful woman in a dress with a high collar. Jewels, trinkets, and skeleton keys swayed at the ends of silk ribbons, and little spheres held tiny toys. Children's faces adorned some of the little portraits. I wasn't sure what all this meant, but a shudder rippled up my spine.

I paused again to look at one of the little oval portraits that twisted in the wind. On the back, someone had inscribed the words,

Come away, O human child!
To the waters and the wild
With a faery, hand in hand,
For the world's more full of weeping
than you can understand.

The sadness of the words coiled deep inside me, and it took me a moment to realize I'd seen them before—in a Yeats poem called "The Stolen Child."

"Is it just me," I whispered, "or is this place creepy?"

"Not just you," Shalini whispered back. "A forest full of children's pictures hanging from trees is unquestionably creepy as fuck."

"Ava..." Torin's low voice floated on the wind, making my heart speed up.

I followed the flickering lights, until we crossed into a clearing. Crooked tombstones jutted from the snowy earth like monstrous teeth. When I looked closer, I saw the death's head carvings above the text.

All around the clearing, ribbons and trinkets hung from the trees, some of them tinkling together in the wind. In the shadows of an oak, Torin stood next to Aeron.

He stepped forward, and I caught a glimpse of two rapiers in his hands.

I hugged my cloak like a shield. "What are we doing out here?"

He held up one of the rapiers, then tossed it to me. It arced through the air, and I darted forward to catch it by the hilt, surprised to find it was much heavier than what I was used to. Now this was a *real* sword, not the modern kind I'd practiced with.

"Not really into fencing safety protocols, are you?" I said.

Torin marched through the snow, stepping over a tiny tombstone that looked disturbingly like it might belong to a small child. He crossed into an open area, a cleared snowy circle within the tombstones. Once, maybe a temple or church had stood there.

The corner of his mouth curled. "I know you are a fencing champion, but that was among humans. I need to see how you compete at the fae level."

I stopped myself from arguing that of course I was good, because the truth was, humans were not as fast, strong, or dexterous as the fae. Perhaps he had a point.

"Why are we in a cemetery in the woods?" I asked. "What is this place?"

"We're here because no one ever comes here." Torin prowled closer in the cleared circle, graceful as a cat. When he was only a few feet from me, he stopped and looked around, as if noticing the strangeness for the first time. "It's the old burying ground for the curiosities from long ago."

"The curiosities?" Shalini asked. "What does that mean?"

"It's what we used to call humans we brought here. Long ago, wealthy fae would bring young human curiosities to our realm and raise them." He shrugged.

"It was fashionable, hundreds of years ago." He glanced at me. "You were raised among humans."

"You two would both be considered curiosities," added Aeron. "Exotic creatures from another world. Even if one of you is technically fae."

"No," said Torin, his eyes locked on me. "Ava is a changeling, of course."

"Hang on," I said. "So, the fae...kidnapped human children?"

Torin sighed. "They were very well looked after." His gaze slid over a row of tiny gravestones. "At least, attempts were *made* to look after them. Humans are so fragile that it's confusing to us. They really die very easily."

"It was a different time," added Aeron with a shrug.

Torin nodded. "And the fae who took the curiosities usually left behind a fae changeling with the human parents. The changelings were usually demented, wild fae who served no purpose here in Faerie. But they were glamoured to look like human babies, so the families never knew." He cocked his head as he looked at me. "Like you, Ava."

"Okay, that's really not what I am," I snapped. Fuck. It wasn't, was it?

Torin lifted his blade and inspected it in the moonlight. "Honestly, it was a real improvement on fae–human relations from a thousand years ago, when we used to cut out the eyes and tongues of any humans who spotted us in the forest."

"Perfectly reasonable, then." *This fucking place...* "Can we just get on with the fencing?"

He nodded and pointed a few feet away from him. "Start there." He glanced at Shalini and Aeron. "You might want to move out of the way. We will be moving around quite a bit."

"Okay." I stepped closer to him, lifting the sword with feigned awkwardness. "Is this right? I'm easily confused, because I've only spent time around curiosities and not real people." I waved it around like it was a flyswatter.

Shalini snorted a laugh.

King Torin sighed. "I honestly can't tell if you're joking, so I will go ahead and explain. Your goal is to not get stabbed."

I stared at him. This was not my experience of competitive fencing, which was not actually lethal. "Sorry, what? What are the actual rules here?" For foil, the strike zone was the lamé, the full-torso vest. For épée, the target was the whole body. For sabre, it was above the waist. Sabre was a slashing weapon, but foil hits had to be with the tip. I was used to a *very* specific set of rules.

With this sword, in Faerie? I had no idea what we were doing.

He cocked his head. "I told you the actual rules. Try not to get stabbed. And try to stab me. When you do, you get a point."

Okay. I began to walk toward him. He held his sword out in a casual grip, and when I was close enough, I tapped my blade against his.

"Don't go for my sword," he said. "You will want to hit me."

I didn't wait for him to finish. As fast as I could, I slashed the end of my blade at his chest, slicing an eight-inch gash through his cloak.

King Torin jumped back, staring at me, then a slow smile turned the corner of his lips. "Good." He attacked immediately.

This time, I parried hard, driving his blade toward the floor. Then, before he could react, I grabbed the hilt of his sword and wrenched it clean out of his hand. I threw it, and it skidded across the icy snow. I whirled and pressed my blade against his throat—lightly.

Okay, so that was not a standard fencing move, but nor was this standard fencing—and it seemed like these swords were the actual, medieval dangerous kind, and not the light foils I'd practiced with.

I arched an eyebrow. "How am I doing?"

His blue eyes blazed in the darkness. After another moment, he returned my smile. "Perhaps you did learn some things among the curiosities, then. Or you adapt quickly." He raised his hand. "Aeron. My blade."

Aeron was already standing by the rapier. With the tip of his toe, he expertly flicked it up into the air, and Torin caught it effortlessly.

"All right," he said, leveling the rapier at me. "This time, I know who I'm fighting."

He held up his left arm, pointing his sword at me with the right. I did the same, sliding my feet into the starting position, my right foot pointed at him. He advanced, fast as lightning, stabbing with the end of his rapier. I parried it, driving the blade up and above my head. With a quick twist, I thrust my blade forward and skewered him neatly in the shoulder. Just a *tiny* little stab through his cloak, but I stared at it, my stomach twisting. "Sorry."

The weapons I'd trained on weren't actually designed to skewer anyone, but in Faerie of course they were.

"Don't apologize." He grunted. "Best of seven."

"Three for Ava, zero for Torin," Shalini called out in a tone that could only be described as gloating.

This time Torin was more circumspect in his approach. He carefully circled me, stabbing and feinting —testing my reflexes. I waited until he'd lunged a little bit too far and parried hard, slashing at his knee. Quickly, Torin jumped out of the way, cursing under his breath.

"Any other techniques you want to fill me in on?"

He smiled back at me. "Stay alive."

He began to circle me again, feinting and testing. I kept up my defensive strategy, parrying his strokes, staying out of striking range. Even though he needed me to be good, I could tell he was competitive as hell. He wanted to even the score, and I was more than willing to make him work for it.

"All right." Torin flashed me a mischievous smile. "Let's try this with an offhand. Aeron, toss me a dagger."

Aeron, who apparently had been prepared for this request, tossed a short dagger in Torin's general direction. Torin reached out with his free hand and caught it.

"And what about me?" I said. "Can I get a parrying dagger, too?"

"Is your counsel ready with one?" Torin continued to circle me, like a hunter with his eye on his prey.

"She would have been," I said, "if anyone had told us why we were coming here."

"I gotcha, Ava," shouted Shalini.

Out of the corner of my eye, I saw silver arc through the air, then a dagger plunged into the snow at my feet.

At this point, the fight began in earnest.

Now it became clear that King Torin was used to fighting with two blades, and I was not. Among the *curiosities*, fencing was a popular sport—but it was done in a modern style, and with a single sword. I was already out of my league, not being on a fencing strip, and doing all this circling on the snow. Adding an additional weapon into the mix was stretching the bounds of my ability. Still, I put up the best fight that I could.

I defended well, but Torin fought hard, herding me to the edge of the clearing. At any moment, I was going to fall backward over the row of children's graves.

As I faltered, he stabbed, and my parry missed. The tip of his rapier nicked my shoulder.

He cocked his head. "There."

Irritated, I raised my sword. "You're still down two points."

Torin stepped back into the circle, assuming the starting position. I lunged forward in a surprise attack, but he was somehow ready. With ease, he caught my blade between his off-hand dagger and his rapier, and ripped my sword from my hand. In an instant, he'd nicked my other shoulder.

I gritted my teeth, feeling my irritation simmer. But

I kept my mouth shut because I knew better than to be a sore loser.

"Three-two." Amusement gleamed in the king's eyes. "Next touch ties it."

Torin's sword was up, and his little smile suggested he had full confidence. I sensed that he knew he'd figured me out, that this final point would go in his favor. I'd do my best to make sure it didn't.

I raised my blade, and Torin immediately advanced. His rapier weaved around in a serpentine motion, but I wasn't used to looking out for a dagger, too. I backed away, unable to watch the two blades simultaneously.

His rapier slashed, and I parried it. He counter-parried, and I leapt to the side to avoid being caught by his blade. He lunged at me with his dagger, but I ducked under his blow and slashed up with my own. Sadly, Torin was ready, deflecting my blade away with the hilt of his rapier.

"That's not going to work," he said with a cockiness that ignored the near miss.

As I steadied myself, he whipped forward and stabbed with his dagger. Somehow, I managed to defend, catching the tip of his rapier in the guard of my own. The blades of our daggers sparked against one another.

Torin pushed, driving my dagger arm down and his own dagger toward my throat.

"Yield," he commanded in a low, velvety tone that brought to mind the feel of his magic inside me.

"No." My arm shook, and his dagger inched closer

and closer. He was going to use his size and strength to score the final point. He knew it, and I knew it.

What he didn't know was that I always fought to win, and that included with more than just a blade.

I lifted my leg and brought my foot down hard into his kneecap. A disturbing *crack* sounded, and the king dropped his blades.

Slowly, Torin stooped to one knee, the muscles in his jaw working. The wind whipped over his hair, and I had the sense that he was mastering control over himself.

I leveled my blade at Torin's throat. "Sorry, darling. No rules. You yield."

I knew it had hurt, but as a fae, he'd heal exceedingly quickly. After all, he wasn't like the fragile humans buried here.

Torin looked up at me, his jaw working. Slowly, his lips slid into a charming smile. "Looks like I absolutely picked the right person."

High-pitched laughter floated on the cold wind, and I turned to see that a newcomer had joined our group.

Orla stood in the shadows by an oak, her blonde hair whipped by the wind. "Dearest brother, it sounds like you have picked a vicious one. Take care to keep her safe, though."

Torin rose, flashing her an indulgent grin. But when I looked back to see her, she was gone, already blending into the night around us.

I COLLAPSED INTO MY BED, MY TOES AND FINGERS numb with the cold. A fire crackled in the fireplace, the only light in the room. Under the warmth of my blankets, my muscles were starting to melt.

The fencing tournament would be the final event, several weeks from now. But as the *only* fae here without magic, Torin was determined to make sure I had every advantage possible when it came to skill. I'd be training with him every night.

The day had exhausted me. This was, quite literally, more exercise than I'd gotten in a week back in the human world.

"Shalini!" I called out. "My whole body hurts."

"Fifty million," she called back.

Right. Fair point.

And whatever else Andrew and Ashley were doing, I couldn't imagine it had been half as interesting as my day.

Tonight, I hadn't the energy to look for dragons in the sky. I gave the stars a cursory glance through the mullioned windows, then closed my eyes and fell into a deep, deep sleep.

❧ 18 ❧
AVA

By my sixth day of sparring with the king, my muscles ached and bruises covered both our bodies. As soon as I'd slammed my heel into his knee, Torin had stopped holding back.

Alone, I trudged into the shadowy cemetery, where the moonlight silvered the snow. I was learning to ignore the cold and fight without the cloak so I could move more easily. As long as we were sparring, the exertion kept me warm enough.

I found Torin standing by himself in the cemetery clearing, the wind whipping at his cloak. As always, he'd brought two rapiers with him. Once I stepped into the snowy ring, he tossed one through the air at me. Caught off guard, I only just managed to grab it by the hilt.

"Give me a minute, Torin." Annoyed, I yanked at the button on my cloak. I knew he'd pull some kind of sneak attack, so I ripped it off quickly and tossed it into the snow behind me.

Torin stiffened, his gaze sliding down my body as he

took in the form-fitting black clothes I wore underneath.

Was he checking me out? How many of us contestants had he checked out over the past week? The king, surely, was a bit of a player—and that was why he could never get married for real. As long as it was merely a business arrangement, he could cheat all he wanted, guilt free.

His gaze met my eyes again, and I was advancing, lunging across the snowy earth.

As our blades clashed, he kept his gaze locked on me, his eyes shining with something like excitement. I was starting to get the sense that he enjoyed this, that it made him feel alive.

Even more strangely, I was starting to feel the same way...

Andrew had made me feel safe. But Torin? He made me feel like I was standing on a precipice, about to fall off. Heart racing and blood pumping, I'd never felt more exhilarated. The problem? It was just a quick thrill, a blazing candle that would burn out quickly. It wouldn't do to dwell on these thoughts, even for a moment. Clearly, the man wasn't relationship material.

No way in hell I'd set myself up for more disappointment. I'd hardly recovered from the last heartbreak.

Torin's breath clouded around his head as he thrust his rapier closer, nearly nicking my waist. His expression was fierce, eyes glinting.

I leapt back and was nearly taken out by a snowy branch.

Damn.

My mind had wandered, and Torin had backed me up against a tree trunk.

I blocked his attack, and his sword pressed against mine, pinning me against the tree.

The corner of his lip curled. "It seems I have you exactly where I want you, my favorite changeling."

"Favorite?" I returned his smile. "Have you forgotten we hate each other? Because I haven't."

"But Ava." His face was close to mine now, the moonlight and shadows sculpting his cheekbones. "Your utter contempt for me is what makes it all the more exciting when I have you under my control." His knee slid between my thighs, his face close to mine now. The edges of our blades pressed closer to me.

"It makes it more exciting," he whispered. "Thinking of your complete disdain for me."

A fierce, competitive flame lit inside me. Marshaling all the strength I could muster, I shoved him away from me. But I was already growing tired, and I stumbled a little.

Torin slashed, and I parried, but the force of his strike snapped my blade. I stared at the broken sword for only a fraction of a second before dodging out of his way.

By now, I knew him well enough to understand he had complete control of his sword, and that he'd never attack if he thought he'd actually hurt me. But the thing was, I didn't want to lose.

I shifted to the right and gripped him hard by the wrist. A sharp kick to his inner thigh had him doubling over, and I twisted his arm back until he dropped the rapier in the snow. He quickly ripped himself out of my grip and spun, raising his fists like we were about to start boxing.

I arched an eyebrow. "Are we about to fist fight?"

"Why not? There are no rules here."

"So, in Faerie, it's okay to punch a king?"

"No, that's a death penalty offense. But I won't tell if you won't. Here, in this clearing, there are no rules." A sardonic smile. "And as your king, I am commanding you to play the way I want you to."

"Not my king, but okay." I lifted my fists, not entirely sure what I was doing. Truth be told, I was strangely enticed by the idea of hand-to-hand combat with a high king of the Seelie.

Just the thing to help a person forget a bad breakup.

And perhaps I had a *tad* bit of aggression to work out.

I darted forward, striking first. He blocked, again and again, and my knuckles felt like they were breaking against his forearm.

With a devilish smile, the king swung at me, but I lifted my arm, and the blow landed hard near my elbow. I winced as pain danced up to my shoulder.

He heard my catch of breath and went still. His smile faded, hands lowering slightly. "Are you all right?"

I slammed my fist into his cheek, knocking him back. But when his face snapped up to mine, it was with that exhilarated look once more. "Gloves are truly off, then."

"Oh, yes. As a changeling, I'm too wild for this kingdom, of course. No sense of propriety whatsoever."

The wind toyed with his cloak, and his eyes blazed with icy light in the darkness. A smile ghosted over his lips.

I moved forward once more to hit him, but he caught my wrist in an iron grip and contorted my arm. Now it was his turn to twist my arm behind my back. The position and sharp movement hurt like a bitch.

"You're surprisingly skilled," he murmured next to my ear. "For a changeling."

I gritted my teeth. "Turns out I've had some anger issues since the night I met you." I slammed the back of my head into his face, and he released me. "And pretty men are my target."

Exhausted and bruised, I whirled to face him.

"There you go again." He arched an eyebrow. "Calling me pretty."

At that, the air went even colder, the ice cutting down to my bones. And from the way the air shimmered, I had no doubt it was the king's doing. But how could I complain about magic when I'd declared the gloves were off?

I forced myself to move, trying to heat up again, but an all-consuming darkness slammed around me.

Stunned and disoriented, I stumbled back, my heart beating against my ribs as panic slid through my chest. Fuck. This was a vulnerability I'd never felt before.

But in a moment, my senses returned. As a fae, I could always smell much better than humans—but this. I detected every scent for a mile around me: the bark of the oaks, the pine needles and owl nests, the frozen moss, even the scent of the snow. And the sounds: my chattering teeth, the wind rustling through the trees and sweeping across the gravestones—and the sound of Torin's pounding heart beating almost in time to mine.

And there was his scent, richer and earthier than the forest around me, with the faintest notes of a clear, rocky mountain stream.

I didn't feel like a mere changeling right now. I felt like a hunter. And I knew exactly where Torin was, just a few feet away, his heart a hammer against his ribs, just like mine.

I blocked out the piercing cold and lunged forward, striking for his face again. The moment my hand connected with his jaw, the magic slid away, and I could see the feral look in Torin's eyes once more.

He gripped my arm, wrenching it behind my back again, and pressed me against the trunk of a tree, his enormous body close to mine. The bark was rough against my face, but exhilaration lit up my nerves. Sparring with Torin was truly addictive.

"What do you have to be angry about?" I tried to catch my breath. "You have everything anyone could want. Or you will soon, anyway."

"And you?" he whispered in my ear. "How much responsibility weighs on the delicate shoulders of a marginally employed bartender?"

I brought my heel down hard into his foot, and his grip loosened. I thrust my hips into him, throwing him off.

I whirled and took a swing at him, but he caught my fist, then snatched my other wrist, pinning both arms above my head against the tree trunk.

Right where he wanted me—again. My core tightened with his face close to mine, his breath hot on my
throat. With my wrists pressed against the trunk and
his muscled body firm against mine, I felt desire coil
tight within me. I breathed in his earthy scent, my
blood heating. Torin's head nestled into the crook of my
neck, and I heard him inhale deeply, drinking in my
scent. He stiffened, pressing harder against me, his knee
between my thighs.

And here was the thing I knew—among humans,
sniffing each other like this was very fucking weird. But
it was a fae instinct, one I hadn't known I had. And
while it was natural, deep down, it was also shockingly
intimate.

"No responsibilities?" My breath was coming fast.
"You don't know the first thing about me," I gasped, the
cold air stinging my lungs.

He raised his face again, and our clouds of breath
twined together in the frozen night air. "Nor you me.
That is why you are perfect, my changeling And that is
why I crave your company." His eyes closed, and his lips
brushed against mine.

Even though the touch was light, it sent molten heat
sliding through my core. The effect was instant, like I
was melting over the ice.

With a short gasp of breath, he pulled away, dropping his grip on me.

"Sorry," he whispered. "I should not have done that."

I stared at him, wondering what the fuck had just
happened.

It was hard to breathe. "What are we even doing

here? You choose the winner. Why do I need to practice so much?"

He turned, moving into the shadows, then paused to look back at me. "Do you want to see something? A view of my kingdom? I have whiskey."

"And will you tell me all your secrets, and why I'm here?" I followed him down a winding path we'd never taken before, slightly overgrown with brambles. Moonlight pierced the branches above us, and silver light danced over the snow beneath our feet.

He flashed me a wry smile. "Maybe. I will tell you this, Ava. I need to make sure you survive this tournament. The final trial can be bloody, and it's my job to ensure you make it through alive. I don't need any more deaths on my hands. I don't want the ghost of Ava Jones to haunt me." He pulled out a little silver flask and took a sip. "I have enough vengeful spirits on my case as it is."

I huffed a laugh, and the cold air stung my lungs. "How many deaths, exactly, do you have on your hands?"

His jaw clenched. "If I don't choose a queen, the numbers will be in the hundreds of thousands. And as for the past..." He met my gaze, his eyes blazing in the dim light. "A king is expected to participate in duels in times of peace, and I have. A king is supposed to show that he has the power to defeat the demons and monsters, but it's really to prove to the clan kings that none of them should think of rising against their high king. So I have killed noble fae in duels, a bloodletting to keep the peace. Here in Faerie, the high king is like a god. But I must prove it to them over and over."

I swallowed hard. "And a queen should be able to do the same?"

He glanced at me sideways. "And that's why we keep practicing, yes."

"So, the deaths that haunt you, they're from these duels?"

His eyes glittered in the darkness. "There's one death that weighs most heavily on my mind, and that, my changeling, is a secret that will die with me."

Of course, that was the very secret I *had* to know.

He handed me his flask, and I took a long sip. The peaty taste rolled over my tongue.

The dark forest started to thin as we moved up a steep slope, and the wind whipped through the trees. At the top of the hill, the craggy land sheered off and sloped down. The view from here was breathtaking—a mountainous region surrounding a valley with a frozen lake, silvered under the moonlight. Snow dusted black slopes around the valley, and towering castles jutted from their peaks, windows beaming with warm light in the distance.

I stared at the beauty of Faerie. "Holy shit."

Torin climbed onto a large rock, dusting off the snow to make a spot for me. Oak boughs arched over us.

I took another sip of the whiskey and handed it back to him. "You're in charge of all this?"

He pointed to the dark mountains across the valley, where a black castle seemed to rise from the jagged slopes. "The Redcap petty kingdom is found there. So far, six young redcap princes have challenged me in duels."

"And six died?"

"Four died. Two survived, but they can no longer fight. And consequently, their father, the Redcap king, executed them."

"He killed his own sons?"

"I don't go to the Redcap kingdom unless it's absolutely necessary. The king is horrible." He pointed to a pale stone castle on the slopes to our left. "The Dearg Due petty kingdom. Once, they dragged humans into their realm to drain them of blood. Now, they make do with hunting deer and elk." He pointed at the crystalline lake. "The Kelpie clans live around the lake in marshy fields. They could once shapeshift into horses, although they don't anymore. We can't see the other clan kingdoms from here."

"It's a beautiful place."

"But fractious. The clans were once at war with each other, and they have little in common to this day. It's my job to keep them united. Having a queen, restoring life to Faerie, is absolutely necessary." He passed me the flask once more.

"What if you want to marry for real one day?"

"I won't."

My teeth started to chatter, and Torin leaned in to me. He radiated warmth through his clothes, and I relished it more than I'd like to admit.

"You know, Ava," he said softly, "I thought you were a mess when I first met you. Obviously. But it wasn't fair to judge you when you lived in a world where you never belonged."

"I'm not sure I belong here, either." I sighed.

"We belong with family. And we don't have that, do we?"

My mind crackled with fragments of memories of my mom and the warmth I'd felt when I was little. I'd always wanted to get as close to her as possible.

A bolt of loneliness shot through me, and the cold bled down to my bones.

I stood, rubbing my arms for warmth as I searched the snow for my cloak. "I'm going to head back. Are you coming?"

"No, thanks. I'll stay here a while longer."

I pulled on my cloak, casting one last look at him before I trudged through the snow. He sat, shoulders slumped, in the dark shadows beneath an oak. Snowflakes spiraled down around us.

The king—the most powerful fae in existence—looked completely and utterly alone.

19

TORIN

I sat at the end of a long table, my gaze sweeping over the fine woodwork in the hall and the crimson walls above the wainscoting. Ancient suits of armor hung against the mahogany, and a black and white checkered floor spread out before me. A fire burned in a vast stone fireplace, making my back uncomfortably hot.

My gaze flicked to the gruesome tapestry on the wall—the Seelie conquest of the demons three thousand years ago. In the image, King Finvarra held up a severed demon's head, one with golden horns and black eyes. What the image didn't show was that the demons had cursed us. After the conquest, the demons condemned us to endless winters until we learned how to keep them at bay with the power of a queen and a throne. The demons cursed us again with the Erlkings, who arrived every hundred years to spread their icy death.

And when we'd tried to make peace with them one

final time, they'd cursed my entire family. They'd blinded Orla. They'd sentenced my parents to death. And they'd condemned me to murder any woman I loved.

Even without the tapestry in this Great Hall, I could never forget the horrific horned demons and what they'd done to our world.

I poured myself a glass of wine, my thoughts dancing with death.

My parents had battled the demons in this Great Hall, had spilled blood across the tiled floor, but it had hardly been the first massacre here. Over a thousand years ago, High King Trian, ruler of the six clans, had held a feast here with two Dearg Due princes. The young men had threatened to take back their ancestral lands, and Trian had promised peace. Midway through the dinner, servants brought out the severed head of a black bull—our symbol of death. And within twenty minutes, the severed heads of the Dearg Due hung speared on our castle gates.

And this was how a Seelie high king kept the peace: keeping bellies full and slitting throats when necessary.

But none of that history could compare to the horror of what lay before me today.

And as the human TV crew began rolling in their equipment on the far side of the hall, my stomach was already turning.

Never in a million years would I have agreed to this —meals with each of the princesses and Ava—except it had been a very specific part of the contract. Without this, the deal was off, and I'd be stuck with the mountains of debt again. The humans wanted to film us as we ate together and broadcast it out to their nation of voyeurs. They called this "the dating portion" of the show.

I scrubbed a hand over my jaw, watching in silence as they set up their equipment before me. Once, on a visit to Versailles in the human realm, I learned that King Louis XIV allowed all of his courtiers to have intimate knowledge of his life. They watched his wife give birth. They watched them fall asleep and wake up.

This was what people wanted, apparently—access into our world. To feel like one of us.

And as much as I hated it, I'd do what I must to keep the Seelie fed and happy.

My thoughts wandered as the humans bustled around me, setting up lights and attaching a microphone to my indigo suit.

I sipped the wine again, my gaze flicking to the door. The producers hadn't told me which woman I'd be meeting with first, and I found myself hoping it would be Ava.

Had they told her what to expect today? She was supposed to cook for me. It was ridiculous. A fae queen did not cook—royals had people to do that for us. Nor could I imagine Ava cooking, considering she seemed keen on takeout.

I needed to get my mind off her. How, exactly, had I let Ava get under my skin? And why? There was the way she looked, of course—that beautiful pout, her large eyes framed by black eyelashes, her perfect body...the way her heart raced when I got close to her and her cheeks flushed.

But many fae women were beautiful, and they hadn't set up home in my mind like she had. Maybe I craved a woman who didn't give a fuck that I was the king. And then there was the fact that she seemed to be at war with herself over her desire for me, which made me want to do the filthiest things possible to her, to hunt her through the forest until she gave in to her lust for me and stripped off her clothes—

Of course, I couldn't crave her too much, so I clamped down on those thoughts hard and shoved them away.

As the door opened at the far end of the hall, I found myself staring at Moria. She really did know how to draw the eye to herself.

She wore an ivory column of a gown. Her burgundy hair, threaded with vibrant wildflowers, was a sharp contrast to her creamy white skin. I stood as she crossed the room, the cameras panning to take in her elegant movements as she glided over the floor like a wraith.

She looked so much like her sister...but I couldn't afford to think about that now.

Instead of food, she was carrying a bottle of wine. Moria slipped behind the table and took a seat next to me.

I sat up straight, trying to ignore the cameras pointed directly at me. "Thank you for joining me, Princess."

She smiled. "I am delighted to see you again. We are

old friends, aren't we?" She lifted the wine bottle. "Servant? Open this."

A male servant scrambled from the shadows, brandishing a corkscrew.

"You couldn't really expect me to cook, Your Majesty." She leaned on her hand, smiling at me. "What a ridiculous thing."

"I only expected your gracious company." Once, I'd felt remarkably comfortable around Moria. But now, I only felt the sharp-edged blade of guilt.

"Well, that's not all I brought, of course. The wine is from a vineyard that has been in my family for thousands of years. At one point, it belonged to Queen Melusine, one of my ancestors."

"Your family history is truly noble." Noble...and full of a long history of blood drinking. Which, frankly, gave me pause when it came to the wine, though I could hardly turn it down.

"I'd love to show you around our castles sometime, Your Majesty. And the vineyards in the Dearg Due lands." Moria smiled. "I've heard that you are remarkably skilled at archery on horseback. Is that true? We must hunt together."

"I love horses."

The servant poured two glasses of wine and slid them across the table.

She lifted her own wineglass, leaning back in her chair. "Hunting is my absolute favorite. I practice every afternoon. I have the most beautiful horse, Nuckelavee. Unlike the other princesses, I ride and shoot as well as a male fae. I am quite discerning in my judgment of other females, and I have heard you are as well. It's why you haven't yet married, is it not? You have discerning taste."

"I have exceedingly high standards." *Namely, I cannot be around anyone I might love.*

Was I making a mistake with Ava, then?

No—she'd made her opinion of me quite clear. For someone in my position, it was strangely liberating being around someone who didn't respect you at all.

A pretty, rich douchebag... It's all fake.

Moria's gaze sharpened, and I realized she must have sensed I hadn't been listening.

I raised my eyebrows, encouraging her to keep going.

"For my part," said the princess, "I do not adjust my opinions of accomplishments to accommodate the weaker sex. A female High Fae must be as skilled as a male in order to impress me. She must ride and shoot with perfect accuracy. She must have exquisite knowledge of the fae classics. She must be free of any scandal or public disgrace, of course."

"Of course." What was she saying?

She stifled a laugh. "Any grotesque displays of public inebriation and vulgarity, for example, would strike someone off my list. I would never expect to find you in that state."

If she'd seen me two weeks ago while planning this event, she'd never say that. And after today, I fully expected to be a drunken mess. But I was expected to be pleasant and charming here. Boring.

"Quite right," I said blandly.

Then I wondered if I'd just conspired with her in publicly insulting Ava.

"An impressive woman must have a voice like a siren," added the princess, "and she must be classically trained on the harp. But beyond all that, she must be graceful and elegant, regal in her bearing, and a brilliant and witty conversationalist. Of course, hardly anyone meets that description. Excluding your sister, Orla, of course, but I can't think of any others." She sighed dramatically.

"There is you, of course." I sipped the wine, fully aware I was supposed to say that. Moria had always delighted in flattery, and I'd always indulged her, like a younger sister I wanted to please. But now? It was desperation to make up for what I'd done. "Of course, I may add another crucial item to your list. She must be a ruthless fighter who is willing to do whatever it takes to win."

I'd meant this as another compliment for Moria, but as I said it, an image blazed in my mind—a stunning and ferocious fae with violet eyes and cheeks rosy in the cold...

The princess's cheeks glowed pink, and she touched my arm as she spoke. "I see we share the same world-view, Your Majesty. We are well matched, indeed."

Distantly, a bell rang, which I understood to be the end of our *tête-à-tête*. I rose, bowing slightly. "Thank you, Moria. I always enjoy our time together."

As Moria glided away, servants bustled about, clearing the table again.

And already, Etain of the Leannán Sídhe, a type of

female fae known to break a man's heart, leaving him a shell of his former self, was crossing into the Great Hall. There are males in her clan, too—the Gean-Cánach—though they keep their distance from me. Etain's hips swayed as she approached. She carried a bowl of cherries, and she smiled at me from under her eyelashes. Her violet and apricot hair cascaded over her bare shoulders, and her black gown hugged her curves.

When she sat next to me, her knee brushed my thigh. I stared at her mouth as she popped a cherry between her lips and pulled out the stem. She was speaking to me, but my mind kept drifting back to last night, sitting under the oak with Ava—until Etain put her hand on my thigh.

"I really don't give a fuck what other people think," she said, her hand moving further up my leg. "I take what I want. And if I want to fuck a king on a table, I don't really care who's watching."

Heat followed in the wake of her touch, but I was imagining Ava saying those words to me, thinking of her full lips against mine. I'd pressed her against the tree, my beautiful and wild captive, the sound of her heart racing, her breath hitching, music to my ears.

I struggled to keep my composure. In the presence of a Leannán Sídhe, my thoughts were aflame with desire. I was thinking how Ava would look naked in the curling steam of a hot lake, imagining how her bare skin would taste. She hated me, but perhaps, if I could make her moan my name anyway—

What was wrong with me? Apparently, I only wanted someone who loathed me. Even with this absolutely gorgeous woman sitting close to me, gripping my thigh, my thoughts were on the fae who'd called me a fake twat, making it clear she hated men.

Interesting.

Maybe this was because deep down, I hated myself.

"The other fae here are fucking insane," said Etain. "You see that, right? I'm a lover, not a fighter."

The show's host stepped in front of the camera, smiling. "Apologies for the language, folks." He laughed nervously. "But the fae can't be controlled, can they? And that's why we find them so fascinating. Now, King Torin has chosen another princess as his next date—Princess Cleena, a clear front-runner in these trials. As part of these dates, we've asked the women to bring an item of food to the king. In fae tradition, a queen is responsible for managing the castle's kitchen."

He looked to the side, frantically motioning for someone to take Princess Etain away. As she left, Etain lifted her middle finger at the camera.

"Now, in the human world, I'd get in trouble for saying that we want women to stay in the kitchen these days." He adjusted his cufflinks, chuckling. "Apparently, I'm not allowed to call them the 'good old days.'" He laughed a little too loudly as the doors opened once more and Princess Cleena entered.

She was truly beautiful in a daffodil-colored dress that perfectly flattered her dark skin. Sparkling makeup shimmered over her high cheekbones.

She crossed to the table, moving languidly. Just as I was used to being obeyed, it was clear that Princess Cleena was used to being admired.

The reporter said in a low, awe-struck voice, "Princess Cleena of the Banshees is widely considered to be the most beautiful fae princess of the last century, and she is here representing the Banshee clan. Now, let's just hope she doesn't scream at me, because we all know what that means." He grinned. "It means death."

She sat next to me and smiled. "It's so nice to see you again, Your Majesty."

"It's nice to see you again, too, Princess Cleena."

She sighed. "I had something made for you, Your Majesty." She beckoned to someone off camera. "I have it right here." A servant scurried over with what appeared to be a miniature version of a wedding cake, covered in a gold dust. "Gold is my favorite color." She beamed at the cake. "It's made with caramel layers." She smiled at me for a moment before returning her attention to the cake. "If you don't eat it, I will."

She picked up a fork, which, frankly, impressed me. She'd come here with a delicious cake, and she was going to eat the delicious cake, and she didn't really give a fuck what I thought.

She scooped a forkful of cake and froze, her fork suspended in the air. Her eyes darkened, and her muscles stiffened, her gaze sliding to the camera crew.

Oh, *gods*. My heart went still.

Princess Cleena rose from her chair, staring at the camera as she swung her legs over the table, her yellow gown trailing behind her. She slid to the floor, her movements elegant as she approached the camera.

Opening her mouth, she unleashed a haunting sound, an otherworldly song, like hell was being harrowed, and all the souls were mourning on the way out. The eerie horror of the sound slid all the way down to my bones.

"Christopher?" she called out. "Christopher, where are you?"

The camera twisted to a skinny, brown-haired man holding a boom mic. A look of absolute terror was etched across his features. Princess Cleena moved towards him, calling his name again. "Christopher?"

He dropped the boom with a loud clatter, but the princess ignored it. She stood over him, and the trembling noise in her voice grew louder and louder until it became an unbearable, caterwauling scream.

Either Christopher or someone he loved dearly was going to die.

When the camera panned back to Cleena, she seemed to have recovered herself, her expression calm again. With a little smile, she returned to the table and picked up the golden cake. She smiled at me wistfully. "This really looks very good, doesn't it?"

Looking pleased with herself, she crossed out of the room.

But poor Christopher wasn't being given a second thought by the producers, because a footman was already bringing in the next princess.

Alice, princess of the Kelpie clan, hurried into the room, holding a silver tray with a dome. Her hair shimmered over an emerald dress studded with tiny pearls. As she scuttled over next to me, her eyes were wide, nervous. She slid the platter onto the table.

"Your Majesty." She dropped into the chair, beaming

at me, but her smile seemed forced. "I have brought you a gift."

I returned her greeting with what I hoped was a reassuring smile. "Delightful, Alice."

She pulled the dome off the platter. "It's a cake made with peaches. I've been told peaches are your favorite. I baked it myself." She picked up a large silver spoon and began to scoop some of the cobbler onto my plate with shaking hands. "I collected the peaches from the trees in the eastern greenhouse." She was stumbling over her words. Then her face fell. "I had intended to bring some clotted cream to go with it, but unfortunately, the milk went rancid." She shook her head. "Maybe I shouldn't mention rancid—"

"The milk was spoiled?" I cut in, a sense of dread weighing on my shoulders.

"Yes." She took a deep breath. "It keeps spoiling."

I nodded grimly. "The boggarts, I'm afraid. They'll be gone when we have a new queen, along with the other dark magic."

The firelight warmed her pale features. "I'm so pleased you allowed me to participate, even with my scandalous past."

I stared at her. I had literally no idea what she was talking about, and Alice didn't strike me as a scandalous person. "Well, the past is the past."

"He was a pirate, you see. From the Selkie clan. And he nearly stole my honor, but you have nothing to worry about, because my father rescued me before I was ruined forever. I cried for weeks, Your Majesty. I wouldn't eat or get out of bed. My heart was entirely broken. Because I really thought he loved me, but it turns out he'd ruined many a naïve kelpie, and he was after my money. He left me nearly destitute."

"You don't need to tell me this," I said, more abruptly than I meant.

"But now I have a second chance at love, don't I? And I would dearly love to have children. As many as possible. A whole brood of tiny fae, running around, getting into things. I'd teach each of them to ride a pony, then horses. And I'd read to them every night."

But dear Alice, true love is not on the agenda here.

As the bell rang and Alice rose to leave, my mood darkened. This entire charade was ridiculous, just as Ava had said when we'd first met.

My gaze flicked up at Sydoc crossing into the room, carrying what looked like a raw steak on a platter.

There was no way in hell I'd be touching that, and I was afraid it could have a human origin.

She wore a little red beret over her sleek black hair and a sleek red dress. The heels of her formidable black boots clicked on the floor as she walked. Reaching my side, she slid the meat in front of me, and the rusty scent of blood curled into my nostrils.

Her eyelashes were black as coal and unusually long. "Your Majesty. Do you remember saving me years ago? In the Karnon forest, when you were out hunting. Some unruly Redcap brigands were chasing me. You slaughtered them all."

A dim memory arose from the recesses of my memory—a woman with black hair, her dress torn.

Running through the mist at full speed from three wild Redcaps, their bare chests streaked with blood.

My eyebrows rose with surprise. "That was you?"

She nodded. "And I knew then that I must marry you. Because you were someone who could keep me safe."

My blood went cold.

Oh, no, Sydoc. That's not me at all.

"And you know how things are in the Redcap kingdom," she went on. "When my older sister, Igraine, showed that she was not sufficiently bloodthirsty, my father had her drowned in the lake and her body hung from our castle walls."

The blood drained from my head as I started to wonder if I'd allowed the petty kingdoms too much leeway in developing their own laws.

"But the culture here is so lovely," she said. "There's art and music and books. It's not only about who you can slaughter."

I cocked my head. "Only during the duels."

She touched my arm, her eyes shining. "I have loved you since the moment I saw your portrait hanging in our castle. And when you saved me in the Karnon forest, I had no question. We are meant to be together. I'd never in my life felt so safe. And you slaughtered them so quickly, so expertly."

I motioned for the servant to bring back the bottle of wine that Moria had brought me, and he poured me another tall glass. "Well, let's hope the tournaments help me decide who is the best queen for all the Seelie.

Because she will not just be my wife, but queen of the six clans."

She drummed her long fingernails on the table. "But you must see there is something *wrong* with Ava, don't you?"

Now *this* surprised me. "Ava?"

"More than just being around the humans. It's the way she moves...as a Redcap, we are hunters. We are in tune with movement. And she doesn't move like humans, or like us. She stands too still, sometimes. Like a statue. It's *unnerving*."

My changeling...

I wondered if these were merely the desperate words of a princess who craved nothing more than escape from her sad world.

I have loved you since the moment I saw your portrait.

But I knew she hadn't. She saw me as her ticket out of a grim fortress where her sister's corpse had hung from the walls.

By the time Eliza, princess of the Selkies, entered the chamber, I'd finished more than half of Moria's bottle of wine, and I was in danger of defying Moria's prediction that she'd never witness any grotesque or public displays of public inebriation from me.

Eliza wore a blue-green ballgown, excessively ornate, that trailed over the floor as she walked in. Her green hair was swept up on her head, decorated with pearls and seashells, and the firelight wavered over her bronze skin. She walked with a determined frown, her lips pressed into a line. She did not look any more thrilled to be here than I was.

She carried a pie with grim determination.

I pulled out her chair, and she sat next to me. Without making eye contact, she began cutting into the pie. "I have been told that you have an exemplary sense of taste. And for my part, it has been many years since I have tasted a berry as fine as these, without the vulgarity of too much sweetness."

A servant quickly dropped two porcelain plates onto the table, then dodged out of view. Eliza used the knife to slide a piece of pie onto my plate, then frowned as it fell apart.

"It looks amazing."

At last, she met my gaze. "I have studied your interests, Your Majesty. I have been working through a list of your favorite books, though poetry is not something I understand, but I will strive to appreciate it."

I poured myself another glass of wine, letting my mind drift again. Where would anyone find a list of my interests?

"I do note that your eyes wander as I speak," she said hurriedly. "But I am also of the opinion that a king cannot appear too eager, for fear of showing weakness. I commend you in your strength and wise decision-making."

I'd never in my life felt as relieved as I was when the bell rang once more and Ava strode into the room. She wore a delicate dress the color of pewter. The material was sheer but layered just enough that I felt desperate to see her body underneath...in fact, I wanted to order everyone out of the room, tear right through that delicate fabric, spread her thighs wide, and explore every inch of her beautiful body. Somehow, I thought I knew what she'd like. And I wanted to teach her what it meant to be fae, to submit to a king's power and lose herself in ecstasy...

No, if I weren't cursed, I'd make her forget whoever it was who'd taught her that there was something wrong with being fae. Ava had the air of heartbreak about her, and I could make her body pulse with a sensual thrill until she completely forgot the human idiot responsible and only my own name filled her thoughts. If I weren't cursed, I'd fuck her until she forgot his name—

Oh, gods. I must stop. *Fucking focus.* I was losing it. Because the fact was, I was cursed.

But surely this was only lust running out of control. And a king's impulse to conquer, to tame, to make my subjects worship me, body and soul.

Wasn't it?

❧ 20 ❧
AVA

I strode into a great hall, one of carved oak walls and an enormous table shaped like an angular U. My gaze moved to a gruesome tapestry, a demonic creature decapitated in the forest.

The camera crew stood in the center, the lights and camera aimed at King Torin. He stood when I entered, giving me a slight nod, his pale eyes lingering on me.

Dimly, I heard the TV host introduce me, and to my absolute horror, he reminded viewers of my messy, drunken outburst.

I slid down into the free chair, wishing I could disappear.

"And surely none of us expected to see Ava here. After all, she declared herself a fae who plays by human rules and the trials themselves embarrassing. If anyone knows what's embarrassing, it's Ava Jones. Her slurred outburst went viral, earning her scorn and mockery from all corners of the world."

I dropped my head into my hands, wishing I could disappear.

"In her exact words," the host went on, "King Torin's life is the nadir of human civilization. Don't ask me what that means, but I don't think she meant it as a compliment. Particularly when she called him a pretty and rich—" The host turned to Torin with a grin, then looked back at the camera. "Well, I'd love to finish her thought, but I'm afraid it wouldn't be allowed on daytime television. The real question is, will Ava drink all that whiskey and treat us to another sloppy—"

"That's quite enough, thank you." Torin's commanding voice from my right surprised me.

I glanced at him. Irritation was etched on his features, and his pale eyes were locked on the host.

"It seems our royal bachelor is eager to try his drink," the host said with a smirk. "Far be it from me to stand in the way of a king."

He stepped out of view of the cameras, his smile instantly fading.

I felt frozen for a moment, my mind still whirling with the image the host had painted. Of course, for that one snapshot in time, it was a completely accurate image, broadcast out to the entire world.

But one night wasn't *all* of me.

I could not for one moment let myself linger on what Andrew might have thought about that introduction right now, or it would throw me completely off.

I dragged myself from these spinning thoughts to find Torin looking at me with something like concern, his eyebrows raised. "I'm excited to see what you have in store for me, Ava," he said quietly.

I took a deep breath. Pulling my gaze to the cocktail ingredients laid out for me, I went into bartender mode.

Before me stood a large bottle of rye whiskey, a smaller container of vermouth, a bottle of Angostura bitters, an insulated container of what I hoped was ice cubes, a stainless steel shaker, a Hawthorne strainer, a jigger measuring cup, a paring knife, a bowl containing lemons, a coupe glass, and to my relief, as directed, a small container of Maraschino cocktail cherries.

"Have you ever had a Manhattan?" I cleared my throat. "Your Majesty?"

"No." Torin's eyebrows rose. "Named after the human city, I assume?"

I smiled back at him. "That's where it was first developed, long ago. In the old Victorian days. And I know you like whiskey because it's what you ordered in the Golden Shamrock."

"I didn't realize you were paying attention."

"Oh, you had my complete attention." I smiled at him, actually starting to forget about the horror of that introduction. "I was very curious to see what you were going to order."

"Scotch is a favorite."

I nodded, and it occurred to me that he smelled faintly like a peaty Scotch. "This is rye, but I think you'll like it. And I'm the perfect marginally employed, responsibility-free bartender to make you your first one."

He actually flashed me a genuine smile.

I cracked open the bottle of rye and poured two jiggers of whiskey into the shaker. "This is what the humans call a cocktail shaker. One of their greatest inventions."

"We do have cocktails here, of a sort. But we make them with magic."

"We don't have magic in the human world, and that's where all the tools come in." I poured a jigger of vermouth into the shaker. "This is wine that's been fortified."

Torin watched quietly as I added two dashes of the Angostura bitters, then picked out five ice cubes.

"Stirring is traditional," I said. "But like the great James Bond, I prefer mine shaken."

"Interesting," said King Torin, watching me carefully. It was clear to me he'd never seen anyone mix a proper cocktail.

I put the clear glass top on the shaker and began to shake it. The noise seemed awkwardly loud, ice cubes slamming against the metal, but at least I felt comfortable once more. Shalini truly was clever, setting me up with something she knew I didn't have to think twice about.

After shaking up the cocktail, I popped off the top and poured it into the coup glass using the Hawthorne strainer.

"You're not going to mix yourself a cocktail?" he asked.

I shook my head. "The entire world already thinks

I'm an alcoholic. A cocktail at ten a.m. won't improve that situation."

Torin laughed. "Considering all the wine I've been given this morning, they should be judging me."

Who was he kidding? A rich and gorgeous man could get away with far more in the public perception than I could.

He reached for the glass, but I pushed his hand away. Strangely, as our fingers touched, a little electric thrill raced down my arm.

"I need to garnish it." I plucked out one of the cocktail cherries, and then, using the knife on the platter, sliced a thin ribbon of peel off a lemon. I gave it a twist over the glass, then dropped it in.

"Are they important?" asked Torin.

"It improves the aroma."

"Fascinating." He lifted it to his nose and inhaled, keeping his eyes on me. "I do appreciate a good aroma."

The velvety tone of his voice made desire heat my skin, and I found myself blushing.

He closed his eyes and took a sip, letting the drink roll over his tongue for a moment, truly tasting it. At last, his startlingly pale eyes opened again. "Delicious, Ava." He inhaled a sharp breath. "Now, why don't you tell me exactly what happened in the Golden Shamrock?"

I stared at him in dawning horror. If he'd really wanted to ask about it, why would he bring it up now, in front of the cameras? Didn't he know I wanted to move on?

I glanced at the camera and swallowed.

"I'd like to hear your side of the story," he said. "Because you've been here for over a week, and I've seen a very different side of you than the person I met on the first night."

Ah. I held his gaze again, and it occurred to me that he was trying to give me a chance to redeem myself before the world. As much as I just wanted them all to forget about that video, there was no way they would.

I took a deep breath and reached for his cocktail. "I'm going to need a sip of this after all if I'm going to get into that." I closed my eyes as I drank from it, savoring the faint burn in my throat.

When I opened my eyes, I found Torin watching me with curiosity.

Where to begin?

"The night I met you, Torin, was my birthday. Or at least it was the day my mother, Chloe, decided was my birthday when she adopted me. We never really knew the date because someone found me outside a human hospital when I was maybe six months old. And I think because my mom was always so determined to make me feel normal, like I belonged, she used to go very over-the-top with birthday parties. Enormous cakes, magicians, twenty-five kids...I think she thought it would help me make friends. Even in high school, the birthdays were extravagant, with trips to the Caribbean or Paris. She didn't need to do all that, of course, but we made some great memories."

I stared at the Manhattan, realizing I'd started this story much further back than I'd intended, and now my heart hurt. "Anyway. When I was in college, my mom died. It just came out of nowhere, and..." I took another sip of the Manhattan. "But I had a boyfriend by then, and he took over making my birthdays special so I wouldn't feel too sad about my mom being gone. He'd make me dinner and cakes. As the years went on, the birthdays weren't as big a deal, but that's what happens when you get older. So I'd just pick up some takeout, and we'd watch a movie. Fine by me. What really mattered was that we were going to form our own family. My mom wasn't around anymore, but we'd make a new family with little kids I could spoil on *their* birthdays."

The hall seemed strangely silent, and I couldn't quite believe I was saying all this in front of the cameras. Except I didn't feel like I was telling the world. I felt like I was telling Torin, and with the way he was listening so intently, he was somehow the perfect audience.

"He said we were soulmates, and we had all kinds of plans," I added. "I was working in a bar to put him through business school. I was paying his mortgage. Then he was going to help me invest in my bar. And I'd name it after my mom. 'Chloe's.'" I smiled. "That was my plan."

A line formed between Torin's eyebrows. "And what happened on your birthday? The night we met?"

I picked up his Manhattan again and drained half of it, no longer caring what the rest of the world thought. "On my birthday, Torin, I came home to find my boyfriend naked in bed with a blonde he'd met on vacation two years ago. Apparently, they're soulmates now, and everything I'd planned for was gone. The family, the kids with the elaborate birthdays, the backyard barbecues, and the bar named after my mom. So I went to the Golden Shamrock and got drunk enough to forget about everything. At least, I tried."

King Torin stared at me, a muscle working in his jaw. "But you paid for this scoundrel's mortgage."

"Oh, I know." I snorted. "He said I should be happy for him because he'd found true love."

"He broke a contract." There was a quiet fury in his voice that put me a little on edge.

"I mean, we didn't have an official contract."

He raised an eyebrow. "But you had his word that he would invest in your bar. And he lied to you for two years. What sort of miserable cad does that? Give me his name, and I will have this dealt with."

My eyes widened with rising panic. "No, thanks. Look, silver lining, right? I'm here now, in Faerie after all. It worked out for the best."

He paused for a moment, like he was considering his words. "Do you like it here?"

My own answer surprised me. "I do, really. When I first got here, I had a sense that I didn't belong. Like the castle walls themselves objected to my presence. But I'm starting to enjoy being around other fae."

It took another moment, but at last, a smile curled his lips. "We are wild creatures, and that is precisely why you belong here," he murmured. He reached out to touch my wrist, but when he did, it felt as if pure ice had been injected straight into my arm.

"Ouch," I gasped, yanking my arm away.

King Torin's eyes widened, but I saw that deathly cold flicker within them. A chill spread through the room, and I didn't quite understand what had just happened.

But before I could say another word, the bell rang, signaling the end of our date.

21
AVA

That night, for the first time in eleven days, Torin failed to show up at my room for training. To my surprise, I realized that I was disappointed.

I didn't know why I missed him. He'd told me in *very* clear terms that he had no interest in true love, that he wasn't even capable of it. That he'd simply chosen me on the basis of disliking me. In Shalini's words, he was a fae fuckboy.

Maybe I just liked the thrill of sparring.

Tonight, the castle felt empty.

The cold air chilled my skin, and I pulled my blankets over my chin so just my nose peeked out. I'd spent most of the day reading books with Shalini, and Torin hadn't come to find me for training.

Shalini had been scanning social media and the online tabloids to see what they were saying about me. While I really didn't want to know, after today's televised date, I'd become a favorite of audience members.

Seems they despised cheating, and public opinion of my outburst had softened. They'd already dug up Andrew's identity, and I felt a pang of guilt about that. I was angry, but it was no fun at all to get raked over the coals so publicly.

I stared through the diamond-paned windows at the coal black sky. Tonight, clouds hid the moon and obscured the stars.

The fire had simmered down to a few embers. Honestly, I really loved it in this little room. The coziness, the view through the tiny window. It was a safety nook—a marked juxtaposition to all the giant rooms and long hallways of the castle. I really was starting to feel more like I belonged here.

My gaze returned to the window, where snowflakes were landing and melting in tiny beads.

I snuggled under the sheets, happy to be warm, and my eyes drifted shut.

❧❦☙

I CAN'T SAY WHAT WOKE ME. NOT A DRAFT—THE room was just as cold as it was when I fell asleep, and I liked a cool room for sleeping. Nor was it a change in the light. A sound, maybe? A creak of the floorboards, or the squeak of a door hinge...

Except it wasn't just a noise. Something felt fundamentally wrong.

I scanned the room, but I could hardly see a thing. Outside, the sky remained cloudy, and the light was dim.

Quietly, I opened the door to Shalini's larger room and surveyed the space from the doorway. A low fire still burned in her fireplace, and everything seemed in its right spot—Shalini's chest rising and falling as she slept, shadows pooling in quiet corners.

The hall door slowly opened without a sound, and I slipped back into the darkness of my room to watch. A silhouetted figure stood in the doorframe. What the fuck?

The intruder studied me for a long moment, and I slunk back a little, going very still. He inched toward Shalini's bed, tall and cloaked in shadow.

My breath caught when I saw the dagger glinting in his hand.

Fuck. I didn't have a weapon.

I could shout, but then he might panic and lunge for her. I didn't want to warn him. The figure glided to the foot of the bed, his black shadow creeping over the sheets like billowing smoke.

I snatched the little vial of magic fog off the bedside table and darted into the other room. "Shalini, wake up!"

The figure spun to face me, and I hurled the potion in his face. Instantly, thick mist slid through the room, hiding Shalini and me from our attacker. Shalini screamed—which made sense, given that she'd woken into complete chaos—but I could no longer see her through the cold, damp mist.

"Shalini!" I shouted back. "Are you okay?"

Footfalls echoed off the stone, and a door slammed.

"What's happening?" Shalini shouted.

I stumbled through the thick cloud of fog until my fingers brushed against one of the bedposts. "Someone broke in."

The door opened, and Aeron's voice pierced the mist. "What the fuck is going on in there?"

An icy wind swept through, clearing some of the fog away. Goosebumps rose over my skin, and I turned to see Torin standing in the doorway, surrounded by silvery magic. He carried a sword. And with a shock, I realized he wore only a pair of black underwear.

The sight of his sculpted, muscular chest and the dark tattoos that curved over his shoulders and biceps, weaving together above his collarbone, left me speechless. The designs were abstract, reminiscent of the sinuous, rugged lines of oak boughs.

"What happened?" Torin asked. And as his gaze swept down my body, I realized I was nearly as naked as he was—just a pair of black underwear and a thin camisole.

Guess we were all really getting to know each other now.

"Someone was in here with a dagger." I sucked in a sharp breath, hoping I hadn't dreamed all this. "I couldn't find a weapon, apart from the magical fog, but I'm sure I saw him standing by the foot of Shalini's bed. I'm almost positive I heard him run off after the fog filled the room."

Aeron had already begun searching, looking under furniture and behind curtains. Like Torin, he wore only his underwear, and he gripped a sword in his right hand.

His right arm was tattooed with a flock of crows taking flight.

Torin crossed to me over the stones. The dim light from Shalini's fireplace lit up his bare chest from below, and shadows kissed the contours of his muscles.

"I will put a ward on the door," he said. "You and Shalini are not to leave your quarters without an escort. Aeron will stand guard outside the room tonight, and I will have the castle searched. Is there anything else you can tell me about what he looked like?"

"I think he was wearing a cloak." I rubbed my eyes. "I thought the door was locked."

Torin took a deep breath. "Maybe he's skilled at picking locks, but he won't be able to get through my magic." He turned back to the door and pressed his palm against the wood. He began to speak in the magical fae language, and the air around his hand began to glow with a cold light. Brighter now, tendrils of frost crawled over the wood. King Torin spoke more quickly, and the frost began to twist and turn in strange patterns. When he stopped, the frost flashed with a blinding light. Once my eyes had readjusted, I realized the glowing frost had disappeared.

He stepped back and turned to look at me. "Only the four of us will be able to enter now. I'm going to set patrols all over the castle looking for him, but Aeron is the one fae I trust the most."

I caught Shalini staring at Aeron, the look on her face like a starved woman seeing food for the first time in months. I *hoped* I didn't wear the same expression.

Torin rested his sword by the door, his blade against

the wall. "I'll leave this here. Aeron, will you be able to stand watch all night, or should I send others to take shifts?"

Shalini raised her hand. "What if he was inside our room? I mean, where it's more comfortable."

"No," said King Torin. "For one thing, I need him searching for the intruder before he gets to the door. And for another, we wouldn't want anyone getting the mistaken impression that he'd forsaken his vow of chastity."

"His *what*?" Shalini's face twisted into a horrified expression that reminded me of the time I'd told her my WiFi password was "password."

Torin's gaze met mine—but for just a moment, it swept down my body, and I caught the faintest curl of his sensuous lips. "I hope you sleep well. I will return in the morning to check on you."

🕷 22 🕷
AVA

Pearly morning light tinged with amber streamed into my room. I rubbed my eyes, still feeling like the events of last night had been a dream. Who the fuck had been in here with a dagger? I shuddered at the thought and pulled open a drawer in the dresser.

For women in Faerie, there were basically two options—beautiful gowns or leather leggings with blousy shirts and leather vests. I went with brown leather pants and a silky white shirt with billowing sleeves. When I'd dressed, I pulled my hair into a ponytail.

As I entered Shalini's room, she was already dressed, drinking coffee in her bed. She sat with her phone in her lap. Steam curled from her cup, and her blankets formed a twisted nest around her brown leggings.

She stared at me over her coffee. "A vow of chastity? Who *does* that? It's supposed to keep him focused on protecting the king. Honestly, it's the worst thing I've learned about fae culture so far."

I moved to the little table by her bed and poured myself a cup of coffee with cream. "There are plenty of other fae, you know."

"I know. But I liked him. I talked to him through the door last night. He has a cat named Caitsith, and he bakes bread. And he's read so much poetry, Ava. He reads poetry books under this sycamore tree by the river. He said he'll show me the place."

"And the vow?" I perched on the end of her bed, sipping my coffee.

She was sitting cross-legged, her long dark hair falling over a silky blue shirt. "Vows can be broken, and you know I like a challenge. He's like...a hot priest." She smiled at me, looking so stunning that I had no doubt she would succeed—until her smile fell, and she lifted up her phone. "I wasn't sure if I should tell you this, but Andrew is sending me text messages in all caps."

I stared at her. "Why?"

"Since your fans on Reddit doxed him, he's been getting harassed in the street, and I think maybe some death threats?"

I gasped. "Fuck. I mean...I'm mad at him, but I didn't want him to get death threats. I didn't know they'd figure out who he was."

"It's not your fault, Ava. He's a douchebag, and he's reaping his douchebag consequences."

A knock sounded on the door, and I opened it. The king stood in the doorway, fully dressed this time in a gray shirt, black pants, and high boots. A crown gleamed on his head, made of silver strands twined and spiked like thorny tree branches. Aeron stood by his side, looking exhausted. "Good morning, Ava," said Torin. "I tried to dismiss Aeron to get some sleep, but he seems very committed."

Aeron's eyes were locked on Shalini. "I don't care if you want me here or not. I will be keeping you safe today."

Shalini shrugged. "Fine. How about a tour of a castle, then?" She rose from the bed with catlike grace, flashing Aeron the same dazzling smile she'd given me earlier.

Aeron shook his head. "I'm not sure if it's safe to move around like that."

"We came here for adventure," said Shalini.

"I'll join you," said Torin. "No one would dare attack in my presence."

I snatched up my white cloak and pulled it on over my shoulders.

Aeron opened the door. "What would you like to see?"

I stepped into the drafty hall. "Can we see the magic thrones up close?"

"Whatever you like, changeling." Torin started to lead us down the hall, past towering lattice windows with a view of the snowy courtyard.

He turned into a narrow stairwell. "King Finvarra built this castle three thousand years ago after uniting the clans and claiming the land from monsters. I don't know that I've even seen all of it. I suspect I'll die before I finish discovering every passage in the place.

And that is exactly why we haven't found the assassin yet."

"There are legends..." Aeron spoke up from behind me, his voice echoing off the stone. "That once a long spring blessed the land, and the castle grew from the earth itself, sung forth by the vernal goddess Ostara."

Torin glanced at me as he led us into a hall at the lower level. "If you believe in the gods."

I shrugged. "Why not? I've seen enough strange things here that we might as well add gods to the mix."

"If you believe in the gods," added Aeron, "then you must believe they ordained Torin to rule."

"Will the Ostara ordain the reality TV queen to rule as well?" I asked.

Aeron snorted. "Personally, I think her annual spring festival was just an excuse for the fae to fuck in the forest—

"Aeron," said Torin, cutting him off.

"Sorry," Aeron said. "To *fornicate* in the forest."

Torin slid him a sharp look. "We may have to rethink your vow of chastity. I have a feeling it's doing the opposite of keeping you focused."

Torin led us out into the white, sparkling courtyard. My gaze roamed over the dark stone castle walls, which were adorned with icicles and carved with images of stags and serpents. "It really doesn't look three thousand years old."

"Because it's blessed by the gods." When Torin turned to look at me, the late morning light washed over his skin, giving him an otherworldly glow.

In the icy air, I pulled my cloak more tightly around me.

Aeron looped his arm through Shalini's, and he began giving her a tour of the courtyard, explaining the mystical meanings behind each of the sculptures on the walls. Just like I'd expected, camera crews had taken locations in some of the towers, and I caught the glint of their lenses in the winter sun.

"This isn't normally how these shows work," I said. "The cameras are so far away."

"I'm king of Faerie. I'm not allowing them to intrude on my privacy any more than they already have. I refused to wear a microphone or allow them to follow me twenty-four hours a day. They can film me from a distance and get their entertainment. I'll get the money I need. And it will all be over soon."

I fluttered my eyelashes at him. "You're so romantic. Sounds like every girl's dream wedding."

He gave me a sly smile. "You're not exactly every girl, though, are you? You've sworn off love, just as I have. We both know that love won't feed you through the winter when ice encases the crops, and it won't fill your children's bellies when they are starving to death."

"I couldn't agree more. Love is for idiots. But you know, if you needed more children, you could always start stealing humans again."

He moved in closer to me. "Ah, changeling. But we've long since decided that anything from the human realm isn't worth the effort. Too much chaos."

I glanced at the cameras again. "It must be annoying to need them."

He cupped my chin, then brushed his thumb over my lower lip. The sensation sent a forbidden shudder of pleasure through me. "Once this is done, we won't need a thing from the humans anymore." He leaned closer, whispering in my ear. "Three weeks on the throne, changeling, is all it will take. Our lands will be restored, and our worlds will part ways. The way they were always meant to be."

Was that a hint of regret in his tone, or was I imagining it?

He pulled away from me, sliding his hand into one of his pockets. And as he stepped back, I felt the loss of his heat.

The biting winter air reminded me of Torin's magic, and I turned to him. "I have a question for you, Your Majesty. After I made the Manhattan for you, your magic did something to me." I lifted my wrist and tugged up my sleeve, then pointed to a mark on my wrist. About the size of a fingerprint, it was a pale rose color, circled in white—like frostbite. "What is that? And why isn't it going away?"

Shadows slid through his eyes as he stared at it. And though it didn't seem possible, I felt the air growing even colder.

"Sometimes, when I'm very tired, I lose control of my magic." He met my gaze, his preternaturally blue eyes seeming to take me in completely. "It will never happen again, Ava."

I felt as if thorns were growing in the silence between us. There was something he wasn't telling me.

But before I could ask for more details, he turned to

walk away from me. "You wanted to see the thrones. Let's see the thrones."

Clearly, I'd annoyed him, but fuck if I knew how.

He crossed to an enormous oak door studded with black metal and heaved it open. Aeron and Shalini followed in after him, and I hurried to catch up.

Torin led us along a series of corridors until we reached the hall, where two thrones jutted from the center of the stone floor. One larger than the other, they appeared to be carved from a single block of marble, white mottled with dark streaks.

I pointed to the larger of the two. "Is that the king's?"

"That's the queen's." Torin turned to me, arching an eyebrow. "The magic of a fae queen is more powerful than a king's, and she is the one who will bring life to this land once more."

I felt as if the throne was pushing me away—a strange sense of dread warning me not to move closer. And yet, I couldn't take my eyes off the pair. "Fascinating," I said, and walked around the thrones.

"How long have these been in the castle?" asked Shalini, her footfalls echoing off the flagstones.

"The thrones have been here since before the Kingdom of the Seelie was founded, and the castle was built around them. We believe they're made from the bedrock beneath us. Some of the carvings around the castle suggest that our earliest ancestors considered the stones to be representatives of the gods. Like immovable angels. Over the millennia, they were chiseled and carved to refine them more."

Shalini reached out to touch one, and Aeron reached out and gently took her hand. "You mustn't touch them. The magic of the thrones is very powerful, and if a human touches them, there is no telling what the magic might do."

I circled the stones, entranced by the energy they emitted. Even from here, I felt the thrum of their power. Their magic made the air shimmer and my skin go cold. When I'd first come into the castle, I'd felt the uneasy sense that the stone itself didn't want me. And here, by the thrones, the alarm bells were ringing even louder in the back of my brain.

I stepped back from them and hugged myself, shivering.

From the other side of the throne, I caught Torin's eye. I couldn't help but wonder what I was and why the magic here warned me away. Had my birth parents loved me and died in tragic circumstances? Had they thrown me out because I wouldn't stop screaming? Was I really something like a changeling—too unruly to keep?

This was my chance to finally find out the answer.

I took a deep breath. "Torin? How do I find out who my fae parents were?"

One of his black eyebrows arched. "We find the birth records. Ava Jones, we will learn who you are at last."

AVA

Shalini wanted to see the armory—or more likely, to go somewhere alone with Aeron.

Torin led me down a long hall with gothic arches and dark statues of fae kings and queens. As we walked, a chill prickled my scalp. I had to uncover the truth, but I might really hate the answer once I did.

The further away we got from the throne hall, the more my chest unclenched.

"What if I really am a changeling?" I asked quietly. "What if I was too much of a nightmarish baby for my parents to keep? What if I screamed nonstop?"

Torin turned, giving me a perplexed look. "I think all babies scream and keep their parents awake, Ava. You weren't born with anything wrong with you. I promise. The nickname is just me teasing you. You know that, right?"

I hadn't expected him to have such a kind response. "What happened to your parents, Torin?" I knew they'd died young, especially for fae.

He sucked in a sharp breath and glanced at me. "Monsters brought them down. Slowly."

I stared at him. "What do you mean, *monsters*? Like, a dragon?"

"Worse." He slid me a sharp look, his pale eyes glinting with a warning. "Humans might call them demons. But I can't really say more. Even speaking of them could draw their twisted attention."

Curiosity danced up my nape, but clearly, he didn't want to talk about his parents' death, and I really shouldn't have asked. "Of course. I shouldn't be so nosy."

"It's fine." But the air had seemed to thin, until at last, Torin broke the spiky silence. "I remember my mother. They say you're not supposed to remember things from before age three, but I do remember her. I don't remember my father. I remember crawling into my mother's lap, and she'd sing to me. She had a necklace I played with—a little locket with a picture of me. I loved toying with it. When you're so little, you don't differentiate between you and your mom, and I remember crawling all over her. Trying to chew on her hair or sleep on her shoulder. I remember how desperately I always wanted to sleep in her bed..."

He trailed off, and I felt his sadness twisting my heart. "I know that feeling well—missing the one person who always made you feel safe."

He glanced at me with a sad smile—the tiniest flash of vulnerability for the first time since I'd met him—before he schooled his features again. A mask of composure. "I don't know why I'm telling you all this."

It struck me for the first time that apart from Aeron, Torin seemed deeply isolated. But it was his own doing, wasn't it? He'd built a prison for himself to keep everyone away.

My throat tightened as I realized the truth. "You're telling me this for the same reason you already chose me to win. I'm the one without any risk—the person you don't have to worry about falling for. Because you don't like me, and that makes me a safe person for your secrets. No messy feelings."

He paused before a grand library entrance with towering stone columns. "And you don't like me, either." He quirked an eyebrow. "Right?"

A sharp blade slid through my thoughts. I already knew which answer he wanted. "Right."

He inhaled deeply and pulled his gaze away. When he looked back at me, his eyes burned with intensity. "Good. And that is what makes you my perfect bride. Which reminds me—about tonight. Do you know how to dance like the fae? In our court, it's sort of a ballroom style."

"I literally have no idea. The two ways I know how to dance are your basic noncommittal hip sway and a tango."

"A tango?"

"I signed Andrew and me up for classes together because I thought it would be fun for..." I closed my eyes, feeling the heat rise to my cheeks as I realized how pathetic I was, envisioning our wedding dance when he'd never proposed. "I just thought it would be fun. Two years of tango classes."

"Good. I think I can work with a tango. Just follow my lead, Ava, and we'll look nice and romantic for the cameras."

"Of course."

He led me between the towering columns into a magnificent library with two stories of books connected by spirals of stairs. The ceiling above the mahogany bookshelves was arched, with painted images of fae dancing in grassy fields, wildflowers threaded into their brightly colored locks. Looking up at them, I felt a sharp longing for a past I'd never known.

Down the center of the room, green shaded lamps stood on rows of desks. Leather chairs sat waiting for use. Simple wooden circles hung from the ceiling, lit with flickering candles that had to be the worst fire risk in the world.

Torin turned to me. "Wait here for a few minutes. I'll return with some of the birth records from your year. You're the same age as me, yes?"

I nodded. "Twenty-six." Figuring out the age of a fae baby left on a hospital front entrance wasn't an exact science, but I was fairly sure of the year and month.

When Torin left me on my own, I wandered between the bookshelves, enthralled. There were thousands upon thousands of volumes with swirling gold designs on the bindings, all written in a language I couldn't read. Other volumes in shining leather covers were in modern human languages.

I walked through the library until I finally caught sight of a willowy, silver-haired fae sitting behind a mahogany desk. "May I help you?" she called out in a thin, reedy voice.

"Can people check out books here?"

"If you have a library card." Her eyes were a remarkably bright shade of green, and they studied me with an expression that wasn't entirely friendly.

"I don't have one, I'm afraid."

She drummed her fingernails. "Nobody may borrow books from the Royal Library without a library card." She slapped a small piece of paper on top of the desk in front of me and thrust a fountain pen at me. "Sign here."

I signed and dated the contract. Just as I finished, a bright light flashed from the paper, and it disappeared. "May I take out anything?" I asked.

"Limit of ten at a time," said the librarian. "If you don't return them in fourteen days, your brand gets activated."

"My...brand?"

"Well, technically, it's a royal binding," said the librarian. "If you don't return your books on time, a glowing letter L appears in the middle of your forehead. Burns the skin until the books are returned."

I stared at her. "That could have been explained ahead of time."

"As long as you return the books, there won't be a problem." She handed me a small golden card with my name inscribed on it. "What kind of book were you looking for?"

"What do you recommend about fae history?"

Though I wasn't really sure I wanted to borrow one anymore.

She turned in her chair, mumbling in a fae language, and a red book flew through the air and into her hand. She dropped it into her lap. The red book was followed by a brown one and another bound in faded blue cloth. She spun her chair back around and slid the three books onto the desk. "There's *A Short History of the Fae* by Oberon, *A Slightly Longer History of the Fae* by Mistress Titania, and of course, the classic *The Complete History of the Fae* by R. Goodfellow."

I glanced at the titles, but they were illegible to me. "You know what? I won't be able to read those, so I'll just—"

The librarian closed her eyes and began to incant a spell, her fingers moving with jerky insect-like movements.

Light burst before my eyes, and I felt as if a nail had been driven into my skull. I clasped my head, staggering at the pain.

"Stay still," hissed the librarian, "unless you want to end up with mush between your ears. I'm helping you."

Holding my breath, I forced myself not to move even as strange voices hummed in my ears. My vision swirled with images of the fae language. I gasped as an overwhelming amount of information wove itself into my thoughts: each of the forty-two letters in the alphabet, the importance of the silent P, and the five words for magic.

Then, as suddenly as it had started, the flood of

information slowed to a trickle. Dizzy, I pressed my hands against the desk, trying not to pass out.

The librarian pushed a book across the desk at me. "Well, can you read it now?"

My gaze swept across the text, and the title came into focus. "*A Short History of the Fae.*"

Oh, my gods. I could read Fae?

"Ava?" Torin rounded the corner of the bookshelves, carrying a large wooden box. "These are all the birth records in Faerie from twenty-six years ago..." He fell silent and stared at me. "Madame Peasbottom," he said in a deathly quiet voice, "what did you do to her?"

Her face paled, and she stammered, "Just the usual security protocol. We can't have books being stolen."

"I will take personal responsibility for any books that are damaged or lost. But there will be *no* branding of my guests." Icy air raced over my skin.

"I'm sorry, Your Majesty," she said, stumbling over the words.

Torin's attention was on me. He spoke quickly, another spell, and a moment later, the skin on my forehead flashed with heat, then cooled.

"There. I've removed the brand." He took a deep breath. "I have all the births from the year you were born, but do you have any idea what your fae name was, Ava?"

I shook my head. "No idea. But I was probably born in May, if that helps."

The librarian pulled the box toward her. "If I may, Your Highness. This *is* my area of expertise." She added under her breath, "A girl born in May..."

She seemed eager to recover from the branding incident. After a minute of shuffling around, she'd pulled out two long sleeves filled with little silver cards and flipped through them at a stunning speed.

"Well, let's see," she muttered, then paused. "Here's a few." She handed a selection of cards to Torin. "But of course, that was the year of the massacre..." Her voice trailed off.

Torin turned to look at me, his expression suddenly ravaged. "Ava. What month, exactly, were you found?"

"August. Why?"

Torin and the librarian glanced at each other, something unspoken passing between them, a sharpness filling the silence.

The librarian cleared her throat. "The month of the massacre."

Dread bloomed in the hollows of my mind. "What massacre?"

She cleared her throat again, then said, "We should not speak their name."

"Is this about the monsters you mentioned, Torin?" His parents had died when he was three at the hands of these monsters—but he'd suggested it was a long, slow death. Did it begin with this massacre?

Torin's expression had darkened. "Yes. Perhaps our parents were killed by the same beasts."

"Many nobles died that night," said the librarian. "But they would not have given a child up for adoption. And plenty of servants died, too. I could search the records of the victims for births of females a few months before, but the births of servant families are not very well recorded."

Of course not. Not in this world.

My chest felt tight. This was probably what had happened to my parents, then, but I was growing frustrated with the lack of information.

Torin nodded, and she began flicking through another set of silver cards, shaking her head, muttering to herself. "Hmm. No. No girls born in May to slaughtered parents." She looked up at the king and shrugged. "But...of course, it was such a chaotic time. Even if we did have records of the servants, some would be lost."

A pit opened in my stomach, but I was sure now that my parents had been killed by these horrific beasts.

"I'm sorry, Ava," said Torin. "We will keep searching."

But already, my thoughts were swirling with nightmarish visions of monsters no one would name.

☙ 24 ❧
AVA

I stood in my room, staring at the tapestry on the wall—the one with the strange, monstrous fae, those with insect wings and patches of green covering their limbs. Fae with claws, antlers, and horns, with fangs and clothing stitched together with moss. Forbidding, jagged trees arched over them. When I looked closely enough, I saw the horrors some of them were committing—severing heads with their claws, ripping entrails from their enemies.

I still wanted to know what had happened to my birth parents, but I didn't feel the grief viscerally. When Chloe died, the sorrow had split me open. This sorrow, I felt from a distance. I didn't have a single memory of them.

Shalini pushed the door open, her face flushed and glowing. "Ava, I just had the best—" She went quiet. "Is everything all right?"

My limbs had gone heavy. "I'm fine. But Torin thinks my birth parents may have been killed by

223

monsters. The same ones who killed his. They couldn't find any precise records, but..." I trailed off. "There was some kind of massacre the same month I was found in the human world. They might have been killed then."

"What do you mean? What kind of monsters?" she asked.

Ice plunged down my chest. "No one will talk about it. It's like a superstition or something." I pointed at the tapestry. "Do you know anything about these creatures?"

She shook her head. "No. Could be just artistic license?"

I turned back to the bed, where three books lay on the top of the blankets. "Want to learn about fae history with me?"

I plopped down on top of the blankets and pulled the bright red book into my lap. "*A Short History of the Fae*, by Oberon," I read. "I can translate."

"How did you learn Fae?" asked Shalini.

I smiled at her. "Magic." I opened the book to the first page. "'*A Short History of the Fae*, by Oberon Quiverstick,'" I read. "'Within this volume, I have done my best to summarize the long and complex history of the fae. No one knows when we first came to Faerie. For a long time, the six clans' ancestors lived an uncivilized existence, for which no written records exist. It wasn't until the first high king of Faerie united the clans that our written history begins...'"

I started to skim, flipping the pages. "Hang on. This is super interesting, but I want to know about the massacre." I skipped past chapters about the six clans:

the Kelpie, the Banshees, the Selkie, the Dearg Due, the Redcaps, the Leannán sídhe. Coming to the last chapter, I took a deep breath. "'King Mael led perhaps the most controversial reign of any fae king.'"

"Torin's father," said Shalini, leaning over the book.

I continued reading. "'Born second in line to the throne, Mael had been trained to be a soldier, the leader of the army. His older brother, Gram, was to succeed to the throne. But at sixteen, Prince Gram was killed by the Erlking while hunting a stag. After that, Mael was named the heir apparent.

"Whoa." Shalini's eyes had gone wide. "It was that grotesque head we saw on the wall. Aeron said King Mael slaughtered it."

"That's got to be the monster, right?"

I turned back to the book. "'King Mael spent the first years of his reign in the forest, tracking the cursed fae. After nearly five years, he found the Erlking's lair and killed him, finally avenging his brother's death. Almost immediately thereafter, the tournaments for his queen began, and he chose Princess Sofie. They soon had two children: a boy (Torin) and a girl (Orla). However, Mael's reign was cut short when...'"

I turned the page, only to find an image of the Erlking taking up the next page, and then several pages that had been ripped out.

"What the hell?" Shalini said. "It was just getting good."

I nodded, swallowing hard. "Whatever happened twenty-six years ago, they don't want anyone to know about it." I stared at the ripped pages. On the other side of them was text about the beginning of Torin's reign, but it was written in a propaganda style, since he was already king by the time the book had come out.

A knock sounded on the door, and my head snapped up.

"I'll get it." Shalini rose and opened the door.

Aeron stood in the doorway, his blond hair falling in his eyes, looking for all the world like one of the TikTok guys who could garner a million followers just by taking off his shirt and chopping wood. He blushed as he looked down at her. "Hello."

"Do you want to come in?" she asked.

He smiled but shook his head, and held up a large white box. "I just came to drop something off. Ava's dress for the ball tonight. She should arrive in the Caer Ibormeith ballroom in one hour." He glanced over her shoulder. "I will send someone to escort you."

"Oh, okay." I could hear the disappointment in her voice as she took the box from him.

"I won't be at the ball myself. Perhaps...if you are not otherwise engaged...we might dine together."

She smiled at him. "I'll be here. And I'm looking for some adventure, Aeron, because right now, Ava is getting it all."

He grinned at her. "I will show you my favorite grove in Faerie. You should dress warmly." With a little bow, he turned and walked away, and Shalini closed the door behind him.

She turned to me, her smile radiant. "I have a proper date with the hottest virgin in existence. Not just the hottest virgin. Maybe the hottest *man*." She crossed to the bed and dropped the box onto it.

"I'm glad you came with me to Faerie, Shalini." I slid the top of the box off and pulled out a long, silky gown —one in deep violet, a few shades darker than my hair. "I'm not getting a romance out of this, but it seems like you are."

She shrugged. "You don't need romance right now. You need a rebound. And since Torin is a fae fuckboy, he seems like the right person to take your mind off... you know...the monster we shall not speak of."

"Andrew?"

"Don't say his name. You could summon him."

I crossed into the bathroom and filled the tub, watching the steam curling into the air.

The problem was, something told me that Torin might be the most dangerous thing around.

25

AVA

I crossed into the Caer Ibormeith ballroom a few minutes after eight and found all the princesses already there—along with the camera crews.

But my eyes were on the hall itself. The soaring arches seemed to defy the laws of physics. Flowering vines grew over the stone, reaching all the way up to the silvery light of a star-flecked sky. Like a beautiful medieval ruin, the ballroom was partly open to the night. But torches hung around the stone columns and arches, and plants twined around them.

Before I'd left the room, I'd found the name "Caer Ibormeith" in one of the history books. The fae believed she was the goddess of dreams, that she ruled over sleep. And this place felt like a temple of dreams.

But given how cold it was in here, the plants must be alive through some enchantment. On one side of the hall, a fire burned in a great stone fireplace—the only heat source—and the frosty night air kissed my cheeks.

I hung by the edges of the hall, and goosebumps

rose over the bare skin of my arms. Fae servants, perhaps the sort my parents had been, were gliding around with trays full of champagne flutes. When a woman with pink hair offered one to me, I took it. As I sipped the wine, warmth trickled down my throat and spread through my chest. The wine was like a rosé, but with hints of honey and orange, and a faint effervescence—like nothing I'd ever tasted before, and with an enchantment that burned away the cold.

I ventured further into the ballroom and felt all eyes on me. It seemed that our little castle tour today had absolutely not gone unnoticed.

And yet, as the wine warmed me, I didn't mind the staring so much. In fact, I don't think I'd ever felt this beautiful before, with my hair twisted and braided with bluebells. If I stood in the right way, the slit in my dress showed off my right leg all the way up to the top of my thigh.

Musicians stood in one corner of the ballroom—all women, dressed in white gowns. Beautiful music floated through the air: a harp, a violin, and ethereal woodwind instruments I didn't quite recognize. The princesses stood around, sipping from little champagne flutes.

Only one of the faces here seemed friendly—Alice, the kelpie with white hair and iridescent skin, was smiling at me, and she lifted her champagne flute. I lifted mine as well, smiling back, and she approached me with a relieved look on her face.

Her brown eyes were big as she leaned in close. "The Faerie wine is helping me relax. I was so nervous."

"I'm sure you have nothing to worry about. This one won't get violent, will it?"

She shook her head. "No, but the last time I saw Torin, it was a disaster. I kept blathering on about rancid milk. It really wasn't romantic."

I shrugged. "He seemed interested in it, though." I lifted my glass, staring at the pale pink liquid with little bubbles. "So what exactly is Faerie wine?"

She bit her lip. "It has enchanting properties. It can make you feel amazing. In love, even. Tonight should be interesting."

My heart fluttered at the thought, and at that moment, I felt a cool, powerful magic fill the room. The air seemed to thin, and the princesses stopped speaking as they turned to the entrance.

King Torin entered, dressed in a midnight suit of a velvety material. A silver crown rested on his dark hair, and he swept his icy gaze around the room, a faint smile on his lips. I could smell his delicious, earthy magic from here, wrapping around me like a caress.

A servant rushed over to offer him a drink, and he plucked a glass off the tray and took a sip.

Cleena was the first princess to go to him, her movements languid and entrancing. She wore a long, beaded gown of amber silk and a crown of her own made from pale pink roses twined with ferns. Glittery gold makeup shimmered over her high cheekbones, and shimmering amber gems gleamed from her hair. She gave a little wave to the cameras before turning to the king.

Within moments, I saw him throw back his head with laughter, and I felt the tiniest pang of jealousy.

I took another sip of the wine, forcing myself to pull my eyes away from Torin and Cleena. What I *really* didn't need right after my horrific breakup was another round of jealousy, so I'd simply refuse to care about another beautiful heartbreaker.

Alice glanced up at me. "How do you always seem so confident?"

"*Me?*"

"Yes. I mean, you weren't afraid to tell the king exactly what you thought. And you seemed so calm and natural on your date."

Because I already know the outcome. Torin and I have no chance of actually falling in love.

I shrugged. "It's just something you learn in the human world." That was absolutely not true, but at least I wasn't raised with all the insecurities about my rank in the rigid fae class hierarchy. "I think you should just relax, Alice. You're gorgeous and sweet, and whether it's Torin or someone else, you'll find the right person for you."

She smiled at me with relief.

I stole another quick look at the king, only to find him dancing with the raven-haired Redcap, who'd dressed all in black with a crimson flower crown. I didn't recognize this dance—it was something entirely from the fae world. They were hardly touching, sort of circling each other with only their hands making contact, until they spun and switched directions. Torin's movements reminded me of his feline agility and grace when sparring, and frankly, it was hard to keep my eyes off him. I stared as one of his hands lowered around her waist.

"What's the human world like?" asked Alice.

I was relieved to have a distraction. "Well, it's not quite as luxurious as all this, and we don't have magic. But some of the people can be very warm." I felt a twinge of guilt about Alice. She seemed sweet, and she had no idea that none of this was real.

I stared as Moria prowled across the ballroom floor, cutting in on Torin's dance with the Redcap. Moria was dressed in a strapless white gown, her long claret hair falling over her bare shoulders. A crown of poison hemlock with delicate white flowers was on her head.

She danced close to him, resting her head on his shoulder, her dark eyes sliding to me as she clasped him. Flashing me a smug smile, she pulled her gaze from me and whispered something in his ear. Her hand slid slowly up his back to the nape of his neck...

My stomach twisted. This was a job. Just a job.

They looked a perfect couple, two regal fae beauties. Clearly, Torin was afraid of falling in love.

Was Moria the one who scared him the most?

❧ 26 ❧

AVA

I took another glass of Faerie wine from the tray of a passing servant and roamed the edges of the ballroom. One of these princesses probably sent that assassin for me, right? People seemed to sense I was the frontrunner, and they'd do anything to win.

Moria was my first suspect, but that was probably just because she was an absolute twat. As I sipped my wine, the musicians started playing a new song. Not a tango, but one with the same meter, and the seductive song floated through the air.

I glanced at Torin, and this time found his pale eyes locked on me, his mouth quirking to the side in a mischievous smile. From the center of the ballroom, he held out his hand to me.

The wine had heated me up now, making my muscles feel lithe and supple. I dropped my champagne flute on a little marble table.

Tuning out the rest of the world, I crossed to Torin. Normally, I hated being the center of attention, but the wine had relaxed me, and I was focused on him alone. And maybe I hated being in the spotlight a little less when I felt sexy as hell in this dress that he'd picked out for me. The violet gown had a plunging neckline and a dramatic slit, seductive and perfect for a tango-style dance. The king had also given me a silver necklace that looked like blackthorn leaves and berries twining around my neck.

I took his hand, my gaze locked on his. In time to the music, we circled each other for a few steps. His gaze was taking me apart. He locked his hand on my waist and pulled me in closer—one sharp, possessive movement. My hips were tight against him, which wasn't at all how he'd danced with the others...but I wasn't exactly complaining. Even if I could never let myself fall for him, there was no point in pretending I didn't like being near him.

Our right hands clasped, and his left hand slid around my lower back, holding me in tight. My left hand rested on his shoulder, and I savored the iron feel of his bicep and shoulder muscles under his velvety jacket.

Despite the cold blue of his eyes, the look he was giving me smoldered, lighting a forbidden flame in my body.

Expertly leading me, he slid his hand a little lower down to the small of my back and guided me in a twist. My right leg slid behind me as he dipped me slightly, and I felt the cool air kiss my bare thigh as my foot shifted forward on the flagstones.

When he brought me back up, he dropped my

right hand, clasping my lower back. With a sensual smile, he held me against him in a way that was slightly more indecent than the tango I'd learned in class...

All eyes were on us, but I no longer cared.

Torin guided my back in an arch as he dipped me, his body leaning over mine, lips hovering over my neck. In the oak grove, all it had taken was one brush of his mouth against mine to light me on fire. Just the memory was enough to make my pulse race, to make me acutely aware of every point where our bodies met, and the feel of his heart beating under his clothes. If we were alone here—if this were real—I'm not sure I would have had an ounce of willpower left.

He guided me up again, and I melted into him as he took complete control.

As I arched my back in another dip, my head fell back, and I closed my eyes. He lowered his head, and I felt his breath heating the top of my breasts. When Torin lifted me, my cheek brushed slowly against his, and I found myself wrapping my arms over his shoulders, nestling my head into the crook of his neck. The music swelled, and the deep throbbing of a drum echoed through the hall.

The king leaned down, nuzzling my throat. I heard him sigh, then breathe in, inhaling my scent. In a slow caress, the backs of his knuckles brushed my ribs, the idle stroke of a man who had everything he wanted right in his hands. Heat raced over my body in the wake of his touch, and I knew he could hear the racing of my heart, my breath speeding up...

He could tell I was turned on. Were we even dancing anymore?

With a sigh, he brushed his hands along my arms, clasping my hands in his again. He raised them above my head, and our bodies pressed together. Dazed, my head tilted back, and I met his gaze.

This was the same exhilarating thrill I'd felt when sparring with Torin in the forest, but with an intoxicating, sensual feel to each movement. Never in my life had I been more desperate to kiss someone. He seemed to be able to communicate and guide me through his movements, like he understood how every muscle in my body worked, and how to get the exact result he wanted...

He could have me begging if he wanted.

I was pretty sure I had the answer to Shalini's question. Yes, fae men were undoubtedly better than their human counterparts in bed. At least, I was almost certain *this* one was. And of course he was, because he was nowhere near relationship material.

With a nearly imperceptible growl, his hands moved to my hips. He crouched slightly, then lifted me up above his head. Holy *shit*.

When Torin lowered me, I was close against him once more, sliding slowly down his body. As my left foot hit the ground, I found my right leg wrapped around his upper thigh. He leaned into me, arching my spine as he pressed over me, holding me firmly in the small of my back. Desire darkened his eyes, and his lips parted.

Maybe it was all for show—but I wasn't so sure anymore. The cameras couldn't see the look in his eyes, but I could. And that look said he wanted me as much as I wanted him. His fingers tightened on me possessively.

With what felt like a supreme act of will, Torin straightened, and I unhooked my leg from him, stepping away. Torin dropped my hand, though his eyes lingered on me.

I stepped back—he had other dances tonight, after all. But my heart was pounding in my chest like I'd just returned from battle.

I stayed, sipping a bit more of Faerie wine, watching as he danced with Alice not once, but twice. Despite her worries, she danced gracefully, and the king was genuinely smiling at her.

Did I have to stay here and watch him dance with one woman after another? I'd already put on the show required of me. It was all caught on camera.

So, as Moria grabbed him for another dance, I slipped out the dark entrance and headed back to my room.

৩৯৩

THE CASTLE WAS HUGE. TWENTY MINUTES LATER, AS I made my way down the empty hall, I was aware of a hollow, aching loneliness. Was he dancing the same way with someone else now? Truly, it was hard not to wonder.

But I'd sworn off men, hadn't I? It was why I was "the chosen one" here.

The sound of footfalls behind me made my heart

race, and it occurred to me that walking back to my chamber alone might not have been the best idea with an assassin on the loose. I heard the other person's pace increase, and I turned, ready to fight.

But when I whirled around, I found Torin behind me, hands in his pockets. He wasn't smiling anymore. "You shouldn't be walking around here on your own, Ava. Not when someone tried to kill you."

I heaved a breath. "Sorry. I was trying to sneak out."

A smile tugged at the corner of his lips. "Why?"

Did he want me to admit I'd felt the tiniest twinge of jealousy? Because I wasn't about to. I shrugged. "I was bored."

He pressed me against the wall, placing his hands on either side of my head. With the look he was giving me, I felt like he was taking me apart, examining every inch of my soul. "You're really not what I expected."

I licked my lips, and his eyes caught the movement, lingering on my mouth.

"Is that a good thing or a bad thing?" I asked.

"Both."

"That's certainly confusing."

He lifted a hand to trace his fingertips over my collarbone. My body sparked at the light contact. "Tell me again how much you hate me."

My pulse quickened. "Is this your kink?"

"Something like that."

In the dim torchlight, I could see clearly how sharp his cheekbones were, how perfect his lips...

So why not play along? A perfect rebound. "You're

arrogant and desperate to give off the impression that you're in control, all so you can cover up the truth."

He arched an eyebrow, his hand sliding around the back of my neck. His thumb brushed the skin of my throat, his eyes burning bright. "And what truth would that be?" he whispered.

"That you're terrified of your own emotions, so you won't let anyone close."

A slow, seductive smile curled his lips. "It sounds like a state you understand well. One idiot broke your heart, and you swore off love forever."

"You are an irredeemable snob who believes you deserve power because of an accident of birth."

I stroked my hands over his glorious chest as I spoke, reveling in the feel of his steely muscles, eliciting a quiet growl from him.

"We would be a match made in hell," he purred, staring at my lips. "Your family lacks a noble lineage, a truth betrayed by your untrained manners at every opportunity."

I reached up and touched his face. "And you're stupid enough to think that matters, aren't you, Your Majesty?"

His knee nestled between my thighs, pinning me in place. "I'm not someone anyone should fall for, understood?"

My neck arched, my body going taut, ready to give in to him. "Loud and clear."

"But I can't seem to stop thinking about you and the way your body feels against mine," he murmured. "Just one kiss, Ava. I want more, of course. I want to take my time with you, to explore all of you. But I can't have that, because none of this can be real. So, just one kiss."

It was almost a question, and I nodded, my lips parting.

At last, he captured my mouth with his, and I tasted the sweet, fruity tang of Faerie wine on his lips. It was a gentle kiss at first, until he tilted his head and his tongue swept in. Heat radiated through me as the kiss deepened, his tongue flitting against mine in a sensual caress.

My body was igniting like wildfire, my core going tight and loose at the same time. Aching for him.

One of his hands stroked down my body—my shoulder, the curve of my breast, my waist. I was desperate for him to caress me all over, and I let out a light moan. His hands moved further down my hips and into the slit of my dress. He reached around the curve of my upper thigh, and lifting my leg around him, he pressed into the apex of my thighs. Gripping me, he moved his hips against me, and I arched into him.

He pulled away from the kiss, letting out a hiss of breath. But he was still clinging to my thigh—one hand pressed against the wall, the other on me. "Have I told you how much I love the way you smell, Ava?"

I threaded my fingers into his dark hair. "Shh. We're not doing compliments."

He'd said just one kiss, but that was a lie. The King of Faerie claimed my mouth again. My hips moved against him, and the quiet rumbling in his chest made my breasts go tight.

I could feel his hardness straining against me, and his kiss had grown frenzied, desperate.

We were tasting each other, and the pleasure of this kiss had swept all rational thought from my mind like a winter wind. But it wasn't enough. The ache between my thighs demanded more.

He caught my lower lip between his as he pulled away, ending the kiss. His fingers were threaded in my hair, and he seemed reluctant to let go. Catching his breath, he rested his forehead against mine. My lips felt deliciously swollen.

"We are a match made in hell, but I have never wanted anyone more, Ava Jones," he rasped. Meeting my gaze one last time, he stepped back. "I'm sending guards to your room, immediately. I won't have anything happen to you."

He turned and walked down the shadowy hall, his crown gleaming like fire under the flickering torches.

27

AVA

I woke with a pounding headache and one arm slung over my eyes. Had thunder awoken me? I wasn't sure if something had actually boomed through the walls or if it was the lingering remnants of a nightmare.

It wasn't storming. Moonlight streamed into the room, and I felt as if someone was screaming in my head.

I hadn't felt drunk last night—just amazing. I'd had maybe two and a half little flutes of the Faerie wine, which I didn't think was that much. But apparently, Faerie wine fucks you up. And as always when I drank too much, I woke at an ungodly hour.

Immediately, my mind went to the kiss with Torin, and my pulse started to race just thinking about it.

The voice screamed in my head again, and I slammed my eyes shut.

But that wasn't in my head, was it? Who the fuck was screaming?

I forced myself out of bed and into Shalini's room. In the moonlight, I could see her sitting up in bed, rubbing her eyes. "What's happening?" she mumbled. "What time is it?"

I crossed to the door, opening it a crack. Screams echoed off the castle walls, and I saw guards running toward the source of the noise down the shadowy hall.

I slid the door shut and turned back to Shalini. "Someone's hurt, I think. But there are tons of guards out there if there's an intruder."

With a thundering heart, I crossed to pick up my sword, left by the door.

Carefully, I opened the door an inch and peered out again. The guards had disappeared into a chamber. Shadows danced across the stones. The screaming had fallen silent.

Silhouetted figures moved about the hall, and in the torchlight, I identified the princesses, pulled from sleep as I had been, their tangled hair tumbling over their nightgowns. I recognized the dark-haired Redcap, her eyes opened wide with fear as she crept over the stone, and the pumpkin and violet locks of Etain.

"What the fuck is happening?" she asked in a loud whisper.

I tiptoed into the hall, and cold dread plunged down my center.

"What's going on?" I crept to the door the guards had gone through and peered over someone's shoulder to see what had happened.

Through the crowd pressing into the door, I caught a glimpse of a woman's body. She lay face down, her white hair spread out like the petals of a broken flower, her white nightgown stained red with blood. The ornate hilt of a knife protruded from between her shoulder blades.

"It's Princess Alice," I breathed. Her body wasn't moving.

Wisps of our conversation earlier twisted and floated through my mind, and sadness coiled through me. Alice had seemed sweet, nothing like the rest of the ruthless fae.

Aeron was crouching over her, his hands held out. "No one come closer!" he barked. Then he raised his face to the other guards. "How did this happen with a guard at the door? With all of us in the hall?"

A soldier with dark hair shook his head. "No one entered her room."

"And none of you saw anyone pass by?" Freezing magic glided over my skin, and my teeth chattered. I turned to see Torin stalking down the hall. "Everyone must return to their rooms at once," he said, one hand on the hilt of his rapier.

I sucked in a deep breath and stepped aside. Torin was right—we didn't need dozens of people trampling all over a crime scene. I turned, and looking back, I caught a glimpse of the TV crew. They were dragging a camera as fast as they could across the stone floor. I didn't want to be there when they clashed with Torin over broadcasting this.

I hurried to my room, thinking of what Torin had said about the castle—even he didn't know every passage in this labyrinth. Once Shalini and I were safe, I slipped the deadbolt into place. "We need to scour this place for entrances," I said. Heart hammering, I pulled aside tapestries and hunted under the beds for trapdoors.

Shalini was running her fingers over the walls. "Why Alice?" she asked. "Moria and you seem to be the front-runners."

"It's probably Moria," I muttered. "And maybe she couldn't get in here. Alice danced with the king twice tonight. Maybe more. She was still dancing with him when I left."

After twenty minutes of searching, Shalini and I hadn't found a thing—except a note slipped under our door from the king:

Search every inch of the room. Aeron will guard you until I return.

You are not to leave under any circumstances.

❦

SHALINI AND I HAD SPENT THE DAY AS VIRTUAL prisoners in our room—albeit prisoners with tons of books, a luxurious bath, plenty of food deliveries, and a brief visit from Aeron, who helped us inspect the room once more. But now it was just the two of us and the books. As we lounged in our room, servants had delivered stews, chicken wings, blue cheese, fruit, and red wine.

Apart from the threat of assassination, I had no complaints, really.

By six p.m., I was hunched over the chicken wings,

which were smoky and flavorful, the meat practically falling off the bone. In my lap, I'd opened a book to read as I ate, *The Castle of Ontranto*, a centuries-old gothic romance that had me completely hooked.

As I paused for a sip of Beaujolais, a knock sounded at the door.

Shalini reached the door first and pressed her ear against the wood. "Who is it? More food?"

"It's the king." His deep voice boomed through the wood. "And Aeron."

Shalini unbolted the door and pulled it open, letting them in.

As Torin came into the room, I could see his exhaustion. His face was drawn, and there were shadows beneath his beautiful eyes.

Aeron held up the black dagger I'd seen jutting out of Alice's body. He glanced at Shalini and me. "You two are the only ones who got a glimpse of the assassin in action. Is this the same dagger you saw in your room that night?"

I took a step closer, staring at the hilt. "I think so. I mean, it was dark. But I do remember that it was black. Like onyx."

"Did you find a secret passage in Alice's room?" asked Shalini.

Torin ran a hand through his hair. "A painting of Finvarra that no one suspected was a door. It opened into her room, and the assassin must have entered while she slept. The passageway leads all the way down to the dungeons, and I have soldiers scouring the entire thing for evidence and interrogating the other princesses."

Curiosity sparked. "Why don't you suspect us?"

Aeron cocked his head. "You wouldn't have made it past me, would you? Several of the other princesses have hidden passages in their rooms that would allow them out. Yours does not."

I took a deep breath. "Let me guess. Moria is one of them?"

"I can't accuse without evidence. It would tear the kingdom apart."

Aeron fidgeted with his collar. "And there is, of course, the history the king has with Moria and her family."

It's not like he'd told me anything about that.

Torin glanced at Aeron for a moment before meeting my gaze. "I have plenty of guards collecting evidence now, Ava. But we only have a few days left, and I need to make sure you'll be able to defend yourself in the fencing tournament."

Despite everything happening, and despite my better judgment, I felt a hot shiver of excitement at the idea of being alone with him again.

28

AVA

Wrapped in my white cloak, I followed Torin into the forest. But he wasn't taking me toward the changeling cemetery, as usual. Instead, we walked on a winding path between the dark, snow-covered oaks.

"Do you really think I need more practice?" The air stung my lungs. "With everything else going on?"

"The fencing tournament is the night after tomorrow. I'm still worried, yes." He glanced at me, his eyes bright in the darkness. "I'm not sure I should have brought you into Faerie."

"Why?"

"Because you were safe in the human world, but you aren't here. And now, it's my responsibility to make sure nothing happens to you, but I don't feel in control anymore. The forces of darkness are spreading here, along with the frost. It started with the boggarts spoiling the milk. Then I hear reports of dragons and the sluagh demons...the dark magic filling the void is taking over, and I suspect the princesses may feel that malign influence, making them more bloodthirsty."

"Isn't that why I'm here? To fix it all?"

"If you live. After the murder, I have no doubt the princesses will try to tear you to pieces in the tournament."

Cold fingers of dread danced up my spine, but I tried to ignore them. "But you need a queen you can't love, or the kingdom will die. So here I am. Torin, where are we going?"

Shadows seemed to cloak the king tonight, and I had the sense that something was weighing heavily on his mind. "To the old temple of Ostara. We're going to practice there."

"Why?"

"It's none of your concern, changeling," he said curtly. "Just focus on trying to stay alive. Tonight, when we practice, I'm going to be using magic. The princesses will do the same, and you need to be prepared for it."

Apparently, Torin wasn't in the mood for conversation tonight.

But as he led me to a towering temple made of stone, with arches that soared up to the stars, I was lost for words anyway. I wasn't even thinking about the cold as I stared at the forlorn beauty of this place. We entered through an open archway into the old temple.

Snow covered the floor and dusted the stones. If medieval cathedrals were twice their actual size and left to fall to ruin in frozen lands for centuries, this is what they'd look like. Moonlight streamed in through open, peaked windows, and the decaying ceiling spread above us like the broken ribcage of a stone dragon. Statues adorned some of the alcoves, many of them of animals like hares and foxes. I felt the rush of magic pulsing off the stones, vibrating over my skin. Icicles hung all around, crystals gleaming with silver. Thorny plants climbed the walls, no longer flowering in the cold, but the effect was forbidding and stunning at the same time.

I had no idea why we'd come here, but I wasn't complaining. It was a privilege to get a glimpse of this magical place.

"Are you ready?" Torin was already drawing his sword, not wasting any time.

Sighing, I pulled off my cloak and draped it over a half-ruined statue of a hare. I lifted my rapier, steadying myself on the icy ground.

I raised my sword, meeting his gaze. Sometimes, when he looked at me, the intensity of his stare sent a shiver over my skin. This was a man with so much power, I almost felt like I was seeing something forbidden when I looked at him directly.

"Wait." He reached into his pocket and pulled out a pale crystal, one that gleamed like ice. "Keep this close to you. It will help you move swiftly when the other princesses are using magic. Take care not to let its power overwhelm you."

He tossed it into the air, and I caught it in my palm. I didn't have any pockets in my leather pants, so I shoved it into my bra.

When it touched my skin, darkness started to unfurl in my chest—a lust for blood. I felt my lip curl my back from my teeth, and I ran my tongue over my canines. It must be the wild magic of the place, or the crystal itself —but I swear they felt sharp as a wolf's. Around me, the moonlight seemed brighter, and the shadows grew thicker.

Maybe I was never meant for the human world. The wilderness was my home. "I'm not quite sure if you're ready for me, Torin."

"I'll do my best, changeling," he purred.

His eyes were flecks of ice in the dark. I tried to anticipate where he'd strike first, and my legs began to buzz with battle fury.

Torin lunged at me across the snowy temple floor. He attacked, aiming for my shoulder, and I parried easily. Swift as the wind, I moved as we flew into a flurry of clashing blades, our swords clinking in midair. I was driving him back already, my heart slamming with the thrill of it.

Had I been excited for Torin, or desperate for the thrill of war? Was this a suppressed side of me I'd never known in the human realm?

By now, we'd grown to know one another's movements and rhythms, which meant I had to do something different to win. I blocked his strike with more force than usual, then spun away from him. I shifted through the dark, fast as a hummingbird's wings. Torin was on the attack again, and he swung for me—but this time, I ducked.

No rules in Faerie...

From the ground, I moved to strike for his legs, and he leapt over my blade. Before I could rise, he swung again, vicious now. I blocked the attack, and his blade pressed down against mine.

Trapped on the ground, I slammed my foot into his knee. He lost the grip on his sword, and it clanged to the ground. As I started to rise again, the king body-checked me with the force of a steam train. I fell back hard onto the rocky earth, my head smacking the stone. Dizziness shot through my skull, and I lost my grip on the rapier.

Magic surged from the crystal into my ribs, and my body roared with violence. But Torin was already on top of me, pinning me to the snowy earth. I lifted my hips and gripped his hair, pulling him off me.

He rolled onto his back, and I straddled him, punching him hard in the jaw. His head snapped back, but with my next strike, he caught my fist in his crushing grip. With a snarl, he twisted my arm away. I flipped off him, landing facedown in the snow. The wind left my body.

The king was on my back now, pinning my hands to the earth. I moved my hips back up into him, but I wasn't shifting him off me.

He leaned down, whispering into my ear, "I can see you have a wild side, but we clearly have more work to do."

He released my wrists, shifting his weight. Catching my breath, I rolled over to look up at him. But the king didn't move. He pinned my wrists again, this time facing me.

"Quite aggressive this evening, aren't you?" Wildness danced in his pale eyes. "Good, but you need to be more aggressive, Ava. Because I will not have your death on my hands."

My breath clouded around him. "Because underneath your grumpy exterior, you actually like me."

He exhaled sharply and released my hands, but he didn't get off me. "Ava," he whispered, staring down at me.

His eyelashes were long and dark, his face a study of contrasts: pale skin, coal black eyebrows, and eyes of the palest blue.

The snow from the stone floor seeped into my clothes, freezing my skin.

He cupped the side of my face, brushing his thumb against my cheek, and pressed his forehead against mine.

That close, the primeval power of his magic pulsed over me, making my skin vibrate. I breathed in his scent. Being near him was like drawing power from a god. Desire swept through me, and my thighs clenched around his. "This is just physical," I whispered, reminding myself out loud.

"Good." He rolled off me onto his side, but he threaded one hand into my hair, pulling me close. The other hand slid down to my ass, tucking me next to him.

Torin turned his head, brushing his lips over mine, teasing. And when his mouth pressed against mine, his tongue sweeping in, he kissed me with the desperation of a man who thought the world was ending and only our desire could save it.

He slid his hand inside my underwear from behind,

cupping my ass. Torin moaned, his fingers tightening in my hair. By the tautness of his muscles, I knew he was trying to restrain himself with every ounce of control that he had.

This was a dangerous game since he couldn't even admit to liking me.

I ran my fingers under his shirt, feeling the carved V of his abs, then tracing a little lower...

His restraint snapped.

There was nothing in the world now but our limbs entangled, our lips moving against each other, and our hearts pounding. Our kiss was the first star in a night sky—a spark of light surrounded by darkness. The kind of kiss I'd craved my whole life and never known. Everything else faded to shadows.

He pulled away, taking my lower lip between his teeth for a moment, and we caught our breath. Gently, he brushed kisses over my jaw, keeping me close to him. For the first time since I'd been around him, Torin's body radiated heat.

He met my gaze once more, and he seemed to be searching my eyes. "Ava," he rasped.

Then, as quickly as the kiss had begun, he pulled away from me. He sat up, turning aside, and ran his hand through his hair.

I sat up, too, frowning at him. My body missed the warmth of his, the feel of him wrapped around me.

He looked back at me, his expression ice-cold. "You do know it's just lust, Ava. This isn't real. I cannot...I do *not* like you."

His words hit me like an icicle in my chest, and I

stared at him, stunned. As he rose from the ground, it took me a moment to remember how words worked. But of course—I'd expected this all along, hadn't I?

I swallowed hard, ignoring the numbness growing in my fingers and toes from the cold. "You don't like me because I'm a common fae."

Of course, Torin also had a history of some kind with Moria—a High Fae blue blood.

"No," he rasped. "That's not why. I took you here for a reason."

My jaw clenched. "And that reason is..."

"I needed to remind myself..." He trailed off. "Look, it really doesn't matter. This was never meant to be real. You knew that."

I stood, brushing the snow off my clothes. "It's fine." I lowered my voice to steady it so he couldn't hear it breaking. "I knew all along you're just another pretty boy asshole, and that hasn't changed. So there have been no surprises on my end." I was pretty sure I was doing an amazing job of covering up the fact that he'd knocked the wind out of me.

Bizarrely—even though he was the one rejecting me —an expression of pain ghosted over his features for a moment.

Then he turned and stalked away into the shadows. I stared after him. He hadn't even bothered to pick up his sword.

I'd known what this was. He never wanted to marry. Didn't want to fall in love or have children. And neither had I, because I was done with love.

But it felt as if my heart was breaking anyway.

❧ 29 ❧

AVA

By the time I returned to my room, furious, my fingers and toes had gone completely numb, and my teeth wouldn't stop chattering.

Even though Torin had disappeared without a trace, he'd sent guards to escort me back to my room, which somehow annoyed me even more.

I found Shalini sitting cross-legged on her bed, hunched over a book. On the table next to her was a bottle of wine and two empty glasses. Soaked through with snow, I felt a sudden pang of jealousy for her quiet, warm evening.

She looked up as I came in. "You look freezing. How did training go?"

"Torin is a twat."

She immediately grabbed the empty wine glass and began pouring. "Is he? What happened?"

"Well, we trained." I pulled off my damp cloak and draped it over a chair. "Then we kissed. And then he told me he doesn't actually like me."

She stared at me, nearly spilling the wine. "What the hell, Torin? I mean, even for a fuckboy, couldn't he just keep that bit to himself?"

I plucked the wine off the table and went to stand by the fireplace to warm up. "I think he's horrified at himself for having the hots for a common fae."

She shook her head. "Surely he's not that shallow, is he?"

I shrugged. "Well, I can't think of anything else." I gave her a wry smile. "Given how often we end up kissing, it seems he likes how I look." I shrugged. "And surely my charming fucking personality isn't putting him off. But it really doesn't matter, Shalini. I went in here knowing that love was bullshit, so I don't feel a thing. Torin is hardly any different from Andrew, is he? I'm here for the money. That's all."

A thorny tendril of accusation wove through my thoughts—*Liar*. Because that kiss had been mind-blowing enough to make me forget all about Andrew and my pledge to never love again. To even forget about the fifty million...

But did I really need to admit that out loud? My ego had taken enough damage lately.

"You are genuinely charming to anyone with sense." She cocked her head. "By the way, Aeron isn't quite as chaste as he's supposed to be anymore."

"You're kidding." The warmth washed over me from the fireplace, drying my clothes a little, and the fire crackled behind me. I returned her smile. "Well, at least one of us found a nice guy."

She slid her empty wine glass onto the table. "That's not the only thing I found."

I rubbed my hands together, feeling the blood pumping again. "What else?"

"You know how we searched the room for secret passages, and we didn't find any?" She swung her legs off the bed and walked over to one of the bookshelves. "Well, we *do* have a secret passage. And it's a fucking classic."

"What do you mean, a classic?"

"Watch this." She tugged at a stone gargoyle on a shelf, and it clicked. The bookshelf swung inward with a creak, a few books tumbling to the floor.

Okay. The bookshelf passage *was* a classic, and I don't know why we hadn't tried it before. "Where do you think it goes?" I whispered.

She glanced back at the door to the hall. "The assassin came in from the main entrance, yeah?"

"Maybe he didn't know about the secret passage." Stepping closer, I could see the outlines of ancient cast-iron hinges. "How did you find this?" I breathed.

"Just looking for another gothic romance. Already finished *Mysteries of Udolpho*." She took a tentative step inside, then paused to look back at me, her eyes wide. "Should we get Aeron?"

I hesitated. "I don't really want the two of us added to the suspect list. Right now, we're in the clear. Maybe we should just...close it?"

"You know we're going in there, Ava. Don't even pretend to argue." She flicked on her cell phone's flashlight and stepped deeper into the tunnel."

"Hang on one second, Shalini." I darted back into the room and grabbed my rapier.

Inside the passage, the beam of the flashlight illuminated the dark stone walls and the low ceiling. I gripped the hilt of my rapier and sniffed the air. Damp stone, a bit of moss, the scent of the rose-scented soap Shalini and I had both been using—

In the human world, I didn't use this primal skill, hunting by scent. But here, it came naturally, a forgotten sense.

Shalini cast her light over the stone. "Ava, you wanted to know about monsters. The ones that might have killed your parents?"

"Did you find anything?" We were both whispering, but somehow, our voices sounded loud, echoing. "Torin has been talking about monsters. Dragons, and something called sluagh."

"But those are the ones people talk about, right? In one of the fae history books, there were creatures with horns and wings. Half fae, half beasts—like the tapestry. The book said they could be a myth. But it sounds like Torin has seen them, right? Supposedly, they're evil, bloodthirsty creatures. The ancient, dark side of the fae, before they became more civilized."

"He seems certain they killed his parents. And I think he said they once ruled this land, before the Seelie took over and built this castle." My heart pounded, my mouth going dry. "What are they called?"

She turned, eyes gleaming in the dark. "The Unseelie."

The name sent cold dread thrumming over my skin. "I've heard of them. I didn't know they were real."

She shrugged. "In Faerie, it seems like monsters are real."

I sighed. "That's certainly true. Torin says that with magic leaving the kingdom, dark magic is filling the void."

"I'm worried about the fencing tournament. Are you really ready for this, Ava? Because these princesses are *not* fucking around." She turned back to me. "What if Moria is secretly an Unseelie, and she's going to rip you to ribbons?"

"I'll be fine," I said as reassuringly as I could. "I've practiced so much with Torin." But who could say, really?

As we walked deeper into the tunnel, my mind flicked back to the first night we'd been given the room. Aeron had suggested that it had been unused for years, and he didn't want me asking about it. Why would that be?

I had this feeling, this sense, that this passage was important. Who had lived in here before?

I had to hunch to keep my head from hitting the ceiling, and I slipped ahead of Shalini to hold the rapier straight out in front of me. Shalini stayed close behind, her breath shallow with excitement.

After another twenty feet, the passage opened slightly. Shalini flashed the phone light around, showing two stairwells before us—one going up, and one going down.

"Up," said Shalini.

"Why?"

"I don't know. Down is going to be a forgotten dungeon or something, and I don't want to find any bodies."

She gave me a gentle nudge, and I moved forward with my sword drawn.

We crept up the stairs until they stopped at a blank wall of solid rock.

"Why would a stairwell lead to nothing?" I asked.

"There must be another door." Shalini shone her light over the stone. "There!" She pointed to a small, raised bump. "That looks like a button. See? I'm good at finding these things now."

Carefully, I pressed the spot, and it clicked. What had looked like a stone wall began to swing outward.

"Be careful," she whispered.

"I am." I allowed the door to open only slightly and peered through the crack to see another corridor. "A hallway." Slowly I pushed the door further open. In here, the floor was dusty, and cobwebs hung from a gilt-framed painting across from us, a portrait of a fae with jet black hair that glittered with jewels.

The stone passage was rough-hewn and grew narrower, as if built in a time when the fae were smaller. The hall led to yet another stairwell—cramped and winding up and up. I ventured slowly up the stairs with Shalini at my heels. The light from the phone barely illuminated the steps in front of me. They twisted round and round until I began to feel dizzy and claustrophobic, the dark walls seeming to close in on me.

We kept climbing, my thighs beginning to burn.

Just when I was tempted to pause and rest, we reached another door, this one made of wood, warped by time. I twisted a dusty doorknob, half expecting the door to be locked, but it turned easily, opening with a dull squeak.

I stared at a hidden tower room, and at the moonlight that streamed over a bed.

✣ 30 ✣

AVA

Light spilled through windows that swept around us in a great curve.

Shalini peered over my shoulder and exhaled. "This place is amazing."

I nodded, gazing out at the frozen kingdom from the enormous windows. After the cramped stairwell, this place was a relief. From here, I could see the ruined temple where Torin had confessed that he didn't like me at all—a tiny, dark thing in the distance, its towers jutting from the forest like black blades. A sea of silver spread out before us, the moonlight gleaming off snowy trees, fields, and the wintry rooftops of the kingdom.

A darkness is spreading in our kingdom.

I turned to survey the room. Above us, the ceiling pitched upward like an inverted ice cream cone. A single bed stood in the room, plus a desk with a chair. In the daytime, the view from the desk would be magnificent, but you'd wake with the dawn.

A dusty book lay on the bed, and I picked it up.

Claimed By the Mountain Fae, it read in English, and bore a silver crown on the cover. When I flipped to the copyright page, I found that it had been published just five years ago. "Shalini, someone in here was reading smut. Recently."

She held out her hand. "Give me that. I need something steamier than the eighteenth-century gothic fiction in our room."

I handed it over. "This place isn't totally abandoned. The book is only five years old."

"Okay. So we're probably in the killer's room. Maybe we should get the fuck out of here?"

"Hang on."

I crossed to the desk, my gaze roaming over a leather blotter on the surface. An old antique lamp with a stained glass lampshade stood beside it, along with a small pewter pencil holder, which had a few old-looking pens sticking out of it. Dust coated everything.

"It doesn't seem like anyone has been in here recently," I said. "There's a few years' worth of dust over everything."

I pulled open the desk drawer to find a single leather-bound book. The leather was old and slightly scuffed, without a name or label, or anything on its surface.

I opened it, and Shalini flashed her phone light onto the pages. I was expecting to see more of the fae writing, but as I flipped through it, it was just blank beige vellum. "That's disappointing."

"Lame."

But as she pulled her phone light away, the blank

pages started to shimmer with light. Here in the pale light of the moon, spidery writing appeared on the pages in bright silver.

"Look," I said to Shalini, "do you see that?"

She turned back, and the light from her phone erased the writing as it illuminated it.

"It has to be moonlight," I said. "It's what makes the text show up."

"Holy shit. Can you read it, Ava?"

Thanks to the librarian's spell, I could decode it. "This looks like a date," I said. "May 5th, and it's dated three years ago." I flipped to the next page. "May 7th."

"Ooh," said Shalini, "a diary?"

"I am sitting in the most wonderful tower that I think only I know about," I read out loud. A thrill ran through me at the first line.

"So nosy, Ava! This is absolutely none of our business. Read on, please."

I turned back to the page and began to read.

❦

EVEN HERE IN THIS QUIET PLACE, I CAN'T STOP THINKING *about him, the cruel beauty of his pale eyes. He tells me he doesn't think he can love, but not why. He tells me there are secrets only he and Orla know.*

But I know it's a lie. I can feel his love on me like a warm spring breeze, and when we marry, I will restore life to this kingdom.

I remember the first day we met, when he saved me from a wraith in the frozen moors. Of course, I knew who he was. The

265

only man in the world with beauty that can break your heart in the span of a breath.

I'll never forget when our eyes met—it was as if my heart broke in two at that moment. What had been whole was halved, and one half was his.

And even if he refuses to admit it to himself, I know he loves me.

—M

SHALINI CUT IN THEN. "WHO IS IT? WHO'S THE writer?"

I stared at the words, feeling as if sharp-clawed fingers were tightening around my heart.

"I don't know," I said. "It just says *M*. But it's about Torin. He loves to say that he can't love."

"We shouldn't be reading this," she whispered. "Go on."

DEAR DIARY, IT HARDLY SEEMS POSSIBLE, BUT IT'S actually happened. I've moved into the castle—in my own room, one hung with tapestries and filled with books. It's not as grand as home, I suppose, but I'm near him, and that is the only thing that makes me happy. I think Torin plans to marry me, but he keeps warning me about danger...

—M

MY HEART POUNDED AGAINST MY RIBS, AND I FELT the thorny vines of jealousy wrapping around my heart.

Was M for Moria? I suppose it was a common enough letter, but...

Who'd written this? And why wasn't he marrying her now?

The silvery writing was hard to read and seemed to grow dimmer as I was looking at it, so I flipped the page and read out loud as quickly as I could.

8TH DAY OF THE HARVEST,

Dear diary, I spent a long day, just him and me. He seemed out of sorts, as if something was preoccupying him. I tried to speak with him about it, but he said it was nothing. He has started to say that we must not touch each other, and I do not understand why.

I TURNED THE PAGE. HERE, THE WRITING WAS MORE scribbled, as if the writer had written it more quickly than usual.

DAY OF THE FAST,

Dear diary, today was awful. The most terrible thing happened. We went for a walk in the forest, just the two of us. It should have been wonderful, but he kept trying to tell me that something terrible might happen. That I was doomed, but without explaining why. Finally, a chance to be alone with him, but when I tried to hold his hand, he froze me with ice. It was the most painful thing I'd ever experienced, and I had to run to my dear sister to fix it.

She told me Torin would be the death of me.

She told me Torin WAS death.

In her premonition, he would bury my frozen body beneath the earth in Ostara's temple, and he would never tell anyone that he killed me. He swallows the secret, ashes in his belly...

It scares me. My sister has never been wrong before. And yet, I don't think I can stay away from the king...

"I'm having trouble reading it," I said.

As I spoke the words aloud, the text disappeared completely, and I was left looking at a blank page.

My breath caught in my throat.

"Holy shit," said Shalini. "Who do you think that was? Do you think Torin could be dangerous?"

"We're fae. We're all dangerous."

"Maybe the assassin killed her, too." Shalini touched my arm. "Ava, I know I told you to come here in the first place. And you told me the fae were terrifying, but I didn't quite listen. I'm starting to think that...you know, maybe it's not worth risking your life over this?"

"For fifty million?"

"What are you going to do with fifty million if you're dead?" she snapped.

I sucked in a sharp breath. "You'll just have to have faith in me not dying."

Because it wasn't just the money.

I didn't want to leave this place.

✎ 31 ✎

AVA

It was the last night before the tournament, and we were all supposed to meet for a nice, civilized dinner before we hacked into one another's bodies with swords. With Shalini by my side and Aeron leading the way, I prowled the castle's dark halls dressed in a pale silver gown. I wore my hair piled up in braids woven with violets, and Shalini was elegantly dressed in white.

My dress shimmered as I walked, and I couldn't stop thinking of the moonlight and those strange, spidery letters. The diary had kept me up all night, even if I couldn't read it. I'd stayed awake, obsessively examining the diary as if the blank pages could give up Torin's secrets.

I blinked, trying to force myself back to the present. When it was time to fight tomorrow morning, I couldn't be daydreaming about the dark mysteries of Torin's love life or what had happened to *M*.

"Stop brooding," muttered Shalini. "You're in a gorgeous castle on your way to a feast."

I cut her a sharp look. "I'm not brooding. Just nervous for tomorrow."

She frowned at me. "You and me both. It's not too late to, you know..."

"Run away?"

"I'm afraid tomorrow will be a bloodbath," she whispered loudly.

"It will. That's what the fae are like. Just have faith in my survival skills because I'm one of them."

It was with a little shock that I realized I was starting to think of myself as fae, not a human wannabe.

I was fae.

After weeks in the castle, I was actually starting to know my way around. We passed the usual collection of gilded portraits, suits of armor, and flickering torches, and I knew we were closing in on the throne hall.

We went through the doors and found tables arranged in a semicircle around the ancient thrones. Aeron led Shalini and me to our seats, and I glanced at the spot Alice would have taken if she hadn't been murdered. My throat tightened.

A servant poured us red wine. As I sipped it, the other princesses began to file in, gracefully taking their seats.

Torin prowled into the room, dressed in black leather—more like a warrior than a king tonight. "Tomorrow, we hold the final event of our tournament," he said. "It will be steel upon steel, blade upon blade. Tomorrow, you must prove to me that you have the noble warrior spirit required of a Seelie queen. Those who succeed in the first duel will continue to fight the other winners."

Moria turned to me with a pleasant smile. "And if the misfortune of a violent death should befall you, you'd be out of the tournament as well."

Torin cut her a sharp look. "The first duel will be between Princess Moria of the Dearg Due and Princess Cleena of the Banshee Clan." He glanced at me, and I felt my heart flutter for just a moment. "The second will be Princess Etain of the Leannán sídhe and Sydoc of the Redcap Clan, and the third duel will be between Princess Eliza of the Selkie and Ava Jones of Chloe's household."

My heart squeezed a little at the fact that he'd thought to mention my mom's name. He could have left it blank. Ava Jones of...*nothing*. Ava Jones of the dead-servant parents and public-drunken disgrace. But he knew what Chloe meant to me, that she was my home. That once, I'd actually had a place.

I glanced at Eliza—a woman with bronze skin and shimmering hair of pale green. Her eyes were a deep brown flecked with green. They narrowed at me as she spoke. "I have been studying since birth with the finest teachers. My education in the field of swordsmanship is unparalleled. In our kingdom by the sea, our finest treasures are our skills. A fae could go many a year before encountering such an exemplary—"

"I look forward to tomorrow." Sydoc raised a glass, interrupting Eliza. "When I shall dip my cap in the blood of my enemies."

Etain frowned at her. "What the fuck, Sydoc? You do realize you are fighting me in the duel. You're not going to dip your cap in my blood. Can't we just...go on points?"

Sydoc's eyes locked on her. "A queen must demonstrate her skill on the battlefield. It is the Redcap way. And yes, I will honor my clan tradition."

A look of horror crossed Etain's face. "Fucking creep."

A murmur rippled over the room, and the back of my neck prickled with unease. I glanced at Moria to find her passing her phone to the redcap, giggling as she did.

"Princess Moria." Torin's deep voice filled the hall. "Am I boring you?"

"Oh, dear." She turned back to him, her eyes wide. "Apologies, Your Majesty, but I thought you should know that one of the women here has disgraced herself." Her cold gaze slid to me, and her expression hardened. "Again." She met Torin's stare. "I know you abhor grotesque public spectacles, as I do. And I am certain you could not abide a bride with loose morals, someone whose naked body the entire world has already seen. A fae queen must be chaste and pure, not used up like a common whore."

Nausea climbed in my throat as I watched her pass her phone from one princess to the next, each of them gasping, their cheeks flaming red.

My heart was a wild beast. What the fuck had happened?

"Princess Moria," Torin growled, his voice low. "What the fuck are you talking about?"

I'd never actually seen him close to losing his temper before, and shadows seemed to bleed from his body.

Glass of wine in hand, Moria rose and grabbed her phone back from the redcap. "It's all in the *Daily Mail*, Your Majesty. Slightly pixelated in key areas. But I think you'll find the text quite interesting as well. Maybe it will give you a sense how suitable *Ava Jones of Chloe's household* might be. Have a look—because the gods know the rest of the world already has."

My thoughts were flashing in my mind like camera bulbs. Nude photos? I didn't remember taking any... except for that time with Andrew in Costa Rica...

But he wouldn't. He *couldn't* have. Andrew hated the spotlight as much as I did.

I felt the blood drain from my face as I turned to Shalini and found her already gawking at her phone. With shaking hands, I grabbed the phone from her and stared at the pixelated image. I'd saved up for a year to take us to Costa Rica, and we'd stayed in a tiny bungalow by the sea, with a beach all our own. For a few days, before he'd met Ashley and I'd started feeling sick, the vacation had been amazing.

With no one around, I didn't always wear a swimsuit, and Andrew had snapped photos, but so what? We were supposed to get married. I'd never dreamed he'd *show* them to anyone, let alone sell them to the fucking *Daily Mail*.

Gripping Shalini's phone, I surged to my feet, nearly knocking my chair over, and marched out of the throne hall. I flicked through the story, trying to read snippets through the stinging blur in my eyes.

...money obsessed...

...alcoholic...

...she'd have these rages....

...certain she was cheating on me...

My mind spun with thoughts too wild to grasp. *Why* would he do this?

Revenge.

Shalini said he'd been furious that I'd mentioned him during my date, even if I hadn't said his name. People had figured it out, anyway, and this was him clearing his name—and getting back at me at the same time.

Right now, I was feeling distinctly fae because I wanted to rip his head off his body.

"Ava." Torin's soft, velvety murmur came from behind me, and I turned to see him.

"Everything he said is a lie."

"I know that. And I will rip his ribs from his body and leave his ravaged carcass for the vultures as a warning to others."

I wiped a hand across my face. "That's...uh...sweet, but it's not how things work in the human world." I wasn't going to admit I'd just been fantasizing about something similar.

He raised a dark eyebrow. "Not how things work in the human world? What do I care?"

"Seems like you need them right now, even as King of the Seelie." I stared at him. "But really, that's a good question, Torin. What *do* you care? We don't like each other at all. Remember that discussion? It wasn't that long ago."

He pulled his gaze away and took a deep breath. "It's just that when I do like people..."

"It doesn't work out? Welcome to life, my friend."

I turned to walk back into the throne hall.

"Wait." His commanding voice brooked no argument, and I turned to look at him.

"What?" I said.

He reached out to touch me, then retracted his hand like he was afraid of being burned. The expression in his eyes was intense, and I felt like he was trying to communicate something he couldn't quite put into words. "You're the wrong one, Ava. I should not have chosen you."

"Because of a tabloid? I thought the whole point was that I was supposed to be unsuitable." Rage flamed over my cheeks. "I think you chose right, darling, because I'm as unsuitable as they get. And I'm so deeply sorry if it makes you embarrassed, but we have a contract, and a fae king can't break it." I smiled at him, suddenly feeling better. "We're going through with this marriage, and I'm getting my money. And you know what?" I leaned in to whisper to him. "I really can't wait for our wedding day. Your embarrassment will only make it all the more entertaining for me."

"You must not touch me, ever, Ava." His words were brutal, but his tone was velvety. Almost an invitation. "Do you understand?"

"Trust me, I have no desire to." It was a myth that the fae could not lie, because I was doing it right now. It was more that lies were considered a terrible sin among the fae. But me? I was raised among humans.

I held my head high as I returned to the throne hall. Cleena leaned back in her chair and smiled at me. "Ava Jones, you should be proud. You look gorgeous in that photo. And your ex sounds like a heartbroken twat."

"Well," said Moria sourly, "I don't care how many times that one has degraded herself. Tomorrow morning, I'll run her through with my blade, either way. Tomorrow, Ava will be nothing more than tiny threads of flesh."

She flashed me a wolfish grin that made my blood run cold.

32

AVA

Aeron led me through the snow, and I kept my cloak pulled tightly around me. Shalini walked silently by my side. She seemed furious with me, unwilling to utter a word. Or maybe it was simply her nerves keeping her silent, but a sense of foreboding hung over both of us. In just hours, I'd be battling the princesses.

Up ahead, a gray stone amphitheater loomed over the horizon—half ruined, like the Colosseum. Twice the size of Rome's arena, the stone was a gleaming black under the glaring sun. Icicles hung from its dark rock.

Today, we'd be fighting like gladiators on a frozen landscape.

Princess Eliza of the Selkie walked ahead, her green hair hanging over silver armor. She glanced back at me once or twice, looking slightly nauseous.

I let out a long, slow breath. Soon, Moria and Cleena would battle in the amphitheater, and they'd already arrived. I think I knew how it would end.

Cleena would yield quickly. Moria? She'd fight to the death if it came down to it.

The icy wind nipped at my cheeks, and my feet crunched over the snow.

I hadn't seen Torin once that morning, but I was putting him out of my head. Today was about staying alive and winning the prize I'd come here for.

When we reached the icy ruin, I followed the guard into a dark tunnel.

"Not too late," Shalini whispered.

"Have some faith," I snapped back.

The guard pulled a torch off the wall to guide us. The firelight danced over carvings in the stone—the names of fae who'd fought here before, their victories over their monstrous Unseelie foes. Images, too—a king pointing a sword at a fae with enormous horns curved like a ram's, his head bowed in submission.

My chest felt tight as I heard the distant roar of the crowd. The serpentine tunnel wound under the ground, the roaring growing louder, until at last, the tunnel opened into the amphitheater itself, and the bright winter sunlight nearly blinded me.

When we stepped from the tunnel, we were greeted by a deafening roar, the sound of fifty thousand fae cheering.

Shalini clutched my elbow, and together we stared, awestruck. The entire stadium was full, every seat occupied, and they were all screaming my name.

"Ava! Ava! Ava!"

I swallowed hard, shocked that I'd become a favorite even among the fae. I'd never actually expected to be forgiven for drunkenly insulting the king to his face, but maybe even the fae liked an underdog.

"Holy shit!" Shalini shouted in my ear. *My thoughts exactly.*

Eliza turned to look at me, her jaw set tight. "Sounds like they really like you. Even though you're not from here. Even though you're not really one of us. There is something about you that's not quite right, Ava, and I think it's more than growing up among humans."

I could hear the tinge of resentment in her voice, and I didn't reply.

As we stared from the tunnel, a crone shuffled into the arena, dressed in red gossamer that looked far too thin for the weather. She wore a silver crown over her rose gold hair.

The TV crew rolled closer to her, which seemed to startle her. Then she raised her arms. "Welcome to the final contest for the hand of the king!" Her voice was deep, booming. Even without a microphone, it echoed off the stone. "Tonight, some of the princesses may die. But they will die for the Seelie kingdom so that it might breathe with life again. And for the Seelie monarch, Torin, High King of Faerie, ruler of the six united clans."

She turned, motioning to him. King Torin sat on a throne made of black stone, looking for all the world like a sinister, wintry Roman emperor.

Without another word, the crone climbed the dark steps and stood behind Torin.

From my position in the tunnel, I watched as Moria

and Cleena entered the arena. Like me, Moria wore dark leather, while Cleena was clad in a thin platinum suit. I could tell from Moria's stance that she was a skilled swordswoman. She held the blade loosely, but it didn't waiver. Cleena, however, appeared to be shaking. I'd never actually seen her nervous before, but she seemed completely out of place.

From the stone platform, the crone opened her mouth and shrieked, "Begin the fight!"

As the crowd cheered, the princesses began to circle each other, blades glinting in the sunlight. Moria struck first, and Cleena's blade flashed up. It was a good parry, but she barely deflected Moria's attack.

She stepped back, holding her blade ready. Moria lunged, and Cleena was hardly able to deflect the strike. Moria, clearly sensing she had the upper hand, began to circle the banshee princess. Every few seconds, she lunged, stabbing.

Cleena continued to defend herself, but her parries were late, each time only just deflecting Moria's blade. Moria's burgundy hair flashed in the sunlight as she controlled the arena. She held her rapier high, pointing it at Cleena's heart.

She darted forward, her full weight behind the strike. Cleena tried to deflect it, but Moria drove her rapier home, stabbing it through Cleena's shoulder. Cleena fell to her knees, screaming in pain. It was the cry of a banshee ringing across the icy landscape, and I covered my ears.

But the fight was still going, and Cleena rose to her

feet. She backed away from Moria, blood dripping from her shoulder. "Moria," she said, almost pleadingly.

Moria ignored her, striking again, this time stabbing low. Her blade punched through Cleena's right thigh.

The Banshee princess shrieked as blood spurted onto the icy ground.

"Two to zero," shouted the crone, her eyes flashing with excitement. She let out a laugh that sounded unhinged.

Moria circled like a vulture over an injured gazelle. I could tell from her body language she knew she'd already won. All Cleena could do was limp away, trying to stay out of range of Moria's sword. Pain etched her features, and she was whispering something I couldn't hear. Probably trying to give up.

Slowly, Moria stalked her, her body tense with excitement. Cleena's injured leg gave out, and she stumbled, dropping to one knee. Moria stood over her, victorious, but she didn't strike. Instead she looked to me. Our eyes met. A faint smile played on her lips, then she slowly winked at me.

She raised her sword, ready to bring it down onto Cleena's head—

"Enough!" Torin's voice filled the arena, and Moria froze.

Torin rose from his throne, holding out his hand. "You've won, Princess Moria. There is no need to execute her now. You have won."

I let out a long, slow breath. If it hadn't been for that wink, he might not have been able to stop it. Next time, I thought darkly, Moria would strike before he could intercede.

I just had to make sure she didn't get the chance.

※※※

ETAIN STRODE INTO THE ARENA DRESSED IN PALE armor, her hair braided on her head. She stood across from Sydoc, who wore metallic boots and a crimson cap over her black hair. With a jolt of nausea, I realized Sydoc had already soaked her hat in someone's blood. Where the fuck had *that* come from?

When Sydoc smiled, I caught a hint of fangs.

But Etain didn't seem scared. In fact, her smile was just as terrifying, and she looked ready for blood.

Etain attacked first, immediately striking Sydoc in the shoulder. The Redcap roared, on the attack now. She was brutal, ferocious, and her black hair flew behind her as she drove Etain back. Etain was fast, but Sydoc was faster. She cornered the beautiful Etain against the wall and drove her blade clean into Etain's neck, severing her jugular.

Blood poured from Etain's throat, her eyes wide with horror. Even from here, I could see the light leaving Etain's eyes. Sydoc ripped out her sword, and Etain's lifeless body slumped to the ground, her blood pooling on the ice.

But it wasn't enough for Sydoc. She brought her metal boot down hard on Etain's ribs.

Etain wasn't alive anymore. This was simply some sort of crazed bloodlust.

The crowd roared their approval.

Holy shit. What was wrong with these people?

At last, catching her breath, Sydoc leaned down and dipped her cap in Etain's blood, soaking up the gore. She pulled the hat onto her black hair, her face beaming.

She lifted her sword, victorious before the crowd, Etain's blood streaming down her face.

IN THE TUNNEL, ELIZA AND I EXCHANGED NERVOUS looks, her previous confidence completely gone. Now, she merely looked terrified. And I couldn't blame her.

Torin's head was bowed, his expression solemn. I stared as someone carried Etain's body into one of the tunnels.

The crone hobbled down the steps again, the wind whipping at her hair. She wore a grin that sent a chill through me.

"The next duel will be between Princess Eliza and Ava Jones."

My heart began to thunder, and I stepped slowly into the arena with Eliza by my side.

The winter winds toyed with her green hair, her locks shimmering in the pale sunlight. She took her position across from me, holding a thin rapier loosely in her right hand, her shoulders slumped.

Maybe this wouldn't be a difficult fight.

The crone ascended the dais, then turned to face us.

Her strangely long, white teeth gleamed as she grinned. She shrieked into the sky, "Begin the fight!"

I pointed to my rapier at the Selkie, and she slowly lifted hers to face mine. I slashed at her blade. The water maiden parried weakly. I tested her again. Again, she halfheartedly deflected my blade.

"What are you doing?" I asked in a low voice.

"Just beat me," she hissed quietly. "I don't want to do this anymore. I just want to go home."

I circled her. "Then why are you bothering with any of this? Why did you sound like you were annoyed the crowd was cheering my name?"

"It's not about the king. I don't even like males. But our clans demand success." She backed away from me. "It's a point of honor among us. That's all this is. You'd understand if you were from here."

We circled slowly. "Fine. Well, if your honor is at stake, I'll let you pretend to get a good shot in first."

Her features relaxed immediately. "Really?"

"Go. Just don't make it hurt."

She stabbed at me. I parried her blade with ease, but pretended that it was more difficult.

"Good one," I whispered. "Now do another."

Again, she stabbed, and again, I parried. After a few more gentle, back-and-forths, I sensed the crowd was growing bored. Some of them started chanting at us to fight.

Our match didn't have the visceral drama of Moria and Cleena, and I wasn't quite sure it looked real.

"Are you ready?" I asked. "I'm going to have to draw some blood."

"Yes," she whispered.

I sliced at her thigh where her armor didn't protect her, a superficial cut, but enough to spill blood onto the snow.

"Ow!"

"Sorry," I whispered back.

At that point, whispering wasn't even necessary. The sight of blood had the crowd roaring with excitement, drowning out anything we might say.

"A blow for Ava Jones!" the crone screamed.

"You, okay?" I asked.

"Yeah," she said. "That wasn't too bad. Just get this over with, okay?"

I slashed again. This time, I scratched her right wrist with the very tip of my blade. The crowd roared.

"All right," I said. "Are you ready for the final blow?"

The water maiden nodded, but she looked like she was about to cry.

"What's the problem?" I hissed.

"This will look like a failure for me. I'll be letting down the clan of the Selkie."

The crowd was chanting my name, but I ignored them.

"Get in another blow, then."

The Selkie smiled at me, her brown eyes gleaming. I circled her, and this time, when Eliza struck, I let the very tip of her blade slash through my left bicep. My blood dripped onto the ice. It hurt like hell, but I'd recover.

She grinned at me, victorious.

And now, I desperately wanted to end this fight for

good. I slashed a third and final time, cutting through her thigh.

Her smile faded, and she clutched her leg as the crowd roared.

The crone lifted up her arms, her expression exuberant. "Three successful attacks for Ava Jones! She has won the round."

Dizzy, I turned to see the cameras closing in, and I clutched my arm, trying to stop the bleeding. I hadn't even noticed the cameras during the fight, and now they seemed intrusive.

I wanted to crawl away and let my bicep heal—alone. But the tournament wasn't over. Not even for the day.

"The tournament demands we continue until we have a winner. Cleena has announced that she has resigned from the tournament." The crone's voice floated over the amphitheater. "Princess Moria of the Dearg Due will now fight against Sydoc of the Redcap."

IN THE TUNNEL, I CLOSED MY EYES, RELIEVED TO GET a moment of rest. I held tight to my shoulder, though I wasn't sure it was bleeding anymore.

I leaned against the wall, trying to forget what I'd just witnessed.

Shalini stared at me. "Did you fucking see that?"

"I told you what the fae were like, Shalini," I hissed. "You're the one who wanted me to come here."

"Okay, I was wrong. I fully admit that. I didn't know it would be this bad. The fae are very secretive."

I took a deep breath. "Torin wants me to win," I whispered. "You saw how he stopped Moria before. He can do it again."

"He didn't stop Sydoc."

In a daze, I watched as Sydoc took on Moria, Etain's blood still streaking down the Redcap's face. But Moria wasn't as easy to beat as Etain had been, and their swords clashed in the bright sun, the sound ringing out over the amphitheater.

I heard the sound of gentle footfalls behind me and turned to see Orla approaching me. "You're hurt," she said quietly. Her pale, milky eyes were half lidded.

"At least I'm alive."

"You won't be for long, Ava," said Orla. "I can hear the blades. You need to know that Princess Moria has a glamoured sword. It's how she's winning so easily."

"She is? How could you possibly tell that?"

"Her blade is enchanted. By my best guess, it's about three inches in front of where her opponents perceive it to be."

I stared at her. "Isn't that cheating?"

She shrugged. "Magic is allowed. But I want you to look out for it."

"How do you know this?" I asked.

"Because I can hear the blades. And whenever anyone parries Moria's blade, they're always late."

"How do you know it's three inches?"

Orla sighed. "Every High Fae has a magical strength. You'll just have to trust me on this."

"Okay."

"You need to be at full strength for the fight against Moria." She reached up to touch my face, and soothing magic trickled from her palm like warm rain.

She pulled her hand away. "Your arm is healed. But I wanted to give you something to keep you safe during your next match."

I inhaled, watching as she pulled a silver chain from her pocket. At the bottom of the chain hung a charm, a stag's head with emerald eyes.

"It has been in the royal family since King Finvarra reigned," she said. "And it has always had the power to protect us from enemies of the king. When the monsters were going to cut off the king's head, they fell dead instead. I always regretted that my parents were not wearing it when the monsters came for them."

I stared at it, entranced. But when I reached out to put it on, I gasped and yanked my hand back. I stared down at my fingers. They were blistered, like I'd been burned. I cursed under my breath. "Is this because Torin doesn't like me?"

She shook her head, and her brow furrowed. "I don't understand. Torin wanted me to give it to you. He wants you to win."

I pressed my burned hand against the icy stone wall to cool it. "I think I get it."

He wanted me to win *because* he didn't like me. I was the king's enemy, and he'd made it more than clear to me that he wanted me to stay away from him.

"Ava!" Shalini called out from beside me, and I turned back to the arena.

Sydoc had lost her sword and was scrambling for it on the frozen stones. She slid over the ice on her hands and knees, but Moria struck one swift blow to the back of Sydoc's neck and severed the Redcap's head from her body.

The breath left my lungs.

I was next.

❧ 33 ❧
AVA

I stared as Sydoc's body was cleared from the arena, leaving a thin river of red behind it.

Was this worth it? For fifty million—was it enough to risk death?

I walked back into the arena, my breath escaping my lips in clouds.

The truth was, it wasn't just the money. I had nothing to return to, did I? Only ridicule, loneliness, and an empty bank account.

And when I'd practiced with Torin, I'd felt like I could take on anyone. If I could hold my own against a king, the strongest in all of Faerie...

The world seemed to grow silent around me, and my gaze locked on Moria. Blood spattered her leather armor, and her hair gleamed in the bright light—nearly the same shade.

My stomach fluttered.

Moria watched me through narrowed eyes, the hint of a smile on her lips. I glanced down at the ground, where Sydoc's blood was already freezing—just another layer of ice.

I glanced at the crone, who lifted her arms in the air, ready to announce the start of the fight.

My heart was a war drum as I raised my sword, and Moria's deep plum eyes locked on me.

The crone shrieked the start of the fight, and her voice somehow sounded a million miles away.

Across from me, Moria began circling with an unhurried sureness. Like a cat walking along a roof's edge, she seemed oblivious to any danger, her sword arm relaxed and steady. She'd cleaned the blood from it already.

The little smile faded from her lips, replaced by a sneer. She started to advance toward me, slowly weaving her blade back and forth in a sort of mesmerizing movement. And it was an absolutely beautiful sword, a rapier with a long silver blade and a gold and diamond-encrusted hilt. A sword fit for a princess.

With a little snarl, she lunged. I whipped up the tip of my rapier to parry, but just as Cleena had struggled with Moria's strikes, I was a hair late. Instead of a clean deflection, I barely pushed her blade aside.

Her eyebrows rose, and she whipped her blade faster, her expression determined. I kept my rapier up in the guard position, my eyes locked on her sword. Suddenly, she lunged. Again, I parried; again, I was late. This time, she didn't wait to strike. She immediately pressed her advantage with a series of blows.

I struggled each time to deflect her blade. It always seemed as though I were slow, like my reflexes were off.

Orla was spot-on with her assessment—a glamour was at work. I just needed to overcome my own senses.

"Gutter fae, you've never fought someone like *me* before," she said, in a taunting voice. "I have been training with the sword since I could walk."

Moria advanced, the blade of her rapier flashing under the sun.

She struck again. I tried to direct her blade, but she twisted her wrist at the last minute, and the very tip of her rapier scratched my right shoulder.

"I struck a blow!" shouted Moria.

It didn't matter if I lost on points. Torin could choose me, either way. What mattered was staying alive for the next twenty minutes.

Moria's rapier gleamed as she moved her feet into place. She thrust, and I parried. But as before, my sword was late, and I barely succeeded in directing the tip of her rapier away from my body.

I didn't know why I could seem to deflect her blade, but I knew I had to take the initiative—to stop playing defense. I leveled my blade and lunged.

Her blade flashed up, faster than I'd ever seen a sword move, and she slashed a jarring parry.

I nearly lost control of my weapon, and as I was steadying myself, she counterattacked. She drove the tip of her blade into the flesh, just above my left hip. I staggered back, clutching at my side, warm blood already wetting my hand.

"A second blow!" screamed Moria.

She lifted her sword above her head, and I stared as my blood dripped onto the ice.

I glanced at Torin, his dark hair tinged with frost. His body was rigid, hands gripping the armrests of his stony throne.

I tried to straighten my body, but the pain was nearly overwhelming. I staggered, even as the announcer shouted that Moria was now up by two points.

Moria faced me again, her rapier raised.

I forced myself to stand straight, gritting my teeth. Moria appeared to have driven the rapier clean through my abdomen, about an inch and a half above my left hip. It hurt more than anything I'd ever felt in my life.

If that charm had worked for me, I'd really be enjoying its benefits right now.

I gripped my side, struggling to stay upright.

I hadn't even raised my blade before she lunged, and pure instinct had me blocking the blow. "Why don't you just give up?" she snarled. "I'd have crawled away to die after the first humiliating video, never mind the photos."

I didn't have the breath to answer her. I was focused entirely on deflecting her blade. It flashed again, and I parried, the shock of her blow vibrating up my arm. I winced as those same vibrations ran down my injured side.

"You can't possibly think you'll redeem yourself?" said Moria gleefully.

"Not giving up." Hot blood filled my mouth. *Fuck, this isn't good.*

I wondered if Torin would stop the fight if it seemed like I was about to die—

But he believed I was wearing the charm, didn't he?

Moria continued to advance, slashing and stabbing with her blade, but only halfheartedly. She was playing with me now, like a cat with its prey.

"You should never have joined this competition," she hissed. "Even for a gutter fae, you are a disgrace. A common whore."

I wasn't going to waste my breath on her. I needed to focus on the timing of her sword.

Moria lunged, driving her blade at my throat, and I brought my blade up. I managed to deflect her strike, but the movement sent me off balance. I still hadn't managed to account for her glamour, and it was throwing me off.

I lost my footing and fell hard onto the floor of the arena.

Moria was going to sever my head from my body.

I could hear Torin screaming at her to stop, but I knew she wouldn't, not until I was bleeding out on the stones.

Rage ran through me like wildfire, melting away the fear. I didn't need Torin's charm because something dark lived in me. And when I was cornered, I was monstrous.

Moria should drop to her knees and beg my forgiveness.

I kicked up hard, driving my foot into her knee from below. Her sharp yelp of pain was one of the most satisfying sounds I'd heard in years—followed by the scream of rage that erupted from Moria's throat when I skewered her in the thigh with my blade, driving it into her bone.

She stared at the end of my quivering rapier protruding from her leg.

"You're right, Moria," I spat. "I am a gutter fae. We fight dirty, and we fight to win. But you're not very different than me, are you?"

I ripped my blade from her thigh, and she staggered back with an agonized grunt. She looked completely stunned.

But she must have another kind of magic at work because she didn't seem to feel the pain long. Within moments, her blade flashed up, shining in the early morning sunlight. Silver and bright, it glittered like a jewel—a jewel, I knew with complete certainty, she would drive through my heart if given the opportunity.

I raised my rapier, matching hers. As Moria began to circle me, I studied the blade in her hand. Its luminescence drew the eye, and I wondered if that was the effect of the glamour.

I listened as Moria moved the blade slowly back and forth like a venomous serpent preparing to strike. I could almost hear a thin hiss of wind through the air.

If I focused hard enough, I could sense what Orla had said—the sound was out of sync with the actual movement of the blade. Moria thrust again, and I tried to predict her movement, listening for the blade. For the first time, I was able to cleanly deflect her strike.

Moria's eyes narrowed, and she attacked again. Once more, I listened for the sound of the blade and was able to anticipate it. With a hard counter-parry, I directed her sword away.

Moria seemed to lose some of the ferocity of her attack.

I struck then, lunging, anticipating the speed of her sword. She parried, but I was still on the attack, and I slashed at knee level. We quickly fell into a pattern, a whirlwind of blades and ice. Confidence filled my body as I knew exactly when to duck, when to block.

Our blades scraped along each other like the sound of nails on a chalkboard. Moria was so close that our faces were nearly touching.

Unexpectedly, Moria spun, twisting her body, and drove her left elbow into the side of my head as she growled. With a brilliant flash of light, an explosion of pain engulfed me, and shadows blinded me. Frantically, I backpedaled, dizzy, unable to see.

Fuck.

I was prey now, about to lose my head like the others.

Moria began to laugh.

I pressed my free hand to my face. When I pulled it away, it was warm and wet. Blinded, bleeding...

Panic clogged my throat. How was I going to fight Moria if I couldn't see?

But I'd done this before, hadn't I. And beasts hunted by smell...

A ferocious animal instinct burned in me, and I listened for the sound of her blade. When she attacked again, I parried.

The world went quiet around me, and I heard only

the sound of her heart beating, her sharp intake of breath.

You were born to rule, Ava.

The words rang, a deep voice in my head, though I had no idea where they'd come from.

But now, I could envision Moria clearly in my mind's eye; the triumphant grin, the confident thrown-back shoulders. Her blade whooshed through the air once more, and our swords sang as they clashed.

I inhaled deeply, smelling her sickly sweet rosewater perfume. And I attacked, thrusting my blade directly into her chest.

The moment I did, the shadows cleared from my vision. Across from me, Moria staggered back, clutching at her breast. I pulled my sword from her, shocked at how close I'd come to her heart. I'd nearly taken my first life, a thought that didn't feel nearly as horrifying as it should.

Moria collapsed to the ground, and somewhere beneath the sound of the screaming crowds, I could hear her whistling breath. I'd punctured a lung, and I knew all too well how that felt. Her skin had gone pale as milk, and she looked up at me with an expression that wavered between fear and rage.

Her heart was still beating, pumping blood all over the ice. But she wasn't getting up again. The fight had ended.

I wiped my hand down the side of my face, then stared at the blood dripping from my palm onto the dark ice.

The crone crossed into the arena, and the wind whipped at her hair.

She nodded at me once, frowning, then threw back her head and screamed, "As the person with the most points, Ava Jones is the winner of our final tournament." She raised her hands. "King Torin, Ruler of the Six Clans, High King of the Seelie, will announce his choice for queen. At sunset, in the throne hall, we will learn the name of our next high queen consort. Our queen shall make our kingdom thrive with life once more!"

The roar of the crowd vibrated off the stones, and I felt their exultant screams in my marrow. Vaguely, I was aware of Orla rushing up to me, healing my ragged wounds with her magic.

I hardly wondered at all why the king wasn't doing it himself.

34

AVA

I slid lower into the hot water, inhaling the scent of herbs that the fae used to perfume their baths. Steam curled from the bathwater into the cool castle air.

When I closed my eyes, my mind flashed with images of blood—of Etain's lifeless body. Of Sydoc's.

I sank beneath the surface, rinsing off the blood that had dried on the side of my face. I stayed under the warm water as long as I could, hoping to clear my thoughts. My lungs started to burn, and I pushed against the side of the tub, rising again. Gasping for breath, I smoothed my hair back.

Blood swirled in the water around me.

Where had it come from, that ease with which I'd survived, even when blinded in the arena? And that voice in my mind, the one declaring I was born to rule?

My thoughts flicked back to that silver charm and how it had burned me. Here, in Faerie, there were puzzle pieces I couldn't quite put together. My understanding of everything felt disjointed, out of place. A picture that didn't quite make sense.

Torin was hiding secrets from me. He hadn't told me the whole truth about why he was so dead set against finding a real queen, or why he needed me.

As the bathwater started to cool, I rose from the tub. Pulling a towel off the counter, I quickly dried my hair and dressed in a pair of leather pants and a deep gray shirt, the material soft as cashmere. Soon, I'd be dressed in a gown of some kind for the Tournament Declaration, when Torin would announce me as his chosen wife.

I crossed into Shalini's room.

As usual, she was sitting cross-legged on the bed with a book in her lap, and she nodded at a box next to her. "Someone dropped this off for you. Sent by the king himself." She frowned at me. "So, what happens when you're queen?"

"I sit on the throne for a few months, and I make spring return. I hope people will be bringing me books and food because it sounds a bit boring."

I lifted the top off the box. Inside was a note on top of a green gown, the color of spring.

Please throw this in the fire after you read it.

You will be our next queen.

I saw what you did today. Most wouldn't have noticed, but I did. You allowed Eliza to strike you so she could leave the tournament with her head held high. I commend your sense of mercy.

But I must remind you, Ava, that I will keep my distance. And you must not come too close to me ever again.

—Torin

"What does it say?" asked Shalini.

Ice pierced my heart, but I kept staring at the note. "A reminder that I'm not supposed to go near the king."

Torin had told me what this would be like from the beginning, but I'd never imagined us *actually* married, in some kind of relationship with each other. That was never what either of us were looking for. We weren't the romantic types. Not anymore.

So why did this hurt so much?

Through the door, I heard the sound of muffled voices—a man and a woman arguing. Frowning, I went to the door and heard the distinct sound of Moria's voice insisting that she needed to see me.

My first thought, of course, was that she'd come to kill me. Apparently, that was Aeron's first thought, too, because I heard him barking at Moria to stay back.

"I've already resigned!" she shouted. "I dropped out. I have no intention of harming anyone."

I picked up my rapier and slowly opened the door. Moria's face snapped to mine, drawn and exhausted. "I need to speak to you."

"I don't think that's a good idea, Moria."

She gritted her teeth. "Fine. Then we'll talk through the door." She slid her eyes to the left, where I thought Aeron was standing. "I just want us to speak alone."

To my shock, she hadn't cleaned herself up. She still wore her leather clothes, and her hair and face were caked with dried blood. Her skin looked blotchy beneath the grime, like she'd been crying. I'd never expected to see her looking like such a mess.

"Why would you resign from the tournament before Torin has announced his choice?" I asked in a whisper, shielding myself with the door.

"Because I know I'm not going to win."

Doubt flickered through me. Had our deal been revealed? "What do you mean?"

She pressed a palm against the door. "It's been a long time since I've had a premonition, Ava. But I just had one. And my premonitions are never wrong."

Now *those* were familiar words.

My mouth had gone dry. "And what was your premonition?"

The corner of her lip curled in a cruel smile. "You will die at Torin's hands."

My breath shallowed. "Of course you'd want me to think that."

Tears shone in her eyes, then started to run down her cheeks, carving little rivers through the dirt and blood. "It doesn't matter what I say now or what I want you to think. It will happen, either way. My sister Milisandia didn't believe me, either. But I told her that Torin would kill her, and he did. I saw it all in my vision, how he'd freeze her to death in the Temple of Ostara."

My heartbeat was hammering. *This* was the sister from the diary. "Where is she now?"

Her tears were flowing freely, her lower lip trembling. "Torin thinks he covered it up, that we all believe Milisandia went missing. That perhaps she ran off to live like a beast among the monsters. But I know the truth. Torin is death," she hissed. "I had the premonition, Ava. I saw what would happen, that he'd swallow his dark secrets. And I dug up her body in the temple. I knew where to find it. The king killed her because he will kill anything beautiful. It's what he does. He's no better than an Erlking, and his touch is death."

I clutched the door tightly. "Then why were you in this tournament to begin with?"

"I wanted to be as close to him as possible. Because if I were queen, I'd remind him every day for the rest of his life of exactly what he was. That he was death. And I would have done anything to make it happen. But now that I've seen the future, I know my plans didn't work out like I hoped."

"When you say you would have done anything... Moria. Are you the one who killed Alice?"

The corner of her mouth twitched. "Now, why would I admit to that?"

The glint in her eye told me I was right on the money.

"But listen, Ava. Maybe it doesn't matter that I won't be queen. I've seen that he will kill you, too, and I don't need to remind him, do I? Because death will follow in his wake wherever he goes, and everyone will see. Everyone will know that the king who sits on the throne is rotten and corrupted down to his bones. Just an Erlking with a pretty face."

"Why are you telling me this now?"

She wiped her hand across her tear-streaked cheeks, smearing them with more blood. "Because I really and truly don't like you. Milisandia deserved to be queen, but you do not. You are a lascivious, filthy social climber. You are a whore who wants a crown, and you have never belonged here. And worse than that, I can sense there's something really wrong with you. Something evil. You don't belong in Seelie lands, Ava. So I want to make sure you don't feel a moment's sense of victory before you die painfully, the way Milisandia did. I want you to realize you are alone and unloved here. I want you to die in terror, knowing that one way or another, you lost to me, and I will piss on your grave."

She turned on her heel and marched through the hall, her loud footfalls echoing off the stone. I closed the door and turned back to Shalini.

My entire body was shaking.

I pulled on the green gown, tuning out Shalini's demands that I fill her in on every last word that she hadn't been able to overhear.

But I needed to speak to only one person right now, and that man was the king of the Seelie.

❦

I HURTLED DOWN THE STAIRS. AERON SAID I'D FIND Torin in the throne room, already preparing for his grand announcement.

This could be a ploy by Moria—a long con. Maybe she'd planted those journals. Maybe she was trying to force me to drop out. But I needed some answers.

And the thing that clawed at the recesses of my mind was that he'd taken me to the Temple of Ostara for a reason. A shadow of guilt had seemed to hang over him there.

Behind me, I heard Aeron's footfalls as he followed

me, pledging to keep me safe before the great announcement. Until I could wear a crown on my head and restore the kingdom to its former glory.

When I reached the throne room, a few people had arrived early and were standing around the edges of the hall. Torin sat in his throne, his face covered in shadow.

A long red carpet ran down the center of the stone hall, and as I moved closer to the king, my eyes flicked around the room. I wanted to speak to him alone, but I was supposed to stay away from him.

Did he know his touch was death?

And yet, for some reason, despite all his secrecy, despite what I'd read in the diary, I *trusted* him. Underneath it all, I was sure Torin was a good person.

My green gown trailed behind me as I walked, but I probably looked little better than Moria had, my hair still damp and my expression grim.

Torin rose from his throne as I approached, his eyes locked on me. I wouldn't say that he looked *excited* to see me, exactly.

As I ascended the steps of the dais, he leaned in and whispered, "What are you doing, Ava?"

"I need to speak to you alone."

He shook his head. "This isn't the time. Unless you want to renege on our bargain?"

I took a deep breath. "Moria told me about her sister," I whispered as quietly as possible. "Milisandia. She says you murdered her. Does that ring a bell, Torin?"

One look at the ravaged expression on his face, and

I knew immediately that it was all true. My stomach sank.

"Why does she say your touch is death?" My voice was hardly a whisper.

But Torin didn't answer me. He looked at me, his expression pleading.

Was this worth the fifty million?

Was it worth not being alone?

I wasn't so sure anymore. I'd be returning home, poor, disgraced, and utterly alone, but at least I'd be alive. At least I wouldn't be constantly looking over my shoulder, terrified that death was coming for me.

"I care for you far more than I should," Torin murmured.

"And yet, you haven't answered my questions." Frustration rose in me, and I turned from him. As I did, he touched my arm.

I looked back at him. His expression was horrified, his cheeks pale. Shadows slid through his eyes, and my skin grew cold where his fingers grazed my bare skin.

He seemed frozen in place, staring in horror at his hand on my arm—and I couldn't move a muscle, either. The air grew glacially cold, and I could feel the ice spreading in me.

Panic climbed up my throat as webs of frost spread over my arm, turning it white and blue. The arm of a frozen corpse...

Fear had its icy grip on my heart. Moria had been telling the truth.

"Stop it, Torin!" I shouted.

But as ice climbed over him, I didn't think he could

move. Hoarfrost swirled in strange patterns over his cheeks and forehead, and it spread out beneath his feet. His eyes were a deep indigo, nearly black, and filled with terror.

Behind him, ice climbed over the king's throne. With a great crack that echoed over the hall, the ice splintered his throne like a glacier moving through a canyon.

"Ava," he whispered. "The queen's throne."

My body felt like ice, and I tried to tear myself away from him, to run. Frost was climbing up my gown, icing my feet and legs.

Pain shot through my limbs, and I pulled away with all my strength, scrambling backward.

For a few terrifying seconds, I felt as if I were falling into an abyss, until I stumbled onto the hard stone throne.

35

AVA

The hall was a scene of utter chaos—the broken throne behind the king, the frost spreading over the flagstones, and fae screaming.

The chill in my body started to fade, and an emerald haze filled my vision. When I inhaled, it was as if I'd been plunged into the depths of a forest. The scent of wet earth filled my nose, and I felt the warmth of the sun on my skin, heard the calls of insects, the chirping of birds. Vines hung from the ceiling; moss covered the dais.

The vernal scene faded once more as the cold overtook me.

The granite throne was icy through the fabric of my dress. The frost was nearly at my thighs, my skin freezing.

"I want to go home," I whispered.

I closed my eyes.

A warm rush of magic flowed through my chest and limbs and into the stone beneath me. My body began to thaw, healing on the throne.

My back arched involuntarily. A summer sun kissed my skin, and the smell of wet moss enveloped me, until the throne itself seemed to dissolve beneath me, and I plunged into warm, clear water.

Home. Take me home.

It lived in the darkest recesses of my mind, imprinted on my soul, the place where I'd been born.

The enchantment of the forest.

I felt myself sinking deeper, my lungs burning. I glimpsed the clear rays of golden light piercing the water from above.

I kicked my legs, swimming up to the light, to life. My fingernails dug into the dirt, and I hoisted myself over the edge of the watery portal, onto the mossy earth. I dropped flat on my back, gasping for breath. Deliciously warm air filled my lungs, the scent of life. Amber light broke through the tree branches above me, flecking the earth with gold.

Home.

I sat up, trying to get my bearings. I'd asked the throne to take me home, and it had brought me here...

But where *was* I?

Thick green vines emblazoned with red blossoms curled around the bases of the towering trees. The air was warm and intensely humid, as if I'd stepped into a sauna. It was fragrant, too, brimming with exotic perfumes and floral scents I didn't recognize.

An enchanted forest.

The scent of the place unearthed a memory buried in the hollows of my mind, the sense that I'd been here before. Déjà vu, maybe.

Water soaked my green dress and dripped into the earth. I should be utterly panicked, but it was simply hard to get past the beauty. Before me were more shades of green than I'd ever seen in my life—emerald, lime, jade, sage, chartreuse, and olive foliage, so rich and variegated, it took my breath away.

And when I looked down at my shoulders, I found that even my hair had turned a gorgeous bluish shade of green.

I scrambled to a standing position and slowly turned, trying to work out where I was, but in every direction, thick undergrowth obscured my view.

Above me, vegetation extended hundreds of feet, twining around massive tree trunks and branches as thick as a Doric column. An enchanted, primordial forest.

I folded my arms, wondering how I'd get back to Faerie, or anywhere familiar.

A distant screech rent the air, and I saw a flash of red and blue wings in my peripheral vision. Something large, a bird maybe, flew between tree trunks, and the forest went quiet. Then there came a distant, cater-wauling shriek. The sound of an animal dying.

This is not good.

Hugging myself, I stepped away from the portal. I spotted movement on a branch maybe ten feet in front of me. It was hard to see through the foliage, but I caught a glimpse of brown fur—a spider the size of a small dog, with six glittering black eyes and a very large pair of fangs.

I took another step backward. Across from me, the spider's fangs began to twitch excitedly.

"Fuck, fuck, fuck," I said under my breath. The spider mirrored my movements.

I turned, heading back for the portal. Maybe it could take me back? Or at least take me somewhere else?

But as I stood over the water, I caught a glimpse of my reflection, and my heart went still.

Because there, protruding from my green hair, was a golden pair of horns.

I couldn't breathe.

A word knelled in the hollows of my mind as I realized why the pendant had rejected me.

Unseelie.

I'd asked to come home, and this was where the magic had brought me.

My *real* home—the realm of the wild beasts.

It seemed I was a changeling after all.

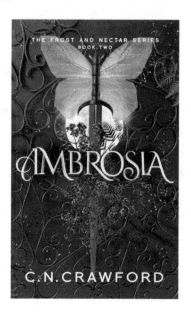

Please read on for an excerpt of one of our other books, **City of Thorns.**

36

SAMPLE CHAPTER FROM CITY
OF THORNS

The bartender slid our mojitos across the bar, and I grabbed mine instantly. I took a sip, letting the mint and lime roll over my tongue. "Please tell me about the City of Thorns. I want to hear about the demons."

"Where do I even begin?"

I raised my eyebrows. "Do you think demons can leave the city walls?"

She shook her head. "I think so, but not for long. As far as I know, there's some kind of magical spell from hundreds of years ago that keeps them mostly tied to one demon city or another. But occasionally, they can travel between them. Why do you ask?"

"That night my mom was murdered—"

My sentence trailed off. I could already feel the air cooling, the atmosphere growing thorny as I raised the painful subject. There was no easy way to say, *One night, a demon with a glowing star on his head hunted down my mom in the woods and burned her to death*. And since the horror of that night felt raw even now, it was hard to talk about it without feeling like I was drowning in loss again.

Sometimes, I thought the only thing keeping me afloat was the certainty that I'd avenge her death. That I would get into the City of Thorns and find her killer.

But this was too dark and weird, wasn't it? Worse than the fox pee beneath my bed.

We were sitting at the marble bar, with the night-dark sea glittering before us. I didn't want to ruin the evening, and so I waved a hand. "I want to hear more about your daily life at the university. What's it like?"

I could feel the tension leave the air again. "Fucking amazing," Shai said. "I might do another year. Any chance you can get the tuition for next year?"

"I'm working on a few ideas for getting in." Wildly illegal ideas at this point. "What's your dorm like?"

"There's a balcony and servants. Even the ocean is more beautiful there. It's not like the Atlantic—it's like this gorgeous tropical ocean made with magic. Okay, so the city has seven wards, each one associated with a demon. And the university buildings are organized the same way. I'm in Lucifer Hall, and it's this enormous stone castle-like place."

Even putting my vengeance plans aside, my jealousy was crippling. "How are your classes?"

"Amazing. They're held in lecture halls that must be four hundred years old, with seats curved all around a stage." She sighed. "I know, it's a huge expense. But I wanted to learn magical arts, and you can't exactly do that at Osborn State. Belial is the finest witchcraft institution for mortals. I'm desperate to stay another year."

"What are the demons like?"

She ran her fingertip over the rim of her mojito. "Well, my classes are mostly with aspiring mortal witches, but there are a few demons, and the professors, obviously. They're beautiful and intimidating as shit. Some of them have horns, but not all. I haven't met anyone who seems particularly evil. At least, no one worse than Jack." She turned and lifted her empty glass, motioning for the bartender to bring us another round, then swiveled back to me. "I've heard the king is evil—him and the Lord of Chaos. They're both terrifying, but I've only seen them from a distance."

My eyebrows shot up. "Okay, start with the king. What's his deal?"

She leaned in conspiratorially. "King Cambriel only recently became king. He slaughtered his father, King Nergal, who'd ruled for hundreds of years. Cambriel cut off his dad's head and stuck it on the gate to his palace."

I shuddered. "That's fucked up."

"The only way a demon king can die is if his heir slaughters him, and Cambriel did just that. Now he's apparently looking for a demon queen, and there's all kinds of gossip about which female he might choose."

As I finished my first mojito, the bartender brought over two more.

"And the women *want* to marry this guy with his dad's head over his front gate?" I asked. "Sounds like quite a catch."

"To the female demons, he is." She slid one of the mojitos over to me. "And the Lord of Chaos is the other eligible bachelor in the city. He's an outsider—a duke from the City of Serpents in England, so he was leader of a demon ward there. No one knows why he left, but obviously, it was a scandal. Dukes don't normally leave their cities. But the most important thing is that he seems to be filthy rich."

"If it was such a big scandal, how come no one knows the details?"

She stirred her drink with her little black straw. "There's no communication between demon cities. Demons can arrive in a new city, but they can never speak about the old one. It was one of the conditions of surrender in the great demon wars years ago, sealed by magic. The Puritans thought that if demons spoke to each other, they could grow strong and rise up against the mortals again, so he can't say a thing about the English demon city."

"Wow."

"So." She leaned closer. "No one really knows anything about him. But here's the scariest thing: on the rare occasion that a demon comes into a different city, they have to pass an initiation called the Infernal Trial. It's supposed to prove that the demon gods have blessed the new arrival. I don't want to say it's barbaric because that sounds judgmental, but it *is* barbaric. In the City of Thorns, the way the Trial goes is that the demons have to run through the forest and try to kill the newcomer. Only those who survive can remain. Most of them die before they can be initiated, but the Lord of Chaos slaughtered fifty other demons. Obviously, all the women want to fuck him because he's terrifying."

I stared at her. "This is all legal?"

She shrugged. "Their city, their laws. They can't kill humans without starting a war, but demons are fair game."

This was *fascinating*. "What does the Lord of Chaos look like?"

"I've only seen him from a distance, but he's shockingly beautiful. Like, fall-to-your-knees-before-him beautiful. He has silver hair, but not from age. It's sort of otherworldly. And he has these stunning blue eyes, devastating cheekbones. He's huge. I have a crush on him, and on a wrath demon named Legion. He has long black hair and these sexy-as-hell tattoos. Both of them are, like...stunning. Legion looked at me once—a smoldering look. Not even joking, I forgot to breathe."

I leaned closer. "What about a star? Have you seen a five-pointed star on anyone's head?"

A line formed between her brows. "What are you talking about?"

And there I was, back to my obsession—my mom's murder.

I shook my head. "Never mind. I just heard a rumor about marks on demons' foreheads. Might be bullshit."

As the pizza arrived, I pulled off a slice for myself and slid it onto a small plate. It looked surprisingly good, even though it was vegan.

Shai drummed her fingernails on the counter. "Why do I get the feeling you're always hiding things?"

"Some things are meant to be hidden." My mouth was watering for the squash and garlic. I took a bite, and while the vegan cheese burned my mouth, it still tasted glorious. I wasn't sure even the magically inspired food of the demon world could compete.

When I swallowed the hot bite, I asked, "Are you going to show me any of the healing magic you've been learning? If I have a headache, can you fix it?"

She wiped the corner of her mouth with a napkin. "I'm not ready yet. And anyway, I'm a veterinary student. I can't treat humans."

I pointed at her, feeling a bit tipsy now. "But if someone shot me in the shoulder, could you fix it with magic, or would you turn me into a cat or something?"

She shuddered. "Probably half-cat, half-human. It would be horrible."

We went quiet for a while as we ate the rest of the pizza.

When we finished, I turned to look behind me and found that the club was starting to fill up.

"Are we going to dance?" asked Shai.

I was now two mojitos and a Guinness into the evening, and so I shouted something about it being my birthday as I took to the dance floor.

They were playing my favorite, Apashe. As the beat boomed over the club, I found myself losing myself in the music. I forgot my college loans, my disastrous presentation, the spiders that crawled over me when I slept. I forgot about Jack and the five-pointed star. I let go of my lust for revenge.

At least, I did so until the music went quiet and tension thickened the air.

Sometimes, you can sense danger before you feel it, and this was one of those moments. Darkness rippled through the bar, floating on a hot, dry breeze. I went still, disturbed to find that everyone was staring in the same direction with an expression of horror. Goose-bumps rose on my arms. The warmth felt unnatural, disturbing. I didn't want to turn around.

When I finally did, my stomach swooped. There, in the doorway, was a demon with otherworldly silver hair and eyes like flecks of ice. The Lord of Chaos? His size and breathtaking beauty almost made me dizzy. He looked like a freaking god.

Maybe it was the mojitos, maybe it was his stunning physical perfection, but I felt magnetically drawn to him. I wanted to slide up closer to him and press myself against his muscular body. As I stared at him, my heart started to pound faster.

Divine. His silver hair hung down to heartbreak-ingly sharp cheekbones. He sported a high-collared black coat that hung open. Under his jacket, he wore a thin gray sweater that showed off a muscular body. It looked soft, but I could tell the abs beneath it were rock hard. I found my pulse racing as I thought of running my fingers over the material and feeling his muscles twitch.

I'd never enjoyed sex—not once in my life. But as I looked at him, I thought *there* was a man who could actually satisfy me.

I clamped my eyes shut. Wait, what the fuck was wrong with me? He wasn't even human. He was another species, one that used to eat humans.

But when I opened my eyes again, I felt like I was melting. In contrast to his pale blue eyes, his eyebrows were dark as night. The effect seemed shocking, mesmerizing.

But when he slid those pale eyes to me, an icy tendril of fear curled through me. His fingers tightened into fists, and he lowered his chin like he was about to charge at me.

I froze. My heart started beating faster now for an entirely different reason. I had his attention, but not in a good way.

This was a look of pure, unadulterated loathing, a look of palpable hatred that sent alarm bells ringing in my mind. He *hated* me.

Holy hell.

What did he think I'd done to him?

ACKNOWLEDGMENTS

First of all, thank you so much to your beta reading team, including Candice, Delia, Debbie, Crystal, and Penny. This helped us to get the story in better shape by focusing on some of the big picture ideas to make it sexier and more engaging.

We appreciate our wonderful editing team, with proofreading and copyediting by Ash and Lexi at Wicked Pen Editorial, and with final proofing by Shelby (@Literary Fairy).

Thank you to the readers in C.N. Crawford's Coven who always brighten our day with bookish discussions and enthusiasm.

And finally, our wonderful promoters, Lauren Gardner and Rachel Whitehurst, who will help get this book into the hands of readers.

Printed in the USA
CPSIA information can be obtained
at www.ICGtesting.com
LVHW010030260923
759259LV00021B/370/J